THE
PROBLEM WITH
crazy

THE
PROBLEM WITH
crazy

Lauren K. McKellar

ISBN: 978-0-9924524-1-4
Cover copyright (c) K. A. Last of KILA Designs
Editing by Danielle Poiesz of Double Vision Editorial
Formatting by Tianne Samson with E.M. Tippetts Book Designs

For fathers, everywhere;
for Mitch's, and for mine

ONE

THE PROBLEM with crazy is that crazy, by itself, has no context. It can be good crazy, bad crazy ... or *crazy* crazy, the kind that makes you turn your head and avoid eye contact, even though you know you shouldn't.

Sometimes it can be thrown about with vicious intent, like when my mum used it against my dad.

"I am going to go crazy at your father, *if* he eventually decides to grace us with his presence," Mum hissed at me. I say 'at' because even though her eyes were darting to all four corners of the full-to-exploding hall, spit still landed square in the middle of my left cheek.

"Mu-um." I sighed. I was pissed, too, though. I could accept his missing my birthday and Christmas last year, after he'd run out of our lives without a trace, but come on; what kind of father calls to say he's coming, and then is late to his only daughter's graduation?

"Kate, it's the least he could do," Mum mumbled. She was taking huge strides down the side of the hall, scanning the hordes of seated parents and students for an empty chair.

Other parents and graduates-to-be milled around, a buzz of excitement filling the auditorium. Up on stage, our principal, Mr McDonald, was speaking to a few class captains. *Suck-ups.*

"I've not had a cent from him in more than a year, and now he thinks he can just walk back into your life to play father at your graduation? If that drunken idiot thinks I'll sit next to him when he finally does get here, he is going to be sorely mistaken."

"I doubt he thinks that," I breathed. Recounting my father's sins, both on the phone to him and in my presence, was one of my mother's favourite activities since he'd left.

"There. There's a seat." Mum extended a maroon-painted talon toward an empty chair in the front row. It matched her freshly pressed suit-dress perfectly. The talon, that is; not the chair. "It'll be a better view for my photos, anyway." I cringed. It was bad enough she was taking photos, but front and centre? Really?

I racked my brain, trying to come up with a contingency plan to get me out of this mess when I felt a cool pair of hands close over my eyes.

"Guess who?" a deep voice asked from behind me.

"Dave!" I spun around to greet him, planting a tiny kiss on his cheek.

"Hey, Kate. Mrs T." He nodded in Mum's direction.

"Hi, Dave. You look just lovely," Mum swooned at Dave's tucked-in white school shirt and firmly fastened navy-blue tie. Even his hair was slicked up into neat little spikes, a change from the usual scruffy mess I loved running my hands through.

"Thanks. Hey, I'm sure my folks would like to sit with you, if you're trying to find a seat." Dave pointed his delicate musician's finger toward an empty seat three rows behind us. His parents waved with fervour, and I said a silent prayer of thanks. "They're just over there."

"That is so kind of you to offer. I'll go on and find them. You two kids get backstage—oh! Mr McDonald has turned on the microphone. They must be about to start."

I turned toward where she was pointing and saw our

school principal had indeed gripped his hand firmly around the microphone. The lights dimmed and the audience slowly hushed. I grabbed Dave's arm and we raced to the door on the left hand side of the room, the one that would lead us to the wings.

Compared to the silence of the hall, backstage was chaos. The other 163 members of our school year milled about, a sea of navy check and white, all talking far too loudly with the exuberance of the released. This was it. In approximately sixty-four minutes, if the dress rehearsal was anything to go by, we would all be officially finished school. And I, for one, couldn't wait.

"You guys! Can you please get into alphabetical order?" Stacey whined from her position at the top of the stairs. Her blonde ponytail bobbed up and down as she brought her fingers to her temple. No one seemed to be listening. Apparently, graduation was the one time she couldn't make our entire year stand still and take notice.

"Oh, Kate. Good, you're here." She bounced over to my side, blue eyes sparkling as she scanned me up and down. "I was getting worried. What took you so long?"

"You know … She couldn't decide what to wear." Dave joked.

"But—it's school uniform today." Stacey tilted her head to the side. I sucked in a breath and ignored the elbow to the ribs Dave gave me. Sometimes, I wondered how Stacey had gotten through high school alive.

"Well, helloooo Stacey." Michael came up from behind, giving her a skirt a quick tug as he scooted his way into our circle. Stacey gave his puppy-dog eyes a quick glare, her hands quickly smoothing the material back down and making sure her assets were firmly covered.

That was how, I reminded myself. With a body like that and eyes that could kill, Stacey had done more than attend high school. She veritably ruled the school.

"Dave, man, how you doing?" Michael asked, clapping his weathered hand on my boyfriend's shoulder.

"I think I'll be better in an hour or so."

"I know what you mean."

"Not to interrupt your male bonding session, but can you please line up in alphabetical? It's im*port*ant," Stacey pleaded, her hands clasped in front of her.

"Your wish is my command." Michael bowed.

"Right." Stacey narrowed her eyes at us, gave a sharp nod, and then spun on her heel. "I'll see you when we're graduates, Kate." She threw one hand up in the air and charged to the front of the line.

"Man, when is that chick gonna notice I'm alive?" Michael turned to watch her go. "Sometimes I think she'll date anyone but me."

"When we're on tour with Coal she won't be able to help but notice you," Dave said. His green eyes came alive, widening at the thought of their upcoming tour.

"You know it. This will be our time to shine." Michael nodded. "It's a good thing your girlfriend is so good at organising things. We'd never have made the tour if she hadn't hit them up."

"It was nothing." I felt the heat rise in my cheeks.

"Yeah, it's not like she wrote the songs." Dave stroked the back of my hair, bringing shiny brown strands of it to rest over my shoulder. "It was probably just seeing her face on our album cover. She's too pretty to say no to."

"Dave." I slapped him playfully across the chest, unsure if it was an insult or a compliment.

"Hey! I'm not saying you weren't part of the reason we got the spot." His hands were up in the air in defence. "And when we're famous rock stars, you can live a life of luxury as payment."

"I can't wait," I whispered, turning to him. He stood deliciously close. He wrapped his arms around my neck and I inhaled his scent—exotic, spicy, and loaded with cologne.

"I can't wait for the first night of tour," he spoke into my hair. "For *our* first night." His words were loaded with meaning. I felt his hands travel a little lower, skimming over the curves of my hips. My school skirt suddenly felt very thin, and very short.

"Guys, get a room," Michael said. I pulled away, my face hot for the second time that day.

"We will. On tour!" Dave laughed, and threw his hand up in the air. Michael laughed and high-fived him right back, and I pretended to ignore their stupid boy banter. Nothing makes a girl feel special like a joke about losing her virginity, made by her boyfriend.

It was lucky I loved Dave—because sometimes he could be a downright jerk.

"Everybody, please line up NOW. They have STARTED ALREADY." Stacey's hands were on her hips as her blonde hair tossed from side to side.

"She's so cute when she's mad." Michael smiled.

"Good luck." I leaned in and kissed Dave on the cheek.

I made my way to my spot in line, leaving the two boys to walk to their allocated places in alphabetical order. They were next to each other, Belconnen and Belmonte. They'd actually met in roll call one year; funny to think they were now co-founders of one of the biggest on-the-verge bands today. I grinned a smug smile. Thanks in part to me, no matter what Dave said.

A blanket of silence settled over the line and I chewed my lip. I wondered if Dad made it, then hated myself for doing so. I hadn't needed him for the past year, and I didn't need him now. Mum and I did just fine without him.

The line shuffled forward and I felt the butterflies kicking around my stomach. This was it. I was going to graduate. My whole future was ahead of me, planning tours and events for the band, spending time with Dave, visiting different countries world over and—

"Tomlinson." Mr McDonald's voice boomed through the microphone, echoing backstage. I looked up. Front of the line already. I smoothed my hands down my blue-plaid skirt and plastered a smile on my face. Father or no, I was really doing this. I was finally going to graduate high school and go on the road with Dave—far, far away from here, from the memories that haunted our two-storey wooden house and this small, seaside town.

I strode out of the wings. In front of me, hundreds of parents gazed up at the stage, expectation written all over their faces. I swallowed. I'd never been great with crowds.

"A reminder that we'll hold all clapping till the end of each letter," Miss Lucas, the assistant principal, disciplined the parents as I crossed the stage to their side. *Because nothing disrupts a school assembly like unruly clapping.*

"Kate Tomlinson," Mr McDonald said. I walked up to him and shook his hand, ignoring the stench of stale sweat seeping from his shirt. I took the certificate from Miss Lucas and stood front and centre on the stage, right in front of the photographer to get my formal shot. On the left-hand side of the floor in front of me, three quarters of my year lined up, holding their certificates, too. Sometimes, being almost at the end of the alphabet was a blessing. At least I had a reprieve on smiling from letters A to S.

"Okay, taking your photo in three, two—"

"Yyyyyyes! That's my daughter!"

The voice came from the very back of the auditorium, accompanied by over-enthusiastic applause. My heart stopped beating for several seconds, stuck somewhere in between my throat and my chest.

What.

The.

Hell.

"Good job, Katie! Good—yob." I hadn't heard it for more than a year, but the voice was easily recognisable. It was my father.

My "dad".

I scanned the room till I spotted him. He was pumping his hands together, standing in the doorway, his mouth slack-jawed, eyes alive with enthusiasm. His voice was slurred and loud, too loud. When he'd left home, he'd been drinking a bit, and Mum and I had hoped his absence would have toned down his boozing.

Clearly, it hadn't worked.

I quickly glanced down to the floor beneath me, hoping that perhaps, by some weird stroke of fate, the parents and students with surnames A to S had failed to notice the display. It was no use. A hall of attentive eyes was flicking from me, to my dad, to the principal—back, back and forward, like spectators on an episode of *Jerry Springer*.

I was stunned. There was nothing in the student handbook about what to do when your father shows up drunk to your graduation. A few titters from students and parents alike spread throughout the room.

"Uh, I must remind you that you need to, uh, hold your applause to the end." Mr McDonald pushed his thick, tortoiseshell-framed glasses back up his nose as he attempted to take control of the situation.

It was no use. Instead of stopping his applause, Dad took this as a sign he should focus on making his vocal celebrations heard, instead of using his hands.

"My! My girl!"

My heart stopped its momentary statuesque state and sprang back into life, beating in double-time, as if to make up for any seconds lost. What was going on? Had Dad lost his mind? Even when he'd been drinking a bit before he left us, it was never during the day, and it was never like this.

No parent was supposed to do this, ever. As a teenager, the embarrassing things you were supposed to worry about included freaking out your mum would pick you up from school wearing slippers and a dressing gown. Or—worse—that you'd go to a party and she'd ask to meet the parents.

Not this.

Never anything like this.

"Yaaaaaaaaaaay Katie!"

This time, one of the teachers walked over to him, no doubt asking him to shut the hell up. My face was a mixed bag of emotion, a smile still plastered from eye to eye, but the corners unsteady, weighted by disappointment and embarrassment.

Why was this happening to me?

It was at that moment, with my face full of unspent emotion, that I was blinded by the photographer's flash and instructed to move on as they announced the next student's name. I shuffled my feet and went to join the crowd of kids already standing in front.

I kept my head down and pushed my way to the back of the group, not wanting to meet anyone's sympathetic eyes or hear the accusation in my classmates' voices. Mostly, they looked away, a few snickers doing the rounds.

"Who gets drunk at, like, ten am?"

"It's eleven, you moron," I snapped, my voice hushed so as to avoid detection and possible detention. I didn't know who'd made the snide remark, but I wished she hadn't. The worst part was their comment was nothing I wasn't thinking myself.

I chanced a look to the back of the hall. Mum approached Dad, reached out to grab his arm, and then took a step back as he jerked away from her touch. He shifted his weight from one foot to the other, like he couldn't stay still. My jaw dropped, ever so slightly. How could one person change so much? This wasn't the father who used to push me on the swing, help me with homework and pick my mum up when he got home from work, spinning her in the air like she was the most precious thing in the world.

This man was a mess.

"Kate, what's going on with your dad?" Stacey said, pushing her way through the throngs of students to reach my side. Her tanned arms were folded in front of her chest, her lips tight with concern.

The collective whispers around me faded to a hush. No doubt everyone was just as curious as she was to know why my father was acting like a first-class moron.

"I don't know." I shrugged. I looked down, studying the cracked, wooden floorboards at my feet. It was simple. When I got home, I was going to kill him. If he was there when I got home, that was. Who knew? Maybe he was going back to wherever he'd been for the past year when the ceremony ended.

I could only hope.

"I've gotta get back to my place up front, but we'll talk about this later, yeah?"

I nodded and tried to swallow the huge lump in my throat. It was hard to breathe. I could feel the makings of a panic attack coming on.

"Ahem." The principal cleared his throat. Unfortunately for me, no one noticed. Everyone, both students and parents alike, watched as my dad was escorted out of the room by two male PE teachers, their hands on opposite shoulders in vice-like grips.

God, if you kill me now, I'll never drink again, I silently bargained. Not that I really drank much anyway, but still. *Also, a hole in the floor would be ideal.*

Silence once again settled over the hall after Mr McDonald completed a sufficient amount of "ahem"-ing and coughing.

"Sean Toohey," he said, and the ceremony proceeded as normal. Well, as normally as a ceremony at a normal, everyday high school can proceed after a parent has shown up drunk and yelled at his kid in front of the whole school. You know: the hushed-whispers-occasional-glances-in-my-direction kind of normal. The crazy kind.

"Ladies and gentleman, I give you the class of 2014." The principal swept his arm in our direction. Around me, I felt bodies stand up straighter, jostle for position.

"You may now clap."

The hall erupted into an outburst of cheering, those with only one child applauding with extra zeal and enthusiasm. I saw Stacey's mum perform a few lazy golf claps. Stacey was the youngest of five. It was no wonder she was such an over-achiever.

After the applause died down, the sea of adults converged upon the mass of students to offer congratulations, hugs and, in some cases, presents.

"A Beemer? Dad! You bought me a Beemer?"

"Yeah, I'm proud, too."

"Can we go now?"

I tried to ignore the rush of voices and focus on getting to the front of the hall and the safety of outside as soon as possible. I felt a few people's stares as I shouldered my way through the masses, but at least only a few of the adults recognised me as the daughter of the drunken guy. Most of my fellow classmates were still stunned, stuck in the safety of our alphabetical-order fold, unable to move for the onslaught of parental congratulations.

I grabbed my phone from my pocket and held it in front of me, pretending I was doing something, anything; anything that wasn't being stuck in this moment. I pushed the heavy wooden hall door, and it opened with a screech.

All I had to do now was bolt to the car park, get in my crappy excuse for a vehicle, and drive. Maybe I'd take a day trip to Sydney, focus on my future life rather than my past. Although I did still have to pack for the boys' tour in four nights, and living on the road for six weeks would require a great deal of preparation.

"Kate! Congratulations."

Hearing her shrill overtones made me cringe. It was all I could do to not throw my arms toward the sky and shout, "Why me?"

Dave's mother was lovely, but she was very over-the-top, seeing me as the harlot who'd trapped her son. Two years ago, when I'd started dating Dave, she'd sat me down to have the "sex talk". I later found out she hadn't even had that discussion with Dave.

"We are all so worried about poor Deborah—I mean, your mother, dear," Mrs. "*Call me Cathy*" Belmonte shook her head. She was a bigger lady, who insisted upon wearing bright and colourful prints that Dave absolutely hated.

"It'll be fine," I mumbled.

"And so embarrassing for you. Come here." She pulled me into her cleavage and I struggled to take a breath under the scent of her thick perfume, a cross between potpourri and the samples aisle at a pharmacy.

"I'm fine, really. I should go, anyway, I—"

"We love Deb, don't we, Dave?" I hadn't noticed him appear by his mother's side. "Please tell her that she can come around any time."

Help! I mouthed the word over Cathy's shoulder to my longstanding boyfriend, but he didn't make a move. His face was blank. I drew my brows; what the hell was his problem? Normally, Dave and I would laugh about his mother's OTT displays of affection. Alarm bells sounded in my head. Image was very important to him. Was he pissed about what had happened with Dad?

"Well, it's been nice seeing you, but I really should be going." I finally managed to push myself out of Cathy's surprisingly strong, pale arms. I looked up at Dave, who stood there, still as a rock. His face was marble, a white sheet. "Are you going to head off now, too?"

"I don't think so." My heart fell through my body till it wallowed somewhere in my freshly polished black school shoes.

"Well, I'll see you tomorrow night at my house, then." I smiled sweetly and stretched up to kiss his cheek. His body stiffened against me. "Stop being a jerk," I hissed in his ear. Like this thing with Dad was my fault.

"Bye, dear." Cathy leaned in for another hug, oblivious to her son's sudden lack of manners.

"Bye, Cathy." I accepted the embrace with a tiny grimace.

"You can come over any time for dinner," she called. I power-walked toward the parking lot. "And don't forget, I'm trusting you to take care of my boy this summer."

I raced through the quadrangle of stale brick buildings to the leafy green trees and loose gravel that framed the parking lot. I jammed a key in the lock of my tiny, yellow Corolla from the 90s, slamming the door behind me once I was safely seated on the cracked brown leather seat. I just wanted to get out of there and drive, drive for a long time and forget this morning ever happened.

I started the car and felt a sense of purpose roll through

me as life took to the engine. Soon Dave would snap out of it, and he'd start getting excited about the tour again—get excited about us. I'd get to leave this town and see the country. Maybe I'd even get to organise another tour, really kick off my event management career.

I'd never have to talk to Dad again, if I didn't want to.

I pulled out of the parking lot and drove aimlessly, a trip around the cliff tops that framed the beachside town where we lived. I let the salt air blow through my hair, sending it streaking behind me like a kite. The music was up loud, almost to the point of distortion: a driving rock beat with big guitar riffs from Dave & the Glories' first EP.

I got home late and went straight to bed, not checking in with Mum beforehand. I was done with family today. The tour could not come soon enough.

TWO

NORMALLY, MY life was incredibly average. The next morning I woke at an average time and ate an average breakfast, while Mum fussed around the kitchen asking all the average mum questions like, "You're definitely not going to college this year?" and "This tour with the rock band … there won't be drugs or anything, will there?" and even, "While you're away, make sure you include a good mix of fruit and vegetables in your diet."

A lot of *yes Mum, no Mum*.

The elephant in the room was my father's drunken display the day before. For some reason, it felt like we were dancing around the topic.

"What happened with Dad?" I finally got a word in. She eyed me suspiciously, her hands poised, ready to open the refrigerator door.

"I haven't heard from him."

"He was drunk."

"I guess so, Katie." Mum took out a bottle of orange juice and placed it on the counter. "You know he'd started to drink a bit before he left."

Memories of those times flashed back to me: Dad, having a few too many beers, his unsteady gait. The slightly slurred speech he'd developed. One night, he'd been so drunk, he barely recognised me.

I'm glad he went away.

But I'm not. Or, I shouldn't be.

You're not supposed to hate your father.

"So, he's not coming back?" I raised my eyebrows.

"I'd like to see him try." Mum's auburn hair bobbed around her shoulders as she poured me a glass of orange juice and placed it in front of my bowl of cereal. She pulled out a wooden chair and sat at the table opposite me, a bowl of yoghurt and blueberries in front of her. She was acting normal, like nothing was wrong. Like people disappeared out of your lives, sent a text saying they wanted to show up at your graduation then appeared drunk-as-a-skunk every day.

I stared at my juice, silent. Just like that. He'd disappeared from my life, come back for a one-morning-only show, and now he was gone again. I hadn't exactly expected a happy family reunion, but I'd expected something. Something more.

Even though I didn't really like him … did I?

"It's no-added-sugar, darling, so go ahead and drink it." Mum pointed to the glass of juice in front of me. For some reason, she thought the idea that I could be dwelling on anything other than the carbohydrate count in my drink seemed rather unlikely.

"You're going out with Dave tonight, aren't you?"

"Mm-hmm."

"Well, just so you know, I've made an appointment with the doctor so we can get you on the pill."

My eyes widened, and I took a huge sip of orange juice.

Screw it, that wasn't nearly enough to give me the brain freeze I required to delete that comment from memory. I drained the whole glass.

"Don't look at me like that! I'm not as naive as you think." Mum shook her head. She speared a blueberry with her fork and delicately placed it in her mouth. "Your father and I used to have intercourse a lot."

"Mum." I drew breath.

"We did." Her eyes glassed over, and she had this weird, wistful smile thing going on. I wanted to be sick. "Not that we would any more, mind. You can't have sex with a drunk man, Kate."

"I won't! I have a steady boyfriend, I'm not going to go pick up some drunk—"

"I mean you literally can't. Physically. Men often can't perform when they've had too much to drink."

That was it. I really was going to be sick. I excused myself, and went to my room to start to pack for tour. I knew I was getting in early, but I always liked to be organised—and besides, what if I needed to wash a few things?

I took out the list I'd made a few weeks ago. I noticed Dave had scribbled the words *those red lacy panties* on the bottom of it. He wouldn't stay mad at me for long, and even though I was pissed he'd acted like such a douche about the Dad thing, I was kind of excited about wearing those red lacy panties for him, too.

I threw them into the bag, along with a bunch of bikinis, dresses and tanks. I rifled through my dresser drawers, discarding some items and adding others to the "maybe" pile until I found it. I shook out the black singlet with gold-embossed letters, reading their name one more time: Dave & the Glories. I clutched it to my chest for a moment, then stuffed it into a ball and threw it into my bag.

By the time I'd finished, it was late afternoon. Mum was at work, and I had the house to myself. Bliss. I grabbed my phone, thinking about Dave and smiling.

> **Hey babe, what are you up to? Wanna come 'round here instead of going out? Mum's not home …**

> **At band prac. Be there later.**

Okay, so it was hardly the "Coming right now, can't wait

to see you" I'd kind of been hoping for. But it was better than nothing.

I danced my way downstairs to make sure the kitchen was presentable. It was completely nerd-girl of me, but I hated having people over when the house was a mess.

After chucking a few saucepans under the sink, I did a quick time check. Perfect: six o'clock. If Mum wasn't home by now, there was a chance she wouldn't be back until after ten, due to the nature of her shift work. Hopefully, Dave would come around well before she got here.

I raced around the living room, turning out all the lights, and then darted into the kitchen, rifling around the pantry for some candles. A bit of mood lighting would definitely help.

I'd hit my head on one of the high shelves and stopped to give it a little rub when I heard the screech of the screen door being yanked open. He was here early!

I tiptoed to the kitchen counter and laid down my candle stash. I'd just have to start my mood lighting in here.

"When we have to, that's when."

The voice was accompanied by the sound of keys in the lock. That was odd. Mum was home early.

"No, now!"

I froze. That voice belonged to my father.

Once more, it was the childish, slurred sound. He was drunk.

Again.

He was in the sanctity of our home, a place he hadn't been for a little more than a year. I closed the pantry door and pressed my forehead against its smooth surface. What was happening? Why was he here?

"Paul, maybe we can put you in care, just for the night. She's going away on tour in three days, then we have weeks to plan how we'll tell her."

What? Plan what? In care? Was Dad going to rehab?

"No care. I want to be here." This last sentiment was accompanied by a *thwack*, as if something had fallen from a shelf, or perhaps Dad had drunkenly slammed into the hallway wall.

"You need to stay calm and concentrate. I'm trying, Paul. I'm not entirely sure why, but I'm trying." Mum's voice was clipped.

My heart slid down to my stomach and I held my breath. What was going on?

Was my drunken father moving back in?

It felt like something out of a movie. I didn't belong in this scene. I delicately tiptoed to the end of the tiled kitchen area. If I was fast enough, perhaps I could slip past them and straight up the stairs, escaping observation whatsoever. But the sinking feeling that had lurked in my belly since Dad showed up at school turned into an anchor. It weighed me down, forcing my feet to stay rooted to the spot.

"Oh! Kate. Hi," Mum said, as she rounded the corner into the kitchen. Dad was draped over her shoulder, leaning on her for assistance. He was worse than I'd thought. "We didn't think you were at home. Why are all the lights off?"

I watched as Mum helped Dad into a chair at the breakfast bar. The whites of his eyes weren't the bloodshot colour I'd expected them to be, and he didn't smell of booze. His posture gave him away, though. He was hunched, bent and slack, like his bones were jellied. When Mum released her support on his shoulder, he slumped forward like a sack of potatoes before righting himself.

"What's he doing here?" I raised my eyebrows. He couldn't just walk back in here, needing our help like this. That wasn't fair. Not when he'd embarrassed me so much and disappeared for a whole year.

"Sweetheart, we'll talk about it in a second. Can you go get me a beer from the fridge outside, please?" Mum dismissed me.

"The last thing he needs is another drink." I pointed at my father's sorry figure.

"It's not for him. It's for me."

I stepped back. For my mother? But she rarely drank. We only kept booze in the fridge outside for special occasions.

So what was so special about this?

"Make that two," Dad's voice was breathy, exhausted.

"No."

"Kate …" Mum warned.

"Not until somebody tells me what's going on." I locked eyes with my mother, engaged in a silent stand-off.

"Kate. Tomlinson. Go and get me a beer from the outside fridge. *Now*." Mum's words were fierce, her eyes flashing with anger.

I sighed and stomped out the back door, walking through the slightly too long grass accompanied by a chorus of cicadas to the garage where we kept the second fridge. It housed copious amounts of water, soft drinks and beer, as well as the occasional supply of ice cream I liked to hide from Mum.

I opened the door and covered my mouth. The room before me was a dirty, dusty mess. I kicked at a wrench lying on the floor near the entrance, watching as it scratched out a path past tools, Mum's car and the window, which offered a twilight view of our empty driveway with its fresh-cut grass. Everything looked so normal out there.

Heat radiated off the engine of Mum's Ford as I stepped closer to it. That was when I realised.

Dad's car wasn't in the garage; Mum's was. I hadn't really expected it to be parked alongside hers, what with him clearly having been on a bit of a bender, but if he really were here for two days or more, where had he left his pride and joy?

How had he even gotten to the ceremony yesterday?

My mind started spinning as I tried to piece it all together. Maybe this had been a long-term problem, the reason he left. Maybe he'd sold his car to pay for drinks, and bought a ticket back to see us when the money finally ran dry?

I shook my head. That was the sort of behaviour drug addicts engaged in, not the sort of thing my father would do.

Would he?

I made my way through the dirt, around the bumper of Mum's car and retrieved a bottle from the fridge, slowly traipsing my way back through the garden. The beer was cool, a nice contrast to the summer air that had my armpits drenched in sweat.

Mum and Dad weren't in the kitchen anymore. They'd retired to the living room, with its almost floor-to-ceiling window draped in floral curtains, and its cream suede couches, which surrounded a wooden coffee table in the middle.

I handed the bottle to Mum then sat on the edge of the couch opposite them, facing the window. Outside, a summer breeze was tilting the heads of the flowers in the garden, their shapes highlighted by a streetlamp as it flickered to life. Night was officially here.

I didn't want to look at my parents. A feeling of impending doom hung in the air.

"Kate, there's something we need to tell you," Mum started. Her hands shook as she flipped the top on her bottle of beer. Her lower lip started to tremble. "It's … about your father."

I turned my attention to him. He was seated apart from her, just a little. His hands were shaking, too, his eyes sallow and sunken. He looked thinner than I remembered him, and every now and then his left knee gave a tiny spasm, as if he couldn't keep it under control.

My earlier thoughts came rushing back.

That was the sort of behaviour that drugs addicts engaged in …

"Are you … are you on drugs?" The words I never thought I'd speak came out. Mum choked on a mouthful of beer, causing Dad to pat her on the back. Tiny droplets of alcohol landed all over the room, over the coffee table and on the stack of old magazines sitting in the corner. Some fell on Dad's leg, which he attempted to pat dry with another unstable gesture.

"I told you it wasn't that ridiculous," Mum said.

"Your mother thought that, t … too." Dad shook his head and stared at the beige-coloured carpet next to his brown scuffed shoes. *Funny.* I remembered them from when he'd leave them at the door after work.

"What is it, then?" I kept my voice level.

Silence enveloped the room, and I widened my eyes,

raised my eyebrows. Any time, now …

"Your father—he's sick."

The words echoed around my head, repeating themselves over and over.

Sick. My father was sick.

"What do you mean? The kind of sick where you get better soon?"

"The kind of sick where you—"

"I have a disease." Dad said the words with pride, like he wore them as a badge. He straightened his posture a little, chin jutting into the air.

I could hear my heart thudding.

My father was sick. He had a disease.

"In the way that alcoholism is a disease?" I bit my lip.

"No." Mum sighed. She was frustrated; her tone gave her away almost as much as the hand on her temple. "A disease that affects his behaviour."

I blinked. It was all I could do not to jump to my feet and scream. What sort of a disease changed the way you acted? Yesterday I'd graduated from high school, and today my parents were trying to tell me that my dad had a disease.

So why was everyone taking so long to get to the goddamned point?

"What *kind* of a disease?"

Please don't say cancer. Please don't say cancer.

I didn't know anyone who'd had cancer, except for one of Stacey's grandmothers. She developed kidney cancer and died six months later.

That couldn't happen to my dad.

Please don't let that happen to my dad.

"It's called Huntington's disease."

"Phew!" I smiled, my lips wide and almost at my eyes. I was an over-animated version of my normal self to counteract the melancholy occurring on the couch opposite.

But even as I tried to be enthused about it, I knew it was wrong. Their grim faces didn't look like the canvases of people celebrating. "I mean, at least it's not cancer, right?"

"It's not cancer, no." Mum shook her head. She placed a trembling hand on Dad's leg. "It's different from cancer."

"Different how?"

"It's a neurodegenerative disease," Mum replied. I narrowed my eyebrows. "It destroys the brain cells that can effect movement, speech, memory and—" Before she could finish the sentence, big, fat tears started snaking their way down my father's face. He held his head, shaking, his calloused veiny hands raking through his grey-flecked hair.

Mum put her arm around his shoulder, and he moved closer to her. After all her comments about him previously, after all he'd done, she was letting this happen. This sickness must be something really, really bad.

A chill ran through my body.

"Kate, your father has a terrible disease. At the moment, he's having trouble controlling his movements and his speech." Mum recited the words as if she'd written them down. "However, in time, he'll lose the ability to control them entirely. His memory is affected. He is going to require constant care and supervision."

My eyes widened. What? My father was going to—

"Dad's going to go … to lose his mind?"

The room fell silent. No one answered me.

"Well, that's it, isn't it? He's not going to be able to control what he does, how he speaks, what stays in his mind and what doesn't. Isn't that kind of the definition of the concept?"

I was on my feet now, shouting. Why was I so angry? I tried to slow my breathing, calm my heart rate, but my body ignored me.

"How could you have let this happen? You're not old enough to be—to be just having this happen. And *you* left. You left us!" I jabbed my finger toward him, stabbing the air in front of his face. I was yelling so loudly I was sure the neighbours could hear.

"Kate, calm down." Mum shook her head. Dad didn't say a word, just kept up his full-body sobs as he cried, tears for a life he would never lead.

Shaking, I nervously backed my way over to the couch.

"So. Okay. How does this work? Why are we only hearing about this now?" I slowly lowered my body, letting the pillows support me as I felt the will to move drain from my limbs. *Take in the facts, Kate. Gather information. Process. Breathe.*

"It started more than a year and a half ago. Small signs, at first. Nothing you or I really noticed, like involuntary movements of his body, depression and slurred speech." Mum's forehead creased. "Or, if we did notice, we blamed it on his drinking."

"It's why I was drinking." Dad raised his head to look at me, his tears momentarily subsided. "A … addiction is a common trait when you have H … Hunting …"

"But you left," I cut him off.

"He did, yes," Mum said. "He knew something was wrong, so he went to get some tests done. He found out he had the disease, but didn't want us to have to deal with—this. The next day, he sold his car to pay for treatment at a care centre, which is where he's been living the past year."

"So, you just didn't tell us? And decided to come back to ruin my graduation?"

Another awkward silence panned out as Dad glanced sheepishly at Mum, then back to his hands that were quietly writhing away, clenching and unclenching in his lap.

"I c … couldn't afford the treatment anymore," Dad said. "I wanted to see you graduate. But I had—I had a few drinks."

Fact check: My dad was back, and he was sick. Real sick. Drinking was a part of the problem. A disease was destroying his brain.

I felt removed from the situation, like I was watching the news. This sort of thing didn't happen. Not to normal people like me.

"Couldn't drinking deplete your brain cells? What were you thinking?"

Dad started to cry again, a new wave of tears, and I brought my hands to the bridge of my nose. What was he thinking? What was I thinking? He was sick, and he was my father. And

I was hardly being understanding.

"Are you—okay?" I tried again, even though it was clear he wasn't. No one answered. There was nothing even remotely okay about this.

We sat there in silence for a few moments, me leaning back in my chair in shock, Mum stroking tiny round circles on Dad's back as he shook some more.

In books, people say that bad news can make you look older. I hadn't really seen evidence of that before, but looking at my parents, I could definitely see the toll of time wearing on their faces and bodies: slumped shoulders, crushed foreheads, tired eyes. My middle-aged parents had become old.

"Katie, I'm sorry." Dad raised his head and looked at me. His blue eyes were surrounded by fiery-red streaks from the tears he'd shed, little spidery veins of sadness.

"It's not your fault."

"Th … there's more."

I clutched the edge of my seat, my fingernails digging deep into the creamy suede material. What else could there possibly be? What could possibly be worse than a disease that was going to make him half a man?

"I'm … I'm going to die."

The words ricocheted through my body.

Die.

My dad was going to die.

"He doesn't mean in the 'everyone-is-going-to-die-one-day' way, sweetie, he means—"

"Mum, I know what he means." I snapped my lips together. "H … how long?"

"Prognosis is good. About fifteen to twenty years." Mum stared at her nails, unable to make eye contact.

"Wow." I thought about all the things that would happen in the next fifteen to twenty years. I'd move out. I'd have a tour management career. I'd get married. I'd have children. They'd grow up, and Dad would be there for some of it, but not all of it. One day, my dad was going to die, and my kids may not ever have known him except as a distant memory.

One day, I was going to have to face the world alone.
Without him.

Even more without him than I'd been for the last three-hundred and seventy-something days.

"This is just—it's a lot to take in." I bit my lip. "I'm sorry, Dad."

I stood from my seat and crossed the room, hovering over him with my arms extended in an awkward sort of way while Mum, reluctant to leave his side, extended one of her hands to my shoulder.

I felt myself still as time slowed down. My hand was on Dad's shoulder, and he wasn't hugging me back. It was surreal, this moment, seeing the drool as it pooled in the corner of my father's lip. Was this really happening?

"How sweet." I heard Dave before I saw him. He'd walked in the door without knocking. For the first time ever, I wished he were a tiny bit less familiar with my home.

"Hi." I quickly disentangled myself from our embrace and smoothed down my shirt, before walking to Dave's side. He gave me a quick peck on the cheek and handed me a weighted plastic bag.

"I bought ice cream," he smiled, "but only for three." The last sentence was directed with a cool gaze in Dad's direction. I elbowed Dave in the ribs. Couldn't he see that my father was upset?

"Deb, do you need me to remove any unwanted guests?" Dave took a step towards my parents. His knuckles were fisted, white bones showing through. Mum shook her head, no.

"Can you help me pop these in the freezer?" I grabbed the plastic bag from Dave's hands and walked to the kitchen. He followed.

The second we were alone, he cornered me against the bench, his arms on either side of mine so my body pressed hard up against his.

"Now I can give you a proper hello," he whispered in my ear and started nibbling against it.

"Dave." I sighed, and gave him a nudge. He ignored me,

pressing closer still.

"Dave. Seriously." This time I gave him a shove, and he stumbled backward. I pushed away from the bench and opened the freezer to put the ice cream in.

"What's your problem?" His arms were folded and his face was grim.

"Dave, it's Dad," I whispered. "He's sick." Even as I said it, the words seemed surreal. How did I describe an illness I barely knew anything about myself?

"Like, a sick idiot who ruined graduation?" I punched Dave on the shoulder. How could he be so tactless when I was trying to tell him something important?

"Stop being such a shit," I hissed. "He has a disease. Something starting with *H*." The actual name escaped me. I hadn't heard of it before today. There was no "day" or "month" to honour it, like there was with cancer or MS.

This disease was going to steal my father from me—and it wasn't like anything I'd ever heard of.

"What sort of disease?"

"It affects everything. He's going to lose control of his speech, his movement—and then he's going to die." I felt tears well in my eyes and forced them back. Dave put his arms around me and I collapsed into him. I breathed in his cologne as he stroked my hair.

"How long?"

"Mum said maybe fifteen to twenty years? He's going to die," I repeated the words, with little to no inflection. I was removed from myself, from this scene.

"You'll be okay."

His words were of no direct comfort to me, but feeling his arms take my weight and support my body helped. I stood there for a moment, losing myself in him, and let my thoughts fly. I was angry Dad hadn't told us, furious he'd run away, and devastated about the whole situation. I'd never felt so many emotions before: mad, upset, protective, confused, and hurt. Was this normal? To feel everything, all at once?

"I have to go back out there." I forced out the words. I

pulled back to look at Dave's face, his pale skin, his electric-green eyes … he looked so steady, so sure. I wanted to stay in his arms forever.

"We'll go together."

Dave placed his hand on the small of my back and led me back into the living room where my parents waited.

"Kate told me." Dave walked over to the couch. "And I'm sorry, man. That's really rough." He stretched his arm out and took Dad's hand, pumping twice before joining me on the opposite couch. Dad's forehead creased up.

"Paul." Dad nodded slowly.

"You've met Dave, dear, that's Kate's boyfriend."

"Dave," Dad repeated, stretching the word out on his tongue.

Everything my parents had said became somehow more real. Dad had met Dave before, many times. And yet, here he was, acting like he was being introduced to a total stranger. Memory loss.

Wow.

"Dude, you like, came to some of our concerts."

I gave a sharp kick to Dave's ankle.

"Kate, I know you must have a lot of questions," Mum said. "So feel free to ask us anything, anytime. I'm still—I'm still trying to take it all in myself."

"O … okay." I'd never stuttered so much in my life.

"And there is something else we need to tell you, dear."

"Deb, not now. Give 'er a rest," Dad interjected, his voice sounding ever more weary with each passing word.

"What? Tell me." My fingers clenched into tiny fists. "What could possibly be worse than what you've already said?" I felt Dave place his arm protectively around my shoulders.

"Maybe we should wait." Mum eyed Dave's hand.

"Anything you have to say, you can say in front of him." I shook my head. "He's family. You know that." Dave and I locked eyes, and he gave me a special little smile.

"Kate, it's not a good time." Mum's voice was shrill. My heart was beating like a jackhammer, *thud-thud-thud*, over and over in double-time.

"If you don't tell me now, I'll Google it. I'll just search the disease and see what I can find. We both will."

Silence. Dave took my hand in his, clasping his other hand around it so I was protected entirely within his palms. Mum and Dad looked at each other, her lips pursed, his still loose.

"The disease your father has …" Mum paused. I nodded at her. *Go on.*

Just tell me. Get it over with.

"It's hereditary."

I struggled to breathe as Dave's fingers slowly unlaced themselves from mine.

THree

WHEN YOUR whole world falls apart, there's not a lot you can do about it. When I found out my dad was going to lose all body control, and Mum told me the same thing might happen to me, I did what any normal person would do.

I walked up the stairs, all zombie-like, and shut myself in my ridiculously neat room. I got into my largest T-shirt. I cracked open my emergency packet of Tim Tams and mixed a bottle of cola with some hideous cheap vodka.

Then, it was horror-movie therapy time. Tarantino, Rodriguez … I rented them all online then watched them, back-to-back, like a junkie. I started to close my eyes once, and then quickly pinched my arm, forcing them back open again.

After two am, I switched from cola to Red Bull to keep the adrenalin pumping through my system. Slash, slash, slash. Stab, stab, stab. All this pain on screen, blood, gore and guts, distracting and enveloping me with its all-encompassing hideousness.

I had to stay awake. I couldn't fall asleep.

You never fall asleep in dreams.

I woke to a piercing shriek, undignified, contrasting and loud. I managed to narrow one eye open into a squint. Light blasted from under my curtains and I saw my room: the boxy shape of my desk, my laptop, the plastic wrapping from the Tim Tams.

I identified the phone on my desk next to the computer as the nearest noise source I could control, and pressed "cancel" on the incoming call. Stacey could ring back another time. My laptop was right next to my phone, so I grabbed it and slammed the lid shut. I had no idea how long the intro music to *Planet Horror* had been looping, but judging from the way the tune continued in my head even after I turned it off, I'd be willing to guess a long bloody time.

"Kate, honey? It's time to get up."

Mum's voice was outside the door. I rolled my eyes. Why on earth would I want to get up? I didn't have school to go to, and I—

The previous night's events came flooding through my mind like a highlights reel on a DVD. Dad had a terrible disease. He was going to lose his ability to speak and move, and be normal. He'd need permanent care. He was going to die. And, oh yeah, it was hereditary. So there was a chance I'd end up with it, too.

I groaned and threw my head back down on my pillow. *Happy end of high school to me.*

"Kate? You go on tour in two days. You need to get up and pack. Have you finished packing?"

I looked around my room, surveying the half-filled suitcase. Was "kind of" a good enough answer?

"Katie, I'm coming in if you don't reply soon."

Mum's definition of the word "soon" appeared to be approximately ten seconds, as that was how long she waited before bursting through the door, concern etched all over her face in her worried eyes, and thin lips. She sat down next to me on the bed, the crinkle of plastic wrappers celebrating under her feet.

"You know, chocolate is never going to solve your problems." Mum picked up the rubbish and placed it in the empty trashcan next to the bed. "I would have thought you, of all people, would know that."

"Mu-u-um," I groaned. "You know I don't care about that stuff."

"I've told you before, you're beautiful now, but in your early twenties … the weight just starts piling on, if you're not careful." She tutted and shook her head.

"What does my weight matter if I'm going to die?"

"Oh, Kate." Mum wrapped an arm around my shoulder, pulling me loosely across her lap. "There's only a fifty per cent chance of that."

"So, it's like flipping a coin?"

"More or less." She sighed and pulled away, studying me. "I know you've got a lot of thinking to do, but you're about to go on tour with the boy you really like—don't let this stop you. Your dad is going to be here when you return."

"He's moving back in?"

Mum nodded, a movement so minute it was almost imperceptible.

"He left, and you're just letting him back?"

"He left to protect us from what was happening to him." I leaned in closer to hear her speak. "And he—he's been through so much by himself. We have to be there for him, now." There was no anger, just hurt in her eyes.

"So, now what? Now we need to live with it?" I bit my lip. He was still my dad; I didn't mean to sound so bitchy, but … I didn't know how I felt, about any of it. "I just don't think it's going to be as easy as 'He moves in, we start playing happy families.'"

"We won't. It won't be. It's going to be a big adjustment for all of us."

I picked at a thread on my bedspread. The black-and-white print was done in William-Morris style, one of my favourites.

"If I have it, when will it kick in?" My voice was tiny.

"It typically hits you when you reach middle-age, so it could be years yet. Dad actually got it quite late. Legally, you can be tested for the disease once you reach eighteen. I've booked you a specialised counselling appointment for tomorrow, so you can ask an expert some questions before you go on tour. Normally there's a wait list, but I told them about your special situation, and they squeezed you in."

My mind was stuck on her first sentence. *Typically*. The average person.

But what about the not-so-average person? What about the one in a million?

"Is there any chance it could kick in … next year? Or the year after?"

I was frightened. I concentrated on biting my bottom lip, so hard I could feel my bottom teeth on the other side of it.

"Kate …"

"It's not fair," I protested. I pressed my hands to my face. "It's just not fair."

"The chance of the gene developing while you're so young is very slim. Besides, you haven't even taken the test yet." Mum rubbed my back. She smelled like fresh soap and clean linen— normal mother smells. Not mother-who-is-married-to-a-diseased-man smells. "Let's talk about this when you get back."

I let her comfort me. It felt like a dream.

"Fifty per cent, huh?"

Mum nodded.

Fifty per cent.

They weren't the worst odds I'd ever heard.

I stood up and scrambled through the papers and books piled neatly on my desk, letting them float softly to the floor as I searched for the coin I knew would be there. I picked it up, balancing it precariously on the back of my hand.

"Heads or tails?" I asked her.

"Kate." Mum shook her head, stood up, and walked to the

door.

"Heads or tails," I insisted, raising my hand.

"That isn't a fair test."

"Heads, tails, or leave me alone."

Mum's eyes glistened, just for a second, and I thought about what a horrible person I was being. Then my instincts kicked back in. This was about my future.

"This isn't a game. We can get you tested properly, but it's completely up to you whether you want to or not. I understand if you'd rather wait. It's a lot to take in—your father coming home, him having a disease, things changing as we adjust to it all. You may not want to know if you're likely to develop it. You're allowed to not want to know."

Silence.

"Would you?"

I switched my attention from the coin to her. She didn't look nearly as happy as she had earlier. She rested her body against the doorframe for support, her freshly ironed skirt pressing against her knees.

"I—I don't know." Mum's voice was quiet. "When I was at an age where I was thinking about having kids? Absolutely. Now, though? I … I don't know."

I hadn't even thought of that. If I had Huntington's, my children could get it, too.

We remained in silence for a few minutes. One part of me felt relief. Leaving, running away with Dave, suddenly sounded a whole lot more appealing. I wouldn't have to deal with it—I wouldn't have to be here for this.

The other part of me was shocked I could try to live a normal life when everything I'd ever thought was real was crumbling.

"Tails, I have it. Heads, I don't."

I flipped the coin. It flew up in the air, circling its way inches from the ceiling then crashing back down to the floor where it landed next to an empty soda can.

I watched it bounce once, twice … then looked away.

"Well?" Mum asked.

I pursed my lips. I didn't want to look anymore. It had seemed like a good idea, but now—now it just seemed scary. I didn't want to know about my problems. Dad's were enough to deal with.

My shoulders started to shake, and I fought to control them. Mum came rushing over, her arms around me, rocking me back and forth as all mothers are programmed to do.

I didn't cry. I just sat there, arms by my side, and let her hug me, stroking my hair like she'd done when I was a little girl. When she eventually stopped she picked up my bin and the empty soda can, taking them outside to empty into the trash.

After half an hour, I managed to swing my legs out from under my quilt and put them on the floor. They felt steady, fine. I was in control.

I grabbed my suitcase from the corner of the room and did a final check, and then zipped it tight so none of the items inside could escape.

I wasn't leaving for two days, but Dave had a show in Sydney tonight, and I was going to watch. Maybe I could stay with him till we left town for good.

Breathe, Kate.

Breathe.

There were eight hours till the gig. I could go downstairs to the house computer, check all the travel arrangements and finalise the band's request lists for the gigs.

As I pulled the door closed, something caught my eye in the middle of the bedroom floor.

I walked over to it, seeing the coin where it had finally landed after its third or fourth roll. I took a deep breath.

I needed to know.

It was tails.

Four

EVENTUALLY I left the sanctity of my bedroom, had breakfast, and mucked around on the Internet for a little while. I checked that all the tour information was correct, that we did indeed have accommodation and transport and funds for petrol organised for the entire two-week trip. Next, I updated the band's social media sites, tweeting and posting that "we are so excited to be on the road soon" and blah, blah, blah, "isn't it going to be amazing, there will be so many babes."

It was so weird. I often wondered if the band's fans would be in such a rush to DM me naked photos of themselves, or shots of their boobs, if they knew the person writing on the website was a girl.

Although, the fact that I monitored it meant the band didn't know about the constant and gratuitous offers of sex, either, and that certainly wasn't something I was about to let slip.

"Where's Dad?" I asked Mum. She was in the kitchen, hovering over the chopping board, bread, ham and tomato in orderly piles next to the knife.

"In the bedroom." She delicately arranged the ingredients and cut her sandwich into two precise triangles. "He's a bit clumsy today."

"Oh." I took a soda out of the fridge and sat at the counter, like it was the most normal thing in the world.

"He'll be out soon."

I took a long gulp, letting the cool bubbles swell in my mouth. I didn't want to be in a house where my father was locked up like a little kid. Tour couldn't come fast enough.

The more I thought about it, the more I struggled to breathe. The air was thick, choking my lungs, invading them with a sense of despair I wasn't sure I could cope with.

I pushed back the hair from my face and clenched my jaw.
Breathe in.
Breathe out.

I had to get out of there. I grabbed my suitcase from upstairs and clunked it down the hall, two steps at a time, rolling it past the kitchen.

"Bye Mum," I yelled, as I slammed the door behind me and headed out to the first show of the tour.

The relief I felt as I walked out the front door, the weight lifted off my shoulders, was astronomical. My steps were lighter. The sun was shining out from behind a particularly dark-lined cloud.

There's something to be said for the art of running away.

After the hour-long drive to Sydney I found an easy park, just around the corner from the club. Stacey and I met out front, arriving what we hoped was fashionably late. Unfortunately, so did the other four thousand fans attending the "intimate" Coal gig that night, meaning four thousand other barely-dressed females stood in line with us, waiting to have their IDs checked and stash their oversized bags, some of which seemed to use more material than their outfits. Apparently, some of the girls attending had taken the term "intimate" as a dress code, not a venue size.

"When are they on?" Stacey checked her watch for what felt like the millionth time. For someone whose boyfriend wasn't in the band, she sure was keen on seeing the start of the show.

"How come? Are you worried you'll miss seeing hundreds of girls screaming at Michael?" I teased, nudging her with my shoulder. Stacey coloured, just the tiniest bit.

"Oh, Kate. Stop looking at me like that." Stacey laughed, and fished around in her handbag for some lip gloss. She found it and reapplied, even though her lips already flashed with the sheen of glossy perfection.

"Well, you know, it is a little odd." I took the proffered gloss from her hand and quickly swiped it over my own lips. "Usually you ignore Michael, or pretend to vomit if he so much as accidentally brushes your shoulder."

"Did you ever think that maybe I miss the attention?" Stacey looked out at me from wide blue eyes as we shuffled forward in the queue.

"Stace, don't toy with him. I know he acts all goofy, but I'm fairly certain he actually does have a heart."

"Tickets and ID," the burly security guard instructed, and I handed them over, noting the tribal tattoos on his incredibly thick arm.

I wondered if he'd have much work to do tonight, shielding Coal and their incredibly hot lead singer, Lee Collins. Then I wondered if he'd have to protect Dave and the band from all the scantily-clad, super boozy girls strutting around the place. The band had played a few gigs lately, and Dave sure seemed to get a lot of attention from the girls. *Would he prefer to be with one of them, and have a no-doubt Huntington's-free lifestyle?*

I shook the thought from my head, grabbed my card and ticket stub back from the security detail and walked inside the club, lifting my feet with extra effort as they stuck to the thin, dirty carpet.

The room was brightly lit with a red-painted bar in the

corner, next to the doorway that led to the room with the stage in it. All around us people were hanging out, draped over railings, slumped against chairs, or milling in the drinks line.

We joined the queue and slipped through the gaps, trying hard to avoid touching other fans and covering ourselves in their sweat.

The main room was more packed than the foyer, people crammed in together near the front of the stage where I could see the familiar amps and drum kit of Dave & the Glories. The ratio of girls to boys was about 70:30. The chance of my toes being trod on through my flat sandals by a girl in stilettos was dangerously high.

"So, did you see your dad after graduation?" Stacey cupped her hand around her mouth to yell at me.

Huh. You could say that.

"Yeah," I yelled back.

"Did he apologise? What was his problem?" A girl dressed in a black, shiny miniskirt rammed into my back, sending me reeling forward till I crashed into someone else's arm. This venue was hardly the ideal location to share my family's deep, dark secret.

"I'll tell you later," I said, and she left it at that.

"Do you want to stand near the front?" Stacey leaned close to me, and I smelled a hint of beer on her breath. She'd been in Sydney all day. Clearly she was ready to party.

"It's okay. It might be a little lame." I didn't like being front and centre when Dave played. It made me embarrassed, which I knew was silly. After all, if he played football I wouldn't have any hesitation standing on the sidelines to watch him at our local clubhouse.

But your local clubhouse doesn't have a 70:30 ratio of girls to boys, Kate.

And the girlfriends at football games attend these outdoor events during winter. They're definitely wearing more clothing than the ones in attendance tonight.

The noise became deafening as the lights dimmed. Stacey gripped my wrist in excitement, flashing me a huge grin. This was it. The moment had come. The boys were going to go on stage.

Dave strode out first, followed by Michael, then Benny, and Nick, the newest member to the group. The girls screamed and squealed, and I saw the flashes of hundreds of cameras go off, highlighting the boys' frames against the backdrop. My heart started to beat faster. That was my boyfriend people were cheering for.

A rush of pride enveloped me, and I screamed out with the rest of them. It was a wordless yell, just noise contributing to noise, but it felt good. I'd helped organise the tour and here they were, on the first night. This was really happening.

"Sydney, you are looking good tonight," Dave said, as if he didn't live just over an hour's drive away. He picked up his guitar and extended his arm ninety degrees from his body, sweeping across the audience. "We're so excited to be here, supporting one of our favourite bands, the awesome Coal!"

If the screams had been loud before, they were deafening once he said the other band's name. Not waiting for the din to die down, Michael struck his guitar, the drums let out an almighty smash and the band kicked into motion. I lost myself in their music, swaying slightly to the beat. It was one of their newer songs, a high-energy, fun number I'd only heard a few times. Dave sung the lyrics into the microphone, his hips gyrating against the stand as his guitar hung, unused, from his neck.

The chorus started and he grabbed the guitar and strummed it, power emanating from him. The crowd yelled in approval, and I saw Dave bounce back from their energy, giving more and more, playing harder, louder, and faster than I'd ever seen him play before.

"*I'm gonna kiss that girl goodbye*," he snarled the hook line of the chorus with no backing behind him. When the music roared back in, the cheers started again. The excitement was palpable.

"That's your boyfriend," Stacey squealed in my ear, shaking her hands up and down.

Dave launched into a guitar solo, ripping through notes and flinging the neck of his instrument around like it was the most consuming musical break known to man. The crowd loved it. I saw the girls at the front of the stage screaming, their hands in the air, reaching up to try to touch him whenever he'd come dangerously near the stage's lip.

The solo finished, and Dave let the guitar hang again, then clasped both hands around the microphone as he sung the chorus one final time. The girls down the front screamed appreciatively once more. I could just see their platinum-blonde hair highlighted in the stage spotlights.

"*I'm gonna kiss that girl goodbye.*"

When the last line was sung, I saw Dave make direct eye contact with somebody in the front row. And he winked at them.

Winked!

My boyfriend … He'd winked at someone?

Was I allowed to be upset about this, or not?

Should I be?

The crowd erupted, jumping up and down and applauding for a band that only two months ago was virtually unknown. I pushed the thought from my mind and instead tried to focus as they launched into their next song, a slower number with a driving bass line, one they'd written years ago.

Stacey thrust her hips in time to the music, shimmying with the beat, and soon, a pair of male arms snaked around her waist. I smiled. Trust her to get the attention of what felt like one of only five males in the building.

I turned my attention back to the set, losing myself in the music as the boys played a short collection of songs I knew like my own personal anthems. When Dave let out his final cry—"We are Dave & the Glories, good night!"—my heart swelled with pride. The crowd was screaming. They'd played well. My boyfriend's first major gig had been a success.

"I'm just going to the bathroom," I said to Stacey, who still had her arms wrapped around her new friend's neck, even though the music had stopped.

After showing the security guard my stamp, I strolled up the stairs, wondering what I'd do to kill time for the next five minutes or so. Of course, once alone, my thoughts flew to Dad.

How much worse would he get?

How long would he have?

And—shit—*what should I expect from this stupid counselling appointment tomorrow?*

A girl in a silver skirt barged my shoulder as she walked past and I stumbled into the wall, catching myself with my blunt nails.

Am I invisible, I wanted to yell.

If I get the disease, will I be? I knew that kind of disappearing act. It was the kind of invisible people are when they're publicly drunk, or have a mental illness; everywhere they walk, people turn away, busy their eyes, their hands and their minds.

I turned around and headed back to the foyer. I didn't want to be alone anymore. I searched out Stacey, and found her with her mysterious new suitor, lips locked.

I just couldn't find the words.

"They're signing autographs."

"The opening band?" A girl standing behind me squealed. I pricked up my ears, full eavesdropping-mode kicking in.

"Yeah, Dave and the something-or-others. They're just inside the doors to the room."

Treasuring this nugget of information, I made my way back toward the stage area. Talking to Dave, feeling his arms around me, his voice telling me everything would be all right was something I needed to get through the rest of the night.

I scanned the room and found a clump of girls surrounding a small table with some shirts and CDs pinned to the wall above it.

I approached, seeing the boys talking enthusiastically to a group of six girls in front of them. They were all smiling and laughing.

I took a deep breath. Was I jealous that the girls talking to Dave were pretty? Or was I jealous that with them he seemed happy and carefree, whereas his last two interactions with me were all about my family problems?

When I was three feet away, Dave leaned over to the leader, a girl with blonde hair wearing a low-cut black singlet. The girl lifted up her singlet, holding the front over her head so she could see out underneath it … as my boyfriend, Dave from Dave & the Glories, slowly signed her boobs with a black Sharpie marker.

He didn't use his hands to hold the Sharpie in place.

Instead, he used his lips.

FIVE

WHEN I saw my boyfriend sign another girl's chest, it was too much. Instead of marching up and confronting him, embarrassing him in front of his newfound fans, I ran to the bathroom, shut myself in a cubicle and concentrated on breathing.

Which was I more upset about, the boobs or his smile?

This really wasn't a big deal, was it?

But why did he look so happy?

Even as I heard the sentence in my mind I knew it sounded lame. What sort of a rock star wouldn't sign boobs? It was bad marketing for him to refuse that kind of attention. And it wasn't like he kissed her, or anything.

The delicate notes of the start of a Coal song filtered into the bathroom, mixed together with the sound of faucets and flushing.

Keep it together, Kate.

I pulled up my pants and pulled myself together, running downstairs to the sold out main room where thousands of girls were now pulsing to Coal's beat. It was easy to fall into their music, and I found myself swaying, hypnotised by the talented lead singer, Lee Collins, the first singer I'd ever had a celebrity crush on. I tried to ignore the sick feeling twisting my stomach into knots and watched the rest of the gig with Stacey and her new friend who, by the final song, were shamelessly making out on the dance floor.

Dave found me leaning against a wall next to the overly affectionate couple when the music stopped, and I was so glad to be getting out of there I'd all but forgotten the incident earlier. This was our night. *The* night.

As soon as his hands wrapped around my waist and his lips pressed against my cheek, I shivered, desire flashing through me.

"Can we get out of here?" I whispered in his ear. Dave snapped his head around to my face and kissed me on the lips, hard and passionate, tasting of beer and sweat and success.

"You bet," he said into my mouth. He grabbed my hand and led me to the backstage door so he could get his guitar, flashing his pass to let me through security.

Backstage was nothing like I'd expected—no red carpet, no chandeliers. Instead, it was stark white light in a messy room with carpet that needed a serious cleaning. A table of untouched food was set up in one corner and an empty cooler in the other. The back wall was covered in graffiti, signatures of bands that'd played at the venue before. I stared at the wall, trying to see what the famous people wrote, how different it was from standard high school graffiti.

Killing Time 4 EVA was scrawled in a script font level with my shoulders. An arrow was pointing to it just underneath, where someone had scribbled *Suck a dick*.

Apparently, high school graffiti and rock star graffiti were pretty much one and the same.

"Nice job, man."

My eyes widened.

That voice.

Was it … Lee from Coal?

"Thanks, dude." Dave walked behind me, and I spun

around, almost falling over in my enthusiasm.

There he was: Lee Collins. He was tall, much taller than Dave, with icy blue eyes and a rough jaw of darkened stubble. His hair was a little too long, and he exuded this animal magnetism that made my heart get all *thump-thump.*

"We've got a really good fan base at the moment," Dave was saying, which was good as it meant I could keep staring and ignore the fact I could barely feel my knees. I was completely star-struck. Lee-freaking-Collins!

"Yeah, seems that way." Lee smiled this slow, sexy smile, and I swallowed.

"We've just gone from strength to strength. It won't be long before you're opening for us, bro." Dave gave Lee a light punch on the arm.

Oh, God.

Ground, please open up and swallow me.

What had Dave just *said*?

You just didn't joke about someone like *Coal* being your opening act. They'd won a Grammy, for crying out loud.

"Kate."

I glanced at Dave, feeling his elbow give me a sharp jab to the ribs. I widened my eyes at him. Why was he being so rude in front of Lee, who was—

Oh. Whose hand was outstretched in my general direction.

Like, waiting-to-shake-my-hand outstretched.

"Hi," I said. I think. At that point, I could have also died, I'm not really sure because I was touching Lee Collins's hand. My knees went weak. It was lucky he was holding my hand, because if he wasn't, I was sure it would be shaking.

"I'm Kate." His eyes were so blue, so deep, I felt I could stare at them forever.

"He knows. I just introduced you." Dave threw an arm around my shoulder.

"Hi … again?" I tried. *Well, this could be less awkward.*

"All right man. We'll see you on the road." Dave grabbed his guitar case and ushered me down the hall, back into the throngs of people outside the venue.

"Maybe don't act so obviously in love with him when we're on tour," Dave muttered as the blast of fresh air hit my face.

"I was just—it was Lee from Coal, Dave," I said. "I'm not in love with him. It was just the initial celebrity thing. You know I'll be cool."

"Good."

We found Stacey and said our goodbyes, and I waved when one of her brothers came to pick her up. Dave signed a few more autographs, and then we walked two blocks down the street, and entered through the sliding doors of a much cleaner, brighter hotel, with white marble floors and sprawling timber ceilings.

I heard a few hushed voices pointing Dave out and felt some glances in our direction but Dave seemed oblivious, only giving a slight nod to the hotel clerk as we walked past the check-in desk and entered the lift.

"You've already checked in?" I asked, once the metal doors closed behind us.

"Of course," Dave replied. He flashed me a tired smile. Any tension he'd felt earlier seemed to have disappeared. My own anger at the boob signing, the star-struck moment meeting Lee—they were gone. Tonight was about us, after all. "What a night, huh?"

"Totally," I agreed.

The doors opened and we walked in silence down a corridor until Dave produced a key and stuck it in a lock, pulling it out and holding the door open for me as I walked in.

The room was beautiful. A huge king-sized bed with a white quilt lay before me, the lights of the city sparkling out the window like little twinkling stars fourteen storeys below. A bottle of champagne was chilling in a bucket at the end of the bed, and pink rose petals had been strewn everywhere, like a scene from a movie.

"They wouldn't light the candles for me, in case it burnt the place down while we were on stage." Dave propped his guitar against the wall then pulled a lighter out of his pocket, darting around the room to illuminate the wicks of the clusters of red candles on the bedside tables.

"It's—it's beautiful." I breathed out, slowly. It was amazing. Dave had done all this—for me?

"You're beautiful." He placed the lighter down, and came over to me once more, his hands cupping my face gently between them. His green eyes glittered darkly in the dimmed light. "I'm so excited for our tour."

He ducked his head, stepped into me. I brought my lips to his, and we kissed. His tongue darted inside my mouth and I felt him, warm and wet. His kisses were lazy, lolling around, but his body pressed against mine with urgency till we couldn't get any closer. I tried to focus, to get excited by it all, and moved my hands to his waist, raising them up his body over the damp stickiness of his shirt, feeling the muscles in his back, the tone of his sides.

Dave moved his mouth to my neck, and I inhaled sharply as he sucked against it. Soon, his hands were roaming all over me, up my back and around to the sides of my ribs.

We stepped toward the bed, him moving backwards but never letting the gap between our bodies widen, always covering my mouth with his, as if he couldn't get enough of the taste.

We reached the bed, and he sunk down onto it, pulling me with him. I lowered myself over his body and concentrated on keeping my weight on my hands, trying not to squash him.

After a few minutes, Dave tried to swap our positions so he was on top. He fell to the side a little, his hand getting stuck behind my back. I giggled, and he held a single finger to my lips, a slight frown on his face. Apparently, this was not a laughing moment.

Seconds later, it was back on. I felt him kissing my neck, sucking and pulling at it, biting my ear. It was wet, and he really was sticky after sweating it out onstage. I found myself staring at the small round lights on the ceiling, wondering if this was how it was supposed to feel, and when exactly I was supposed to take my clothes off. Would he do it, or would I? Would there be an interim time where we were both in underwear?

And *ow!* I was fairly certain he wasn't supposed to grab my nipple so hard *through my shirt* that I wanted to yelp.

I scrunched my eyes shut and tried to get lost in the moment again. No one's first time was great; Stacey had warned me.

We rolled onto our sides, and Dave's hands worked their way down the edges of my top and lifted it up. They explored my stomach, tickling their way over my ribs, until they reached my chest, kneading through my bra and cupping my breasts.

Dave's earlier boob autographing flashed through my mind.

I tried to ignore it, focussing instead on the present.

"Oh, Kate," Dave groaned in my ear. His hands were trying to get inside my bra now, one fiddling with the clasp, the other trying to access from underneath.

What exactly had he written on her chest, anyway? Do you address the autograph "Dear Tits" or use the girl's name?

And why am I thinking about this now?

I pushed Dave away, managing to get a tiny bit of distance between our top halves, our legs still firmly intertwined.

"Okay?" he asked. He was already leaning back in, desperate to close the gap between us again.

"Dave, wait." I placed my hand on his chest. He stopped, a slight frown marring his otherwise ghostly white forehead.

"Wait?" A dangerous edge serrated his voice.

"I just need to ask you something, that's all," I said, chewing on my lip. How on earth was I going to phrase this one?

"If it's about protection, I brought—"

"No, no, it's not that. It's just—" I paused. My pulse started to race again, and not with lust. "—just that I saw you signing some girl's boobs earlier, and I was wondering were you attracted to her, or will you do that at all the shows this summer, and—"

"You're stopping this right now because you saw me signing some girl's boobs?" Dave's words dripped with disdain. He untangled his legs from mine, shifted his arm away from my body. His actions hurt more than his words ever could.

"You saw me doing my job, interacting with a fan, after which you all but threw yourself at Lee Collins, and—"

"I did not throw myself at him." My jaw dropped. "I've just never met someone famous before."

"You looked like you wanted to fuck him."

"I'm sorry." I curled my legs up under me. "I didn't want to—it was just that celebrity thing. It won't happen again."

"But still, you're going to persist, and act like me signing Tara's boobs is a big deal?" He raised his eyebrows.

Tara.

He'd remembered her name.

"It's not a big deal," I said. "I was just wondering, you know?"

"What does it matter whose boobs I sign or touch during the shows if it's you I'm sleeping with at night?" Dave sat up, fire in his eyes.

"Whoa, calm down, babe. It was just … a …" I leaned forward and hooked my hand around Dave's neck, pulling him closer to me. It wasn't that big a deal.

We kissed, and I threw myself into it. I pressed my body against his, I thought only sexy thoughts, and I sucked in my stomach and tried like hell to look hot. When I reached for the hem of his shirt, though, Dave grabbed my hand, roughly pushing it down over his crotch. He squeezed my wrist so tight it hurt.

"Ow!" I pulled back, snatching my hand away.

"What now?" His face was unreadable.

"You hurt me." I gave a half smile and shook my head. He was being so *weird* today. What the hell was wrong with—

"I don't think I can get past this."

I blinked. *What?*

"I am so into you, Kate. I've stayed with you for two whole years, even though you've held onto your virginity like it was your last card in a high-stakes poker game, and you're trying to stop me now? When I've done all this, even after everything with your dad the other day?" Dave gestured to the room around him. I took it in; the flower petals, the champagne, the sweet scent from the candles that had melded with the rose's perfume.

"I appreciate what you've done." My voice wobbled. "And I'm not the one stopping here. I'm ready; I told you."

Dave slowly exhaled and bent over, resting his head in his hands between his knees.

"You know, this isn't easy on me." He didn't even look at me. His eyes were fixed firmly on his big, black boots.

"It's not easy for me, either." He gave no indication that he'd heard.

"When I told the boys and Coal about you and your dad, they—"

"You told the band? You told *Coal*?" I flashed a murderous glance in his direction. I hadn't even told Stacey, and he'd gone and shared this precious nugget of information that was less than twenty-four-hours old with his stupid band mates, and a Grammy Award winning act, all of whom I'd be spending the next two months with on the road?

"Well, how do you think this is for me? Coping with all this, and the tour?"

"The tour I organised?" I sprang to my feet. "Is that the tour you're talking about?"

"Please, don't flatter yourself." Dave raised his hands in exasperation. "You made a few phone calls and booked a few flights. I didn't ask you to. In fact, the only thing I've been *asking* you to do, you keep bloody denying me."

His words were tiny needles, jabbed all over my body. I blinked, and focused on not crying, not losing it right here in the middle of the hotel room.

"Then w … what am I doing here, if I'm denying you that?"

Dave stood up and walked over to me. He placed his hands on my arms, and looked me up and down.

"Kate." He swallowed, staring me straight in the eyes. His voice was flat and hard. "Take off your clothes."

"What?"

"Take off your clothes," Dave repeated, never breaking his icy gaze. "Prove that you were planning on giving yourself to me tonight. Strip for me."

My knees trembled. Dave was my ticket out of here, the way I could avoid dealing with my intense, new family life. We were arguing now, sure, but that was kind of my fault as well as his, and we'd been dating for two years—even though I felt like he was a bit of a jerk right now, we were meant to be together.

Weren't we?

Slowly, I joined my hands to his, lifting them gently off my shoulders and placing them at his sides. I was surprised I didn't send the nervous shudders straight out from my fingers and into his.

I raised my hands to my sides and lifted up my T-shirt, throwing it over my head and letting it land on the floor next to me. Swaying my hips to the side, I threw my hands out in a ta-da movement, like I was the host on a game show.

"And the jeans." Dave nodded and took a few steps back to the bed, sitting down and crossing his arms. His face was blank, and his eyebrows were raised. I'd never seen him look so unimpressed.

I flipped the button and undid my fly, slowly pulling my skinny jeans over my thighs, my knees, my calves, and finally my ankles and feet. There was no way to do it and be sexy, so I settled for not falling over. I stepped out of my pants and stood up straight, in only my underwear.

Dave checked his cell for messages.

I felt sick.

My stomach roiled.

"Go on," Dave instructed. "Sexier, this time."

I raised my hand behind my back, and started to fiddle with the bra clasp. I couldn't get the damn thing to unhook, and tears welled in my eyes. My hands wouldn't work, falling apart in the sort of fumbles I'd seen my dad do the other day.

It seemed like a nightmare, like this was happening to someone else. Was this really what someone who cared about me would make me do?

And why did I feel like he was judging every ounce of flesh on my body?

"Anytime, now …" Dave widened his eyes impatiently. I was surprised he wasn't tapping his foot.

I couldn't do it anymore. I dropped my hands to my side, my bra still very much on.

"I told you, you were never gonna do it." Dave stood and threw his hands in the air. He bent down to grab my shirt and threw it at me. "Get dressed."

"I was! Just not like this." My voice was raw with emotion. I scrambled to get the shirt back over my head and felt my breath release once it covered my stomach.

"There's always gonna be something with you." Dave stepped right in front of me. I felt the spit flying off his tongue land on my face as he spoke. "I didn't ask to have a girlfriend with a crazy father."

I felt as if he'd shot a cannonball out his mouth, and it had landed, smack bang in the middle of my stomach. I clutched at my sides, fighting the urge to double over in pain.

"He's not crazy," I whimpered. "And I didn't ask for it, either." I stood there, still as a statue while Dave walked back to the bed. He blew out the candles on either side of it, flicked on the lamp, and cleared the rose petals out of the way with one fell swoop of his arm till they were scattered all over the floor.

How had this all gone so horribly wrong? And why did my heart feel like it was cracking in two?

"Don't you get it? I mean *I* don't want one. I don't want a girlfriend who might lose her freaking mind," Dave yelled. He grabbed my jeans off the floor and threw them at me, the metal button connecting with my wrist. "Honestly, I was going to let you come on tour, but do you think I could seriously have a girlfriend with a crazy father when we make the big time? Put your clothes on. Go, get out!"

I blinked. This wasn't happening. This couldn't be happening, not after two years of dating and all the work I'd completed on the tour and just—just everything. I felt a solitary tear snake its way out of my eye, over my cheekbone, and down my face, playing kamikaze off my jaw.

"We're over, Kate. O-ver." Dave sucked the marrow out of the word. A flimsy breath shuddered up my throat. "Move."

His word snapped me into action. I threw one leg into my jeans, and then the other, pulling them up so hard and fast I was worried I'd push through the material. I held the sides closed and did up the fly, threw my shirt over my head, and grabbed my clutch and shoes as I ran for the exit, sobs heaving in my chest.

I slammed the door behind me and ran for the stairs, not wanting to risk taking the lift and running into other people, people who would see the ugly mess of tears that had taken over my face.

I charged past the receptionist who moments ago had looked so in awe of me being taken up to the room by my romantic rock star boyfriend, and ignored the now-smug shape of her upturned lips.

When I got to my car, I turned the lock and slammed my body against the seat. I draped my arms over the steering wheel, shoulders hunched as I tried to shut out the world.

I slumped there till the first rays of the sun crept over the horizon, and filtered through the tall brick buildings in the surrounding car parks.

In three days, my dad had embarrassed me at school, I'd learned about his disease, discovered my chances of developing it, found out the guy I thought I loved had told his friends and a Grammy Award winning band about my potential illness, lost my boyfriend, ruined the start of my tour-organising career and said goodbye to my ticket out of this stupid town.

There was nothing I needed saving from more than my past, my future, and myself.

SIX

"SO, HOW come there's no psycho couch?" It was the first question that came to mind when I stepped into the genetic counsellor's office. It was a small room with a big, open window framed by deep-blue curtains on either side. A desk cluttered with paper, books, and a model of a brain with moving parts was in the corner, two slimline office chairs next to it.

"Pardon me?" A woman whose name I'd learned was Leslie asked. She looked to be about Mum's age, maybe a little older, and had blonde frizzy hair loosely pulled back into a bun. Streaks of grey ran through her locks, and tiny wrinkles gathered near her eyes. Was that a side effect of the job? Counselling people who were going through a whole lot of issues would surely bring out the greys in anyone.

"You know, like in the movies. When people go see a psychiatrist, they lie on one of those chaise lounge thingys." I took a seat, a plain black one, close to the window. "Nothing offensive, but this isn't anywhere near as comfortable as it looks."

"Firstly, I'm not a psychiatrist, I'm a genetics counsellor," Leslie explained. "And secondly, if you're not comfortable, I can grab a cushion for you."

"It's fine." I shifted my weight from one side of the chair to the other. "I just kind of feel like maybe if I was super relaxed and at a chaise lounge level of comfort I'd be more inclined to share my deepest, darkest secrets with you, you know?"

"I don't intend to trick you into revealing any secrets, Kate." Leslie leaned back in her own chair. Over her shoulder, I could see her computer, an open Word document with my name at the top all lit up.

"Is that where you're going to write your notes about me?" I nodded toward the screen.

"Yes," Leslie said simply.

"Can I see my notes?"

"If you want to."

"What are you thinking of writing so far?"

"That it might be time to rethink my interior decorating." Leslie gave a wry smile, and I couldn't help but to dip my head with respect in return. Score one, Leslie.

"So, do all the counsellors in here deal with people like me?" I studied the little skull model on her desk. *I wonder if it's so she can point out where the broken hides in people's brains.*

"Not exactly," Leslie said. "We deal with youth and diseases, so a lot of cancer patients, or those who have family members suffering from a life-altering illness."

"Bet you drew the short straw then, getting me."

"Not at all." Leslie raised the corners of her lips. "Firstly, you're in a unique situation and I'd love to help you. Secondly, I happen to specialise in Huntington's, unlike some of the other counsellors here. And thirdly, while you'll see me face-to-face, we work as a team. My colleagues and I discuss all our clients—under the strictest confidentiality, of course—and brainstorm ways we can help you best."

Fantastic. I would be part of a group science experiment. I *so* didn't want to be here.

This morning I'd woken up in my car, driven to a public

toilet block, and changed into the gym clothes I'd had stashed in the backseat from some previous occasion. They weren't any cleaner than the outfit I'd worn last night, but somehow they felt less dirty.

Then, I'd driven the twenty minutes across to the other side of Sydney to make it to this counselling session—the one I really didn't think I needed right now.

"Mum booked this appointment for me." I folded my arms and tilted back in the chair.

"And how did that make you feel?"

"Oh!" I slammed my feet to the floor. "I *knew* you were going to say that. It's like, straight out of the movies or something."

"And how does that make you feel?" Leslie gave a wicked grin, and this time I graced her with a fully-fledged smile. Maybe she wasn't the enemy after all.

I continued to smile and looked out the window. You could see the garden of the hospital, acres of neatly manicured green grass with flowerbeds lining the cream brick buildings that surrounded it, purple and pink hydrangeas bordering the edges.

"So tell me about your experience with Huntington's so far," Leslie suggested gently. Her voice was calm and relaxing. It was no wonder she worked at the state's top facility. I could tell she would be irritatingly good at her job.

"Well, my father came home after a mysterious one-year absence and embarrassed me by showing up drunk at my graduation," I started. "Then, I found out he'd run away when he found out he had Huntington's. Then I learned it was hereditary, my boyfriend dumped me 'cause he thinks my dad is an embarrassment, and that I'm going to go—you know, cuckoo—and it left me with nothing to do with my life, since I'd wanted to plan his tours and be a band manager, or event organiser, or something. But I guess having nothing to do is probably a good thing. You know, since I might die soon, and all."

Leslie nodded and pursed her lips. She wasn't even writing

any of this down. I furrowed my brow.

"Shouldn't you be taking notes as I go? It might be awkward if I bring this up again and you ask me if I'm in college, or something, when I just said I wasn't."

"Let's go back to the part about you having nothing to do." Leslie spaced out her words evenly, a light inflection on each one. She was definitely good at this. Every time I fired up, tried to get a rise, she'd make me feel all relaxed. *Irritating.* "What do you mean you have nothing to do? Sounds like you have a lot on your plate."

"Nope." I shook my head and folded my arms across my chest. "Nada. Zilch. *Nothing.*"

"So you're not helping to care for your father?"

"Well, I will be, a little." I frowned. "It's just—I wasn't even supposed to be here. I haven't thought about it."

"And you don't want to." It wasn't a judgment, simply a statement.

"He left, and didn't tell us what was wrong or where he was going." I hadn't realised I was still angry about that till now. "Then he ruined everything. My graduation, my summer, my boyfriend … *everything.*"

"Have you asked him why he didn't tell you?"

"Kind of." I shrugged. Out the window, a young girl was helping an older man manoeuvre his way across the lawn. I wondered if that would ever be me: the young girl, or the old man. "He said he only came back 'cause he ran out of money."

"So perhaps he didn't tell you before because he didn't want to burden you."

The words clicked.

It made sense.

I hated that it made sense.

"What do you think about that?"

I hadn't really thought anything about that. I'd known I was embarrassed when he told me, and mad, and ashamed of him in public.

I tried to think how I'd feel if it turned out I did have the disease. God, I hadn't even told Stacey about Dad yet. My shoulders slumped. If our situations were reversed, would I man up and tell the world? Or would I run away like he had?

"Kate, this isn't about judging you and your reactions." Leslie rested a hand on her knee. "It's about working out how you feel. Huntington's is a very complex disease, and it brings out a range of emotions in people, from anger, to embarrassment, to depression, to denial. Any and all of these are normal. For both you *and* your father."

I let her words sink in as I continued window watching. Outside, the girl and the old man had reached the other side of the lawn and were sitting down together under the shade of a huge old maple tree, nestled amongst its knotted roots. I wondered if that would ever be me and my dad. If a relationship like that was ever possible for us.

"I'm going to tell you a little more about the disease." Leslie shuffled some papers on her desk and came out with a brochure. I could see from the purple writing on the front it was called *Helping with Huntington's*, or something as equally trite. Fabulous.

"Huntington's causes a deterioration of neurodegenerative skills," Leslie recited. "The disease generally takes about three years to completely set in, although symptoms are hard to diagnose at first, with things like clumsiness, and distant behaviour being common." I let out a breath I didn't know I'd been holding. Was that my dad? He'd always been kind of clumsy, sure. Had he had this lurking monster inside his head for a few years, and I hadn't even realised?

"Addiction is a common side effect, with things like drinking becoming a problem for some sufferers. Control of the limbs and speech will deteriorate at varying speeds for varying patients. General prognosis is fifteen to twenty years from first onset," Leslie kept on reading. "The most common life-threatening complications are pneumonia, followed by heart complications and—finally—suicide."

I blinked. I looked outside at the old man and the girl by the tree. Now the elder gentleman had his arm around the young woman, holding her close in a loving way. I tried to erase him from the picture, imagine him swinging from the tree with a rope around his neck. I tried to replace his face with my dad's.

I shook my head and pushed the picture out of my mind. What was wrong with me? Thoughts like that weren't normal. He was okay. My dad was alive, unwell, but alive. I was a sick, sick person to even think that.

Sick.

Like my father.

"How can I get tested?" My eyes snapped back to Leslie. She placed the brochure down on her desk and pressed her hands together. Her eyes were a cold blue, the kind that made you feel they saw everything.

"Well, you need to see me again"—Leslie counted on one finger— "then I'll refer you to a neurologist, to confirm you have no visible symptoms of the disease already, then you'll see a psychiatrist, and then you can get the blood test." She ticked off her fourth finger.

"Why a psychiatrist? Isn't that pretty much you?"

"It's to make sure you're not a suicide risk, Kate." Leslie's smile was sad. "I'm a counsellor. I'm here to help you along the way, and guide you through this—whether you end up deciding to get tested or not. However, I'd encourage you to wait before taking the test. There's still so much of your life you need to deal with."

"But how can I make plans if I don't know if I'm going to die or not?" I shrugged. "How can I meet guys, or start a career, knowing that in twenty or so years I could fall sick and die?" My hands shook. "What's the point in doing anything until I know? *What's the point*?" I leaned as far forward in my seat as I could, inches from Leslie's face. Unwavering blue eyes met mine. I felt naked.

Leslie reached over to the desk and took the brochure. She opened one of her drawers and took out a small, white paper bag out from its depths, and placed the brochure inside. She pressed it into my hands.

"For you." Her voice was calm as ever.

"I guess I'm dismissed now, huh?" Each breath was a struggle. When did it become so difficult to breathe?

"My next appointment is due." Leslie stood up. She walked over to the door and put her hand over the knob, ready to pull it back.

I grabbed my handbag from the floor and stuffed the brochure inside, like it was responsible for potentially giving me the disease.

"Kate, it's not that there's no point in doing anything until you know," Leslie's words were gentle. "When you know what the point is, that's when you'll be ready."

I raised my eyebrows at her and stormed out. I didn't even stop at reception to pay my stupid bill. I was sure they had Dad's credit card details on file; surely he could spot me one lousy counselling appointment.

As I flew out of the building, I grabbed the stupid brochure and slammed it in the bin next to the doorway. Three words kept flashing through my mind over and over:

Waste. Of. Time.

seven

AS SOON as I'd darted through the front doors of the giant counsellors' building, I turned a corner into a small courtyard and flattened myself against the wall. The dark-brown bricks felt cool, supporting me with their sturdy weight as I pressed my back up against them.

What had just happened?

And what the hell was I going to do next?

I grabbed my phone out of my handbag and shot a quick text off to Stacey, telling her Dave and I had broken up. If only the rest of it—the why, and the telling her about this stupid disease—would be as easy.

What? So no tour?

I felt like throwing my phone against the concrete path that snaked around the building in front of me, but I resisted. Like that was the biggest problem I faced right now.

No tour.

Two minutes later and my phone buzzed again.

Do you still have your flights and the special hotel booked for Queensland?

I thought about it. I'd booked a separate hotel room for Dave and I to spend the first week of tour in, paid for it myself after working part-time at a chemist all year. Of course, I still had the booking and my flights. But I couldn't use them now; I couldn't risk running into Dave. Maybe he'd already tried swapping the room over to his name, anyway, even though he technically had a second room booked by tour management on a less fancy floor of the hotel.

Yes. But I can't use them. I don't want to see him.

Too late. Found flights on sale, we're going. I know you paid for the suite—you're not wasting it! Meet you at the airport at 7 tomoz xx

Apparently, I wouldn't have much choice in the matter. I rolled my head against the building and thanked a potentially deaf God for the fact that I had at least organised the accommodation. I shot off a quick email to the hotel manager—I knew they had a sister property slightly further south. Perhaps I could move our room there, meaning I'd only run the risk of seeing Dave on the plane, and not at the hotel where the band had also booked rooms.

I kicked off the wall and looked at the winding path that led to the parking lot. After being trapped inside that claustrophobic emotion-inducing office I didn't feel like hopping back in my tiny yellow car, and driving the hour-long trip home. I felt like walking, stretching my legs.

No, scratch that.

I felt like running.

I grabbed my ankle and pressed it behind me, stretching my muscles out in the privacy of this tiny courtyard. Birds sang gaily in the branches of the giant willow tree across from me and I tried to block them out.

Next, I kicked my foot out and leaned forward to touch

it. It was a good thing I'd changed into those workout clothes, after all. Maybe I could do a few laps around the building—this giant ambiguous counselling office—before starting the trip home. I switched legs and bent down again. To sweat, to feel exhaustion and pain—I needed the physical accompaniment to my internal turmoil.

"Nice ass," a deep voice said. I jumped and quickly straightened up. Heat rushed to my cheeks as my head spun from left to right, trying to identify where the voice had come from.

"Sorry," the voice came again, only this time I identified its source. A guy stepped out from behind the tree, lit cigarette in hand. He was tall, about six-foot, with floppy brown hair, olive-toned skin and chocolate-coloured eyes. A tiny freckle marred his right cheek. A small smile was twisted on his lips, showcasing a dimple that made something twinge inside of me.

"You can't do that." I frowned.

"You bend over in my presence, and I'm not allowed to compliment you?" The guy stepped forward, closer to me.

"I was stretching." I shot him what I hoped was a withering look. "And you were hiding behind a tree."

"I was relaxing behind a tree." He stepped closer again, and I saw the light dancing in his eyes. "But I do realise I might have come across a little sleazy. I meant it as a compliment. You have a great ass. Much better than some of the others I've seen around here."

"You do this all the time?"

"Depends on what you mean by 'this.'"

"Stand behind trees and check out people's asses." A tiny smile crept onto my lips, and I tried to force it back down.

"Only when I have time." This time, a full-blown grin stretched its way across his mouth and I was treated to double dimples and square, white shiny teeth. "What about you? Do you, er, stretch at counselling centres a lot?"

His words brought me crashing back down to the present. I was at a counselling centre, a specialty one, for people coming to terms with illness. I was here because my dad was dying, and I could be, too. Some random guy had flirted with me, but I'd probably never have a boyfriend again because who would want to date someone with my problems, as Dave had oh so kindly pointed out?

Reality = checked.

"No." I shook my head. "Anyway, I was just leaving." I turned my back and looked at the path in front of me, trying to decide which way to go.

"Great." The boy nodded. "You're going for a run?"

I didn't answer. Maybe if I ignored him he would get the hint.

I chose left and jogged down the path, a slow gait at first while my legs got used to the activity. It felt weird, running in the middle of the day in a park I'd never been in, but I didn't care.

As I turned the corner I picked up the pace, my knees pumping up and down with extra speed. I passed windows in the multi-storey brown building, more giant, gnarled willow trees like the one out front, and brilliant flashes of lime-green grass.

I wondered if anyone inside the buildings were looking out at me, like I'd looked out at the young girl, and if they'd make up stories like I had. If they tried to envision themselves as the stranger sprinting down the concrete path.

A thin layer of sweat broke out on my back and I rounded another corner. The grounds were massive, and I remembered the map I'd seen out front. There was the counselling ward, a care area, and specialty centres. Each building had the same look and feel, the same staple bricks-and-mortar pattern that managed to be both boring and comforting at the same time.

My knees raised higher, my feet hit the pavement faster. I felt a light breeze tickle my neck.

How many other people like me had come in here and freaked out? How many others had this disease?

My legs moved triple time and I could feel the burn start to creep over me. I pushed, pushed harder and kept going, determined to run until it was no longer a possibility.

When I felt the sharp pain move from my thighs to my chest, I turned a corner again and slowed to a stop, my hands on my knees, my breath coming short and sharp through my mouth. I gulped down hungry mouthfuls of air, as my legs shook and my heart ached, ripping through my chest.

It feels so good to hurt.

So freaking good.

"You're—you're crazy."

I shot up and turned around. Jogging over to me was the guy from the tree, cigarette still in hand. Sweat circled his white T-shirt under his arms, and I could see the sheen of dampness on his collarbone. The veins were popping out from his thin, yet lightly muscled arms.

"I'm crazy? *You* followed *me.*" If I'd been unsure of his weirdness before, this confirmed it. You don't follow someone on a jog around a counselling facility after checking her out. It just wasn't normal.

Says the girl with a potential neurodegenerative disease.

The stranger held up a single finger as if to say "one minute", then flopped down on the grass, flat on his back, and stretched his arms and legs out as far as they could go. He was breathing heavily, his chest rising and falling in dramatic peaks and troughs. His left hand was raised, the cigarette hovering dangerously close to the grass.

"You shouldn't smoke." I stared disdainfully at the offending item, orange embers still faintly glowing.

"I'm not … I'm not a smoker." The guy gave me a tiny smile before turning his head to the blue sky above.

"You're clearly smoking." I crossed my arms.

"I'm just trying it," he said, eyes locked on a marshmallow puff of a cloud in the distance. "It's important to try new things." His breath was more controlled now, slowing down to something like a normal rate. So was mine. I focused on not breathing at the same time as him.

"When people say that, I don't think they mean try things that can kill you." I snorted. I eyed the patch of grass next to him. I was exhausted, physically and mentally from the emotional rollercoaster of the past few days, and I wanted to join him.

Or I would want to join him, if he wasn't a creep who had checked me out, and then followed me.

A cute creep.

"On the *contraire*." The stranger grinned. "I think that's exactly what they mean."

I furrowed my brows and turned away. "Look, it was nice to meet you, but—"

"What about 'What doesn't kill you makes you stronger'?" he interrupted. I widened my eyes in disbelief.

"What about it?"

"Well, surely the things that make you stronger have to stand a chance of killing you, hence the distinction in the sentence."

"So you think the more you smoke, the stronger you'll be?"

"No." The boy turned his head and locked his dark eyes with mine. "I'm just saying I'm going to try everything once, and if it hurts, or it gets hard, it's going to be worth it. It's about living in the present. Having no regrets."

I flitted my eyes skyward and turned away. He was "one of those." I knew the type; moralistic, optimistic and incredibly annoying, all rolled into the one Disney-movie package. Next he'd break out into a chorus of "Don't Stop Believing."

"Do you have a list of things you need to try *for the first time*?" My voice was laced with sarcasm.

"Nope."

"Then how do you remember what you've done, and what you need to do?"

The boy pulled something out of the back pocket of his jeans, a small pad of white paper. He waved it in my direction like it was of great importance.

"I capture the image of the best part of the new thing I tried." He waggled the notebook enthusiastically. "And the way the drawing goes, the way it looks—if it's rushed or delicate, soft lines or hard—then I remember the experience, and if I regretted it or loved it."

Right. Because that was normal.

"Well, I hope you don't regret smoking while jogging," I said as I walked away. I didn't look back, but I couldn't hear any sounds that would indicate he'd moved from his grassy bed.

"I won't," he yelled. He sounded like he was smiling.

He was cute—seriously cute—but I had just been dumped, and wasn't interested, anyway. I thought about my lack of career, my new title of single late-teen lady, my weird family situation and my potential time-bomb-till-diseased future status.

I didn't look back.

EIGHT

When I arrived at the airport, the first thing I saw was Stacey's blonde ponytail, bobbing amongst the crowds of other teenagers with their oversized bags and print-out tickets. The Coal tour manager had chosen the most popular time of year for our visit to the Gold Coast, an area famed for being Australia's version of Cancun.

Not 'our.'

Their.

A few of the girls were wearing matching hot-pink or black velour tracksuits with diamantés on their bums, spelling out words like *princess* or *bitch*. I shuddered. Thank God I'd never felt the slightest urge to wear one of those.

"Stace," I called out, and pulled my wheelie bag over in her direction. She was leaning against the flight-information desk talking to a very cute male flight attendant. She looked gorgeous as ever in her simple white tank and denim shorts combo.

"Kate." She threw her arms around me, as if we hadn't seen each other in months, instead of days. "It is *so* good to see you.

I was just telling my new friend Alex here about your stressful day at graduation, what with your dad and all. And about your loser ex-boyfriend." Stacey's face turned sombre as she shook her head in Alex's direction. "Dave & the Glories: never listen to them."

Now that I knew the truth about Dad's little outburst, I didn't want to talk about it anymore. At least, certainly not with Qantas-employee Alex, who looked a little like he thought Stacey's eyes were located somewhere between her shoulders and her waist. And I'm not talking about her bellybutton.

"Stace, let's go check in." I grabbed her arm, hoping to pull her away before the parent talk escalated.

"No! Alex is going to help us with that. He was just saying he wants us to have the best possible start to our trip, especially after—well, you know." Stacey's eyes softened as she looked at me. "It's been a big week for you."

"Which is why it's my pleasure to upgrade you two ladies to first class." Alex hit a final button on the computer and flashed us a giant smile. The guy must have had a whitening treatment; his teeth were so bright, they could have burnt ants if the sun reflected off them at the wrong angle.

"Eek! That's so exciting." Stacey gave three tiny jumps up and down and clapped her hands, thanking Alex as she took the two tickets from him.

"My pleasure. I hope you have a lovely flight, and I look forward to seeing you on your return to Sydney." The words were barely out of his mouth before Stacey had turned and started charging her way through the throngs of people to the baggage check. I quickly followed suit, although I found it a lot more challenging than I'd expected. Stacey expertly navigated her way into the gaps, whereas people seemed to deliberately step in front of me, causing my bag to clip the edge of a chair. Or another bag. Or a little old lady.

We reached our gate with thirty-five minutes to spare and stopped at the end of the very long line.

"I think our tickets give us access to the lounge." Stacey tapped some letters into her phone to investigate. She perched delicately on the edge of her suitcase while I held mine firm, in case my attempt at "perching" ended up with my body in a scrambled mess on the floor.

"Bitch."

As soon as I heard his voice my body tensed, fists tightening and my chest seizing up. Two seconds later I felt a firm grip around my upper arm, bony hands digging into my flesh.

"Let go." I turned to shrug Dave off. He was right up in my face, anger dancing in his green eyes.

"I know you've kept the suite," he spat. "I called to check, and they said you'd transferred it to another hotel."

"I paid for it." I pried his fingers from me and gently massaged the area he'd clenched. "And you have another room, one with the boys. What's the big deal?"

Don't cry.

Don't.

"So what? You paid for it and booked it knowing *I'd* sleep in it." Dave's voice was raised, and I saw a few heads turn to look at us. Apparently eavesdropping at the airport was a non-discreet activity.

"Dave, you have a room to stay in, anyway. Look, I'm sorry it's not …" My voice faltered as he took a step closer. I'd never felt physically intimidated by him, but right here, right now—I was glad there were a lot of people around. Even if they were pretty much all looking at us.

"Maybe you can sleep with one of the girls you flirted with at the show the other night." Stacey stepped in front of me, acting as a physical shield between Dave and me.

"Of course you'd be here." Dave snickered. In the background I heard screams; the sort of screams that signalled Lee Collins and Coal had arrived.

"Oh, look, the main event is here." Stacey smirked. "Why don't you go offer to carry their luggage or something? You know, *support* them."

Dave glanced back. He was tall, rising above the crowd, and I saw him make eye contact with Lee, who was being protected from the masses by four security guards.

"This is *not* over." Dave's eyes shot daggers into me. He grabbed my hand and dug his nails into my wrist, pulling me close to his skinny chest. "You crazy fucking bitch."

He whispered the words gently, but they had their desired effect. When Dave released my wrist I felt my knees go weak, and I gripped my suitcase for support.

I wasn't crazy. Even Dad wasn't crazy. Sick, he was sick, and—

"So, don't look now, but Lee Collins is looking at you," Stacey spoke under her breath. She grabbed my arm and pulled me to my feet, throwing back her head and laughing uproariously.

"Laugh, I'm pretending you just said something funny," she whispered. I managed a weak smile. I tried not to fall apart.

"Just—I need to go." I grabbed my suitcase handle and started navigating my way through the airport crowds again, Stacey hot on my heels. We made our way to the executive lounge. Thank goodness Dave had been booked into economy class.

I slid into a stool overlooking the tarmac and nodded my thanks to the waiter when a tall glass of water was placed in front of me. I threw it down my throat in one, big gulp, swallowing so hard it hurt.

"So, when do you want to talk?" Stacey asked. I looked around. Hundreds of anonymous heads bobbed around us, different colours, shapes and sizes. Their expressions were tense, as frustration and anger filled the air. The line to board wound its way around the terminal like a shoelace.

"Later." My voice was somewhere in the soles of my boots.

I flipped my phone out from my pocket and checked it. No new messages. A pang of nostalgia shot through me as I realised I'd expected to hear from Dave, maybe an apology text for overreacting.

Maybe I was wrong about him.

Maybe he was just a jerk.

A girl to the side of us was twirling her long, brown hair

around her coral-pink painted nail, chatting away in a high-pitched tone to her friend about their upcoming trip.

"It is going to be great." She nodded, batting her mascara-clumped lashes. "We are going to be, like, *so* drunk every night."

I pinched the bridge of my nose. I felt the dizzying waves of a migraine coming on. Was this really such a good idea?

"Excuse me, ma'am?"

I looked up. A waiter was hovering next to me, black round tray teetering in his hand. Two glasses of sparkling wine glittered on it. He stepped to the side and placed one drink on a folded white napkin in front of me, and then did the same for Stacey.

"I didn't know first-class had free drinks." Stacey flashed a smile at the waiter, who pretty much melted on the spot.

"Oh, they're, uh, not free." He cleared his throat. "They're from the gentleman at the bar."

My stomach dropped. Stacey's elbow made contact with my arm so hard, I worried it would bruise.

"Kate!" she squeal-whispered. "Lee—freaking—Collins just bought us a drink."

I spun in my stool to look at the bar behind us. Sure enough, Lee and his four security guards, as well as his two band-mates, were sitting at the bar. He raised a glass filled with ice and amber-coloured liquid in my direction, and I gave a weak smile and tipped my glass of sparkling back.

How was this happening? Why was this happening? Now Lee Collins was taking pity on me, no doubt after hearing about my dad, and possibly the break up. He'd sent me a sympathy drink?

"You have it." I pushed my glass in Stacey's direction, resting my head between my hands. I felt like I was on a rollercoaster, my mind flipping from wishing Dave still wanted me, to wondering what I'd seen in the douche in the first place. Either way, I knew Stacey thought she was helping, but was subjecting me to a weeklong graduation party honestly the best plan of attack? I didn't feel like partying. Maybe I should change my mind about going.

"Check out her rack." I heard a guy yell from somewhere behind me. Stacey tossed her hair over her shoulder ambiguously.

Scratch the maybe. Make that a definite.

The trip went by in a daze. I fell asleep as soon as the plane was in the air, the exhaustion of the airport wearing on my mind. I didn't see Dave once on the plane—the perks of being in first class—and Lee Collins didn't try and extend his pity on me any further.

We landed in beautiful, sunny Queensland and Stacey and I bolted off the plane, making a quick trip through the airport to get to a cab waiting outside. I felt like an outsider from the get-go. How could I go forth and enjoy the sunshine when it felt like I was storming on the inside?

The apartment I'd transferred us to, however, did a little to lift my mood. It was the top floor of a building that rested right on the beach, giving us a 180-degree balcony view of beautiful Surfers Paradise.

Apparently, booking a room for a tour with Coal came with definite perks and upgrades.

"Check out the size of the TV." My eyes widened at the seriously giant flat screen on the wall in the living room.

"That's nothing. Have you seen the spa?" Stacey came bouncing out of the en suite with a giant, fluffy robe wrapped around her shoulders. "And the bed feels amazing!"

I ran through the two-bedroom suite to my room. It was huge, far too big for one person, with floor-to-ceiling windows showcasing views of the city below. In the middle was a giant, perfectly white pressed-down bed. I suppressed the urge to just jump on it and mess it up, but it was hard.

Exploration complete, I returned to the living room and

took my phone out of my bag, checking it again. Still nothing. No new messages. Not even one from Mum.

Who was I waiting to hear from, anyway?

"All right. You're having a shower while I fix us up a little something, before we spend some serious time on the balcony watching the sunset," Stacey ordered.

"Stacey, I don't really feel like drinking …"

"Uh-uh. I'm making you one super-weak, half-strength cocktail. Because I'm a good friend." She marched to her bag, grabbing her wallet and phone. "Go shower. I'll be back in a sec. We need to talk about all this—" Stacey raised her finger up and down in the direction of my body "—stuff going on with you. I just need to grab some supplies."

I smiled and looked at my feet. I was glad she knew I still needed to talk, even though I'd denied it earlier. "Thanks," I said shyly. It was good to know that, even though everything around me was seriously screwed up, my best friend wasn't changing.

I went into my room and unzipped my bag, searching for something comfy to change into. Just before I left the room I checked my phone again and saw a little light flash up on the screen. One new message.

My breath caught in my throat as I fumbled to grab it, a mixture of excitement and trepidation coursing through me. Was it Dave? Maybe he was apologising. Hell, maybe it was Lee Collins, offering me my job back, and … I quickly clicked through and watched as the words blinked over the screen.

> **Hi darling, just letting you know I've put some cash into your account. Try not to stress too much about Dave. If it was meant to be, it will work out. Have a great holiday, Mum xx**

I slowly exhaled. If it was meant to be it would be? So Dad was meant to fall sick and die? I was meant to have my entire career plan ruined?

I dropped my phone on the bed and took my clothes and toiletries into the bathroom.

The shower was one of the best I'd had in ages. The heat of the water pounded against my head, sluicing its way through my hair and warming my lower back. I spent almost twenty minutes in there, soaking up the warmth and the wetness, feeling extra luxurious.

I dried myself with a towel that could have been made from baby rabbit fur it felt so soft. I threw on a tank and some shorts and walked out to the living room.

Stacey was already on the balcony, a bowl of chips resting on the little table beside her, an orange-and-red coloured drink in her hand.

"I made us vodka sunrises," she said, as she handed me a glass from the tiled balcony floor. "Technically, we're watching a sunset, but I figure it's gotta be rising somewhere, right?"

"Thanks." I smiled and took my drink, settling down on the wooden chair next to her. Miles and miles of beach spread out below us, dotted with tiny little spots of humans. In the water, families played, girls floated and guys surfed, tearing up the waves like little miniature men on their surfboards.

In the distance, ships cluttered the horizon, waiting to unload their cargo and get on the move again. Coloured lights twinkled down both sides of the boardwalk, promoting clubs, restaurants, bars and tattoo parlours.

I felt like an alien, watching it all. This world, it went on, even though mine had come to a stop. The surfers moved to the next wave, the ships to port, the people to the buildings. I wasn't a part of the circle. I was stalled.

"Whenever you're ready." Stacey winked at me, before turning her gaze to the vista once more.

I'm not sure I'll ever be ready.

Where to start? How do you explain to someone with no prior knowledge of the situation the problems you're having with a neurodegenerative disease, and your ex-boyfriend's inappropriate use of the word crazy?

"Stace, it's hard." I sighed. "I mean, not to tell *you*, that's not hard, but—"

"Wait!" Stacey held up a hand. She leaned over and passed me the bowl from the table next to her. "This sounds like a story that needs a good chip."

I grinned, and grabbed a handful of the salted potato goodness. I chewed, chewed and swallowed. Repeat.

Chew, chew, swallow. Repeat. Breathe.

Sometimes, my best friend was a downright genius.

"Last week, I found out something pretty crazy." I let the words tumble from my mouth. I told her everything: how I'd overheard my parents from the kitchen, how Dave had walked in, how he'd found out that I might have the disease, too—and how he'd left. How he'd signed some girl's boobs, and before we could have sex, stopped it, and broke up with me because my dad was too hard—dating me was too hard. How I'd had to visit a counsellor, who made me feel about two feet tall. And, amazingly, whether it was due to the vodka, the potato chips, or simply Stacey's calming presence, I managed not to cry.

"Kate." Stacey's voice was quiet when I'd finished. "Wow."

"I know."

We gazed out at the ocean as it ebbed and flowed against the sand. The sky had changed to a deep purple, with tinges of orange highlighting the horizon.

"So he just broke up with you?"

"Mm-hmm."

"Then yelled at you at the airport for stealing his room?"

"Mm-hmm."

"And you haven't heard from him since?"

I checked my phone for the zillionth time.

"Nope."

"He's a jerk. What an absolute idiot." Stacey let loose and yelled her words over the balcony. "How could someone be such a dick? Seriously!"

"Look, I checked out Lee Collins, and he was upset, and

I was jealous he signed this girl's boobs, and my dad—I … I kind of get it."

Stacey leaned over and slapped me, her palm making direct contact with my cheek. I widened my eyes and pressed a hand to my face, feeling the smart where she'd made impact.

"What the hell?"

"Don't you ever say that again. There's nothing to 'get'. He left because he was an asshole." Stacey stood and rested her body against the balcony. "Thank goodness I made you use your flights. I knew it'd be for the best. We're going to find some new guys to distract you." She wriggled her eyebrows comically.

"I'm not interested in that." If Dave didn't want me, who would?

"Ah, young Kate." Stacey shook her head. "You are yet to learn the benefits of the flirting-and-making-out-with males ego-boosting technique."

"Clearly not an area you're struggling in," I muttered.

"Damn straight." Stace shrugged. She took a swig from her virtually untouched drink. "Can I ask you a question?"

I nodded.

"Are you going to take the test?"

The words imprinted themselves on my heart. I'd known she was going to ask, but I'd hoped she wouldn't. Or maybe I'd hoped she would. I didn't know; my mind flicked from positive to negative, over and over again, until I got dizzy.

Was I going to take the test? Was I going to find out for 100 per cent sure if I had the disease or not?

My phone beeped into life, vibrating its way across the table.

"Ah!" I snatched it up.

"Text from an unknown number?" Stacey's eyes were wide. "Looks like maybe you've started the moving on already."

"It's nothing." I felt my face flush warm. I had no idea who it could be.

"Well, Lee from Coal certainly seemed pretty interested, buying you a drink. Maybe he's heard about the breakup, and he's asking you on a date," Stacey said.

"Yeah right."

"It could be true. After all, Michael told me—" Stacey paused. I knew this wouldn't be good. "—he said Dave told him you wouldn't screw him 'cause you were too obsessed with Lee."

Swoosh. Air rushed from my mouth.

"He doesn't believe it." Stacey squeezed my shoulder. "Now check that message. Who knows? Maybe Lee heard the story and is keen, and somehow found you and is getting in touch."

"Sure he is," I said. Stacey grabbed her glass and walked inside. I waited till she'd completely disappeared, and then pulled the phone away from my chest to read the message on screen.

> **This is a friendly reminder about your upcoming counselling appointment next Wednesday at 5pm. To reschedule, contact 1800 628 192.**

My heart sank to somewhere low in my ribcage. That was about the extent of the dates I could expect in my calendar from this point forward.

NINE

"Shot, shot, shot, shot!" the group of people sitting around me on the moonlit beach chanted. It was late, after midnight sometime. I'd stopped counting when I'd had my fifth shot. Then the numbers on my phone got a little harder to read.

"Drink up, Kate." Stacey nudged me as the chanting continued. It was some stupid drinking game, and I'd lost—again.

I threw my head back and let the content of the tiny glass in front of me slide its way down my throat. The liquid was sweet and sticky, Midori and red something-or-other. I shook my head till I was dizzy, trying to clear any remaining slivers of it out of my mouth. The first shooter had been nice. This one just made me feel like I needed to clean my teeth.

"Okay, okay, I got one. Never have I ever had sex on the beach before." Stacey announced, looking around the circle to see if anyone took a shot. We were seated in a circle of ten people from our hotel, an even mix of guys and girls our age. Waves were crashing in the background and a slight breeze ran over my shoulders, making me wish I'd worn more than just the tiny slip dress I'd been lazing in by the pool all day.

"We can fix that right now, babe," A guy with sun-kissed blond hair joked from the other end of the circle. He was surfer-boy hot, the sort of guy Stacey was into. He smiled at her and ran a tanned hand through his hair, showcasing his lean arm complete with toned muscles, no doubt honed through hours of surfing. I swear I heard her breath catch.

"Drink up, bitches." A guy whose hair shone in the moonlight crowed, as he raised his glass into the air. A few of the others raised theirs and knocked them back as instructed. I kept my eyes firmly on the sand. Bottles were passed around the circle and drinks were refilled.

Stacey angled her body so she could talk in my ear. "You okay?" Concern clouded her eyes. She'd been amazing this whole trip, making sure I was okay, that I was comfortable. She hadn't pushed me to discuss the dad issue. Not even once.

"I think I might go to bed," I whispered.

"Hey! No secrets. Group game," Shiny-Hair yelled. The liquid in his glass spilled over onto my ankle. Gross.

"We're going to head." Stacey stood up, stretching her legs and dusting sand off them. I reached up and grabbed on the hem of her dress, pulling her back down.

"Stace is staying. I'm going." I struggled to my feet, swaying what I'd consider to be an acceptable amount, for one who had been sitting and drinking for an hour.

"Let me walk you," Stace said. I shook my head, and grabbed my flip-flops and purse.

"What if something happens?"

I looked around, at the bright lights of town, the thousands of people drinking, dancing, eating and laughing. Scattered through them all were spots of blue, policemen monitoring the activity. It didn't feel dangerous. In fact, here, away from my home, I felt safe.

And besides, Stacey deserved a chance to get to know the surfer boy. She'd been glued to my side since we'd arrived in town; surely, on our last night, she should have a little fun.

"Never have I ever … kissed a guy before." Shiny-hair

cackled with laughter at his own joke. A few girls threw sand, or pieces of rubbish in his direction. Stacey rolled her eyes, and raised her glass.

"There are police and people everywhere. I'll message you when I get to the hotel." I crouched down, grabbing her shoulder to steady myself. "And besides, don't you have some unfinished business here?" I whispered. Stacey's gaze flicked from hot surfer boy back to me.

"If you're sure." She gave a half-smile, and I waved goodbye.

I took two steps before I felt dizzy. A wave of nausea washed over me, crashing just like the tide a few metres away, as I tried to focus.

Look at your feet, Kate. Look at your feet.

Deep breaths.

When I walked this time, I was able to place one leg in front of the other, my feet sinking into the cool, soft sand, until I reached the boardwalk and put on my shoes.

The boulevard was a mix of sky-high buildings, scents of street-fried food and bright lights selling wares, varying from alcohol promotion to the flashing legs of a dancing girl on a sign above one particular club.

People milled about, in groups, as couples and individuals, clutching drinks desperately and phones even more so. They were flooding out of bars and clubs, lining up at McDonald's and snaking in a line forever-long that led to the public toilets. Even though they were Portaloos, thousands of teenage not-yet-quite-old-enough-to-enter-the-club girls lined up to use them. Gross.

I walked past a group of guys, one of whom was wearing a Coal T-shirt. Had they been to the concert? The hairs on my arms stood on end, and I rubbed them down. Was it my imagination, or was he looking at me funny?

Stumbling over my own feet, I gave myself an internal slap on the wrist. Of course he wasn't looking. I was being hyper-sensitive.

Was that a symptom? Maybe I should look it up.

I strolled through the street, heading back to our hotel. A

girl blew a cloud of cigarette smoke in my face, and I coughed. A guy spilt some sticky, red liquid from a plastic cup around my ankles, splashing over my shoes. People laughed, yelled and smiled, a chaos of noise surrounding me.

I crossed the road parallel to the hub of activity, getting closer to the hotel and farther from the extremities of noise and light. It didn't feel unsafe, though; there were still enough people around to make up at least two football teams.

I started counting the buildings to the hotel. Just three bars, one club, a shop selling all sorts of marijuana paraphernalia, two alleys, and one hotel. Now two bars, one club, a shop, two alleys, and one hotel. Then one bar…

I stopped, noticing a chalkboard erected on the sidewalk.

Fortunes told and futures predicted by the mysterious Gypsy Rose

I stared at the sign, studying the curlicue handwriting. A fortune-teller. Someone who could tell the future.

Would they know what would happen to me? What would happen to—my dad?

A group of three girls walked out of the alleyway, laughing loudly and talking so fast it was hard to make out individual words.

"That was so freaky. She was crazy." One girl laughed, linking arms with another.

"Me? Three kids? No way am I ruining this body on babies," the middle girl joked, throwing her arm around her sidekick. They made their way down the street, leaving me alone in front of the sign.

Just me, a sign, and an alley. And maybe some clues to my future.

The kind of clues I could ignore if I wanted to.

That last voice in my head was smaller, quieter.

I shoved my hand in my pocket and searched the corners for some cash. My interest in Gypsy Rose had gone from vague to decided in a heartbeat. Now I couldn't see her quickly enough.

With two twenty-dollar notes balled in my fist, I started down the alley. It was full of shops, all with their shutters down, selling much more normal things. What an alleyway. Bikinis, shoes, handbags and … futures.

The last shopfront on the right was lit up, another chalkboard erected in an A-frame out the front. A counter stretched across the width of the shop's perimeter, a tiny opening to the left and a huge, black curtain behind it, separating the rest of the world from what I presumed was the place where all the magic happened.

"Yes?"

The voice was younger than I'd expected it to be, and brisk. It came from behind the curtain.

I straightened up and took a few steps closer to the counter. It had a bright-blue laminate top, with a scratched yellow border framing it. I'd never seen a psychic before. I had no reason to expect anything. Yet, for some reason, I knew I certainly didn't expect this.

"I was wondering if I could see-the-psychic." In the rush to get the words out of my mouth they all tumbled together, like vegetables clattering into a bowl. I blinked against the harsh fluorescent lights and ran a hand across my brow. It was hot. Really hot. Sweat, from being in this alleyway where the fresh air no longer seemed to flow, covered me.

"What sort of a reading would you like?"

A woman stepped out from behind the curtain, the owner of the mysterious unidentified yet young-sounding voice. She had black hair, the kind of midnight black that almost gleams blue. It was pulled back in a long ponytail, little tendrils falling to either side.

She wore faded denim jeans and a lemon-coloured T-shirt. Tiny purple shoes covered in sequins adorned her suspiciously small feet. Lines grazed her face, creases around her eyes and her cheeks. Her eyes were intimidating hazel-grey whirlpools of mystery. Or maybe I was just drunk.

Either way, she looked nothing like the sort of fortune-teller I'd imagined.

"A … a normal one?" I asked. Mainly because the alternative, turning to run, seemed like a foolish idea. What if she chased me? Or cursed me? Or … worse?

I had no idea what worse would be, mind you. But I knew I didn't want it.

"I do crystal ball, tarot, tea leaves, or palm reading." The woman sighed and tapped one of her tiny, delicately-shod feet. "Palm reading is the cheapest." She shot out the words like being cheap was a crime.

"Which one works best?"

"They all tell you different things." She swatted her hair back over her shoulder. "Personally, I prefer the tarot. I find it gives a more accurate reading."

"Tarot, then," I said. I didn't want her to feel like I was wasting her time.

The woman turned and strutted behind the curtain, flicking it out behind her so it billowed in her wake. I stood there, riveted to the spot. Was I supposed to go, too? I didn't suppose she'd read me out here in the alleyway, but she'd hardly invited me to come with.

I swallowed and took a few steps forward, then gingerly peeled back the curtain to look at the dark shadows behind it.

There was a room, a tiny, little box where Gypsy Rose obviously worked. It was dark, with light coming in dancing shadows from two candles jammed into a rusted candelabrum on a table in the corner. The scent of musk came floating up to assault my nostrils and I tried not to sneeze. The perfume and lack of air created a stifling, heady mix.

A small card table was set up in the middle, two chairs parked on either side of it, one containing Gypsy Rose's small frame. To the left, a huge bookshelf, crammed full of thick books, thin books, old books with deeply creased spines, and new books with crisp binding, was on display. To my right was a small chest of drawers with a crystal ball on top. The bottom drawer was slightly ajar, and I could see it was stuffed full of papers and other junk, all folded and wadded up.

"Never you mind about that." Gypsy Rose slammed the

drawer shut with her foot. I sank into the empty seat, placed my hands on the table and looked her, as close to the eye as I could stand without actually meeting her gaze. I didn't want her to yell at me again. But I also didn't want to have to look at her, in case that got me in trouble, too.

"Now, let me see here." The woman reached over to the top drawer of the table and pulled it open. She retrieved a pack of cards, larger than your normal playing cards, and laid them on the table in front of her.

"I'm going to start shuffling these cards, and you need to tell me when to stop," Gypsy Rose instructed me. She moved the cards about in her hands, rifling through the deck.

"Stop," I said, after a few seconds of finger-fidgeting nerves.

"Okay, now again." She started her shuffling a second time, and I wondered if I'd gotten it wrong, made a mistake. I started to form the question, but snapped my mouth shut when she gave a small shake of her head in my direction.

"Stop," I said again.

The tiniest of smiles inched its way up the corner of her face.

"Okay, let me lay out the cards."

Gypsy Rose placed a series of cards on the table, one after the other. They were brightly-coloured, garish-looking things, full of shapes and objects, some of which I recognised and some of which I didn't.

"Is there anything specific you want to know?"

The words stuck in my head.

Yes, when is my dad going to die?

Sure, will he remember me at all?

Okay, let's start with am I going to have a mental illness and lose control of my words and movements?

"Oh you know, just general stuff." I smiled, and bit my lip.

"Well, let's look at love," Gypsy Rose said, busy studying the cards in front of her. "All you young girls want to know about love.

"Your true love …" She scanned the cards, searching for something in their garish images. "He is someone you have already met." Yes, and his name is probably Dave, and he's left me. "Someone with … a familiar family situation."

That was odd. I racked my brain, trying to think of any kind of tie between Dave and my family. Both his parents were alive and well. They didn't have any diseases, and both of their parents were living still, too.

Maybe she meant parents I knew, and that's why they were familiar.

Maybe.

"What about my family?" The words escaped without my realising.

Gypsy Rose studied my face, squinting those grey eyes. I felt like a rabbit, caught in her gaze, unable to look away.

She turned back to the cards, studying them intently. She was silent for a while as she read them. She picked one up, put it back down. She looked at the remainder of her deck again. Finally, after what seemed like forever, she looked at me once more.

"What do you want to know?" Her voice was softer this time.

"About my dad," I replied. I knew you weren't supposed to give too much away to fortune-tellers. If you told them everything, they'd predict based on information you'd given them.

"Your father … He is … he is sick," the woman said. She didn't meet my eyes, shuffling her hands. They never seemed to stop, those hands. They constantly fiddled and tidied, a flurry of activity.

"Yes." My voice was as minute as a grain of sand.

"Something with … something with his head." It didn't seem like the words were coming to her as she spoke them. The way she looked at me, licking her lips, made me feel like she knew exactly what she was talking about—she just didn't want to say it.

"There are very tough times ahead for your family," the woman said, slowly shaping each word. "It will be a tricky year."

"How tricky?"

Gypsy Rose raised her painted on eyebrows at me and I immediately returned my gaze to the cards on the table. Her look spoke volumes; more than I needed to know.

"Do you have any siblings?" she asked, again breaking the silence. I shook my head.

"Will the sickness—will it get me, too?" The words came out, and I choked back a sob. I prayed to the gypsy gods that I wouldn't start to cry, not here in a ramshackle studio set in an alley with a cranky old fortune-teller.

"It will affect your whole family," the woman eventually replied. She leaned over to the bookshelf and pulled down a box of tissues from the third shelf, placing them to the side of the table next to me. "No one in your family will be the same."

So, was I going to get it, or wasn't I? Did she mean I was going to be affected because Dad was sick? Or affected *in*fected? And what did she mean, tricky? Obviously it was tricky. My dad coming home would be tricky. My dad having an incurable disease was freaking impossible.

The heat in the building got too much, the air too thick to fit in my lungs. I had to get out of there, fast.

Now.

"Look, thanks for your time." I pushed my chair back from the table and stood up, wiping my eyes with the palm of my hand. "How much?"

"You don't want to stay and hear the rest of your reading?" the woman asked. "We haven't spoken of your career, or your money."

"It doesn't matter." I shook my head. "Just—just how much, please."

Gypsy Rose stood up and walked toward me. For a weird second, I thought she was going to try and hug me. Instead, she just lifted the thick, black curtain, and gestured for me to go through.

I walked outside into the bright, unnatural light and immediately felt better. It was going to be fine. Maybe "tricky" would be learning to live away from home. Maybe the doctors would figure out a cure for Dad's disease, and I wouldn't even need to worry about him, or getting tested myself.

"Thirty dollars, please," the woman said. Out here in the light, she looked a whole lot less foreboding than she had in her room. Her shirt had threads loose from the seams, and a tiny stain marred the shoulder. The wrinkles creasing around her face and neck were much deeper, and her eyes a lot more tired.

She wasn't mystic at all; just a middle-aged woman, trying to earn some cash.

I placed my two twenties on the counter and turned and walked away. I figured she could probably use a tip.

My pace was quick, and I all but flew past the remaining bars and shops. When I got to the hotel, I swiped my room card for entry and headed for the emergency exit. I wanted to sweat. I powered up the stairs two by two, a stitch stabbing into my side, until I got to the thirtieth floor, where I stopped and marched down the corridor to our suite.

One swipe with my hotel key card and the door was open. I tapped out a quick text to let Stacey know I was back, and then threw my phone on the sofa. I charged into the bedroom, curled up in a ball on the big, white quilt and hugged my knees to my chest, taking deep breaths and staring out at the lights, the stars and the ocean as the world went in and out with the tide beneath me.

I didn't move from that spot, not for eight hours. Even when Stacey came home, presumably with her surfer-boy, and proceeded to have a way too noisy make-out session in the room next to mine.

In the midst of all this life, there was me.

TEN

MUM WAS waiting to meet us at the airport. As soon as I saw her curly auburn hair bobbing and weaving amongst all the other people waiting to board, I knew something was wrong.

The airport was a simple train ride from our place. Stacey and I had travelled this route together hundreds of times when we went shopping in the city, or to support Dave and the boys at their gigs. So why was my mother waiting for us in the lounge as soon as we stepped off the plane?

"Kate, isn't that—" Stacey started.

"Uh-huh."

We lugged our carry-ons over to her and stopped, waiting as she threw her arms around first me, then Stacey, a huge smile plastered on her face.

"Girls! How was it? You look tired. Are you tired? Do you need a hand with any of your bags?" Mum asked. She was a whirlwind, fast words and even faster hand gestures as she went to try to relieve both of us of our various belongings. I ended up relinquishing my black cardigan to her, more to give her something to do than anything else. Her nervous energy was sucking me dry.

"We're fine, Mum." I tried to muster up a smile, but I knew my eyes weren't in it. "How come you came to pick us up?"

"I … I thought it was a nice thing to do." Mum's hurt showed as her eyes tugged downwards. She started walking a little ahead of us, taking tiny but rapid steps in her taupe, heeled shoes. I stood still, my brow furrowed.

"It was lovely of you, Deb." Stacey elbowed me in the side, jolting me to life. Gosh, what was *wrong* with me? Had I forgotten how to act normal?

"Here, I'll take that," I said, and pathetically grabbed the sweater back from Mum's hands in an effort to try and help. She resisted, and we ended up having this weird tug-of-war in the airport, obstructing the thoroughfare as we pulled at each side of the cardigan.

"Sorry, you can take it," I muttered and let go, falling in behind her again.

"What is wrong with you?" Stacey hissed in my ear. I shrugged, mouthing the words "*I'm trying*" at her, before catching up with Mum once more.

The three of us walked in silence, all the way from the terminal to the car park. It wasn't a short walk, either: thirteen minutes and fifty-eight seconds, according to my phone stopwatch. I don't know why I decided to time it. It just seemed like a good idea. To calculate a given time, so I knew what to expect in life. Knew exactly how long it would take.

When we reached Mum's car, Stacey and I threw our bags in the back and piled in, me in the front playing shotgun. Mum joined us and turned the motor, sitting in silence a few minutes as she waited for the car to heat up.

"I'm sorry to hear about … about everything, Deb," Stacey said. It felt weird, hearing someone bring it up. It made it more real, somehow, even more real than when I'd told Stacey myself.

"Thanks, Stacey," Mum replied. I noticed her knuckles get a little whiter as her grip on the steering wheel tightened. She backed out of the space, not waiting another second to leave the airport.

We spent most of the hour-and-a-half trip home in weird bursts of extremely high energy chatter then silence, Stacey attempting to fill the gaps quickly and then letting them empty as she realised her audience was less than receptive.

She was in the middle of a story about how we made our own meals every night when we pulled into her driveway and Mum cut her off.

"Wow, sounds like you had a great trip. See you soon." She smiled. Her eyes were vacant, as was her mind. You could tell. Mum never cut people off. Not even when they were giving a play-by-play of how they and her daughter made tacos.

"Okay. Bye, Deb. See ya, Kate." Stacey reached around the seat and gave me an awkward hug before jumping out of the car. She ran around the back and retrieved her bag, then waved gaily as we drove off.

The car was silent. The radio was off. The only noise was the subtle hum of traffic outside, and inside, the hiss of the air conditioner and the sound of Mum's heavy breathing.

That.

Was.

It.

"When we made tacos, Stacey didn't use normal beans," I broke the quiet. "She used refried instead of kidney. Gross."

"Oh, I'm sure they weren't that bad." Mum chuckled.

"They were pretty disgusting. I even told her, and she was all 'That's how my family always makes it.'" I laughed. It wasn't funny. It wasn't even a second cousin twice removed from funny. I just needed to try and make my mum smile, needed to make her be present and try to forget about whatever was on her mind.

Huh. Like there was any question.

What was on her mind was Dad.

And possibly me.

We sat in silence until we pulled into our driveway. Mum switched off the engine, but didn't get out of the car. One hand remained on the wheel, the other sat safely in her lap.

I looked out the windscreen at our garage, and next to it, our red-brick house. So plain, so everyday—so suburban. Who knew that, inside, there was a man who was going to die? That we were battling a disease most people had never heard of?

How did Dad fit into our lives, when he'd been absent for so long? How had she forgiven him, let him back in?

It clicked inside my head, like pieces of a jigsaw puzzle falling into place. You couldn't care for people like Dad unless they were your immediate family.

People like Dad.

People like me.

I swallowed, and pushed the feeling of bile back down my throat. Whether I had the disease or not, my whole life was about to change.

Silence swallowed the car. I heard the sound of my steady breaths, Mum's slightly quicker ones. White noise ate us up.

"You're going to need to get a job."

I flicked my eyes across to her.

"I had a job. My boyfriend dumped me, and it ended. Remember?"

"Yes, dear, but you're not going to college, and I don't want you just loafing around the house." Mum sighed, staring down at the beige colour of her neatly pressed trousers. "I'm going to need you to help out and look after your father while I'm at work, then maybe do some part-time work yourself? This thing … it's going to be expensive."

Wow. Mum had just become a single parent, financing two children.

"It's good you're here, darling, not going on tour."

I took in a sharp breath, catching it at the back of my throat.

"Oh, Kate, I didn't mean—I'm sorry." Mum pursed her lips and I felt a twinge of sympathy for her. This was *her* husband and *her* daughter. I wasn't the only victim.

"How did your counselling appointment go?"

"Hated it."

"Kate." I waited for her to continue, but no words were forthcoming. She tightened her grip on the steering wheel again, the veins in her wrists popping.

"Kate," Mum began. It was like she'd been holding her breath. Air exhaled out of her mouth quickly, her lips in an O shape. "I think, while you come to terms with it all, it's best you continue to see someone."

"Right. Get a job, care for Dad and keep seeing a counsellor?"

Mum nodded, her lips terse. I could see the little crow's feet in the corner of her eyes. She'd never looked so tired, so old.

"I don't know how we're going to do this."

I wanted to ask if we had to, but I couldn't make myself say the words. If Mum could welcome him back and deal with me and my potential problems, surely so could I.

"He's been bad today." Mum stared straight at the house in front of us.

I let the words sink in. I studied them in my mind; '*he*', referring to my father. '*Been*' as in past tense, perhaps not relevant now. '*Bad*' as in not good, negative. '*Today*' as in … Well, I was really too stuck on '*bad*' to care.

"How bad?" My voice shook, even though I tried to control it.

"Well, if ten is the highest," Mum started, slowly, "I'd say a six? Seven?"

I thought about what it could mean. Ten would have to be almost all-out gone, an intense display of forgetting faces, uncontrollable movement, and extremely slurred speech.

What did that make a seven?

"He's just—he's not saying sentences properly," Mum explained, as if reading my thoughts. "And he fell over in the shower this morning. I took him to hospital, but—"

"What? Is he okay?"

"Kate, let me finish. He just cut himself on the razor, that's all. He didn't even need stitches. He's back home now."

I processed the information, let it run through my brain

on repeat. So this was not a good day.

"Will there be good days and bad days?"

"From what I understand, yes." Mum nodded. "But we won't know what day is which, until it happens."

We continued to sit there in silence, both of us staring at the house without a word. I didn't want to go in. I didn't want to see firsthand evidence of my dad acting like a different person again.

"He is in there, right?"

"Yes."

More silence.

There was no comfort in our solidarity, no consolation knowing that my own mother didn't want to see her husband just as much as I didn't want to see my father.

Five silent, drawn out minutes ticked by—again, as timed on my phone—and I decided to get out of the car. I felt stretched between relief that it was five minutes of avoided discomfort, and sadness that when my father did eventually die, I'd never get those five minutes back.

I walked around the back and grabbed my luggage, swinging it over my shoulder and walked to the door. Mum followed close behind, house keys at the ready.

She fussed with the keys and it took her three goes to get them in the lock correctly. The need for keys was odd, since Dad was home already. I guess maybe he wasn't allowed out? Perhaps she'd been told by the doctor to lock up when she left, as if he no longer was capable of keeping the house secure while in his own company?

Metal jingled, and I looked down. Mum had dropped the keys on the front doorstep. She could never hide it when she was nervous. Her body gave her away.

Finally, the door swung open, and Mum stood to the left, allowing me to enter first.

I walked inside, dropping my overnight bag next to the couch, and rushed into the kitchen. I wanted to get it over and done with, to rip open my Dad-shaped wound like I was taking a Band-Aid off, and see him at sixes or sevens.

The kitchen was empty, a glass of half-finished orange juice on the counter. Mum was a shadow behind me.

"Outside," she whispered, pointing to the half-open screen door. We raced outside, like he was a toddler who'd escaped the fold. He was a full-grown man, for crying out loud. Surely he'd be fine.

I scanned the yard, eyes running over the top of garden beds, the rose patch and the swing set.

"He's not here," I breathed. I felt my heart start to race as the blood shot at my pulse. What if he'd fallen down again, like he had this morning? What if, right at this very moment, he was lying in a shattered pile of glass, bleeding his life away and unable to stop the flow?

What if ... what if he'd hurt himself on some of his old tools?

I turned and raced toward the garage, my legs pounding over the cracked pavement. The cement was hard beneath my feet, my soles smarting on impact through my thin-soled flip-flops.

Mum followed, hot on my heels, as if she'd had the thought just as I did. I reached the garage door and flung it wide-open, eyes rapidly scanning the dirty old room for signs of life.

My eyes took a few seconds to adjust to the dark. I made out the shadows of toolboxes, bicycles, old surfboards, the ice chest ...

"Girls."

He was crouched down in the corner, sitting in a pile of dust. A grin stretched from cheek to cheek. Aside from the empty cans scattered around him, he looked normal. There was no blood, no limbs bent at an unnatural angle.

But his leg was kicking, tiny jerks into space, just like the genetics counsellor had warned me about.

Kick—pause—kick—pause—kick.

Over and over and over.

The air clawed at my throat, stopping me from breathing. My chest closed in, constricted.

This wasn't my father.

I pushed past Mum and bolted out into the yard again until I was in the opposite corner. I was desperate for air, taking big, needy gulps of it. I couldn't do this. I couldn't *do* this. I jerked my foot out and kicked a paling on our brown wooden fence, as hard as I could.

My toes curled up in pain and I hopped around, biting my lip and cursing. Even through my shoe, it *hurt*. It hurt so damn much.

But at least this was a pain that was real.

At least it wasn't the pain churning inside of me, eating me alive slowly in its wishy-washy fashion. This pain was a release: short, sharp and loaded with hate. And it was sweet.

I limped back inside and grabbed my bag, hauling it upstairs to my room where I started to unpack.

I wondered if I'd be able to keep living like this thing didn't really exist for much longer.

eLeven

THE NEXT morning I woke up and saw Mum had left a yellow Post-it note on my bedroom door. And one on top of my laptop. One on my phone, too. Apparently, she was really keen on me checking the note she'd left on the fridge.

You know, for my first day of babysitting my father.

Normally her OCD made me laugh, but today it made me feel queasy. How was I going to do this alone? I grabbed my phone and shot off a quick text to Stacey.

Are you free today?

The responding vibration came back less than a minute later.

Sorry, on a date.

Then another:

Wish me luck!

I scrunched up my face, trying not to be too jealous. She was allowed to date. She'd just spent a week with me in another state; I could hardly expect her to hang out with me every second of the day.

After the world's quickest shower, I took the stairs two at a time till I reached the kitchen. As promised, Mum's note was stuck to the refrigerator in plain view. I walked over and snatched it out from the magnet's grasp, crumpling the corner in my hand.

To do list:
1. *Clean house*
2. *Get groceries*
3. *Spend quality time with your father*

Seeing the words hurt. *Quality time with your father.* Stab, stab, stab.

I screwed the paper up into a tiny ball and let it loop through the air on its journey to the bin. I couldn't deal with lists, and forced bonding right now.

I made myself some tea and sat on one of the backless stools lined up at our kitchen bench, staring at my mug. Its soft-brown hue was pretty, I decided. Little bubbles of milk gathered at the sides of the cup, and I focused on them, watching them explode into the deep sea of tea, one by one. Concentrating on that felt easier than concentrating on everything that was happening inside this house. Concentrating on that felt real.

I don't know how long I was in my reverie, but when I finally took a sip of tea it had turned lukewarm, and the sun was no longer streaming through the window but rather dwindling in the corner. I let one side of my mouth rise in mild amusement. It wasn't like I had anything to do today, anyway. I didn't have tour. I didn't have any commitments for the year ahead, thanks to my lack of college applications due to full-time rock star girlfriend commitments. All I had to do was within this house.

The stark white walls started to feel very close, the air thick and stifling. My heart sped up and I wondered what was wrong with me. Why was it so hard to breathe lately?

My breath was coming in short, sharp gasps again, and

I could feel a pounding at my wrist that must have been my pulse. I wasn't normally so aware of my body and its movements. This wasn't me. This wasn't … wasn't natural.

I needed to get out. Now.

I jumped from my bench seat and burst out into the yard, clutching my stomach. Out there, the air was cool. I doubled over and sucked it all in, big, shuddering breaths that filled my chest from the top of my lungs to their very pits.

Slowly, I felt my heart drop its frantic pace. Slowly, I stopped being so aware of my pulse, and became more aware of the thin rays of light still streaming into the yard and gently bathing my arms and legs in warmth.

Breathe.

It was going to be okay.

"Hello." Dad's voice sent my heart rate back to regular speed again. He was leaning in the kitchen doorway, resting on the wall for support. He sounded normal.

"Hi." I barked the word out.

He stood there, watching me as I studied the grass and the filtered shadows running through it. This was okay. Maybe this would be a one day, or a minus three day. We could be normal.

"You go on tour?" A stilted sentence. That was all it took. "*K … kiss that girl …*" He sung the words a little. He'd been to almost as many of Dave's gigs as I had before he disappeared. It was almost ironic he was the reason I wasn't with Dave & the Glories now. Nor would I be, ever.

"Nope." I kicked a small stone that lay next to the path and watched it crush a tender blade of grass where it landed.

I hoped it hurt.

"L … let's get coffee?"

I pursed my lips and studied him, his even frame, folded arms. He looked normal in his checked shirt and blue jeans, nothing like the man who'd shown up drunk at graduation.

If I were honest with myself, no, no I didn't. I wanted to stay at home, watch some bad movies and throw a pity-party.

One day, he's going to die.

"Okay, let's go."

I locked up the house, grabbed my bag, and we hopped into my little yellow car. Dad didn't say much as I drove through town, searching for a coffee shop I hadn't been to before, one where I would run the smallest chance of seeing someone from school. I deliberately drove toward the business district, away from the usual places kids my age hung out.

When we passed the building Dad used to work in, I felt his body stiffen in the seat beside me. He averted his gaze to the road in front. Seconds later, his arm started twitch, just like his leg had the day before.

I didn't say anything.

I didn't know what to say.

Our silence wasn't so much awkward as it was forced. I still didn't really know how to act around him, and I guess he either was embarrassed, or could sense my reserved hostility. I didn't know. All I knew was that it was hard.

"So, how was living in care?" I eventually said, chancing him a quick look as we stopped at some traffic lights.

"Good." Dad shrugged. His arm was still on its flicking mission, but he didn't seem bothered by it.

"Were the nurses nice?" *What do you ask someone who has spent the better part of the past year in a home?*

"Not as n … nice-as-your-mother." Dad gave a toothy smile. I pressed my lips together in a thin line. He'd seemed fine before. Why was he acting funny now? Had I done something to bring it on? Was it asking about the home, or seeing his workplace? And if he missed Mum so bad, why'd he run away in the first place?

I parked in a nearby lot and we got out, walking toward the shops like two strangers who just happened to be going to the same place. Dad stayed a few steps behind me. I wasn't sure if it was because I was charging ahead, or if he was deliberately keeping a slower pace.

Either way, it had to stop. I loved him. He was my father.

"Come on." I stopped and motioned for him to join me. He didn't say anything, only nodded and loped to my side.

We walked on in silence, this awkward gait where I'd speed up, and then stop to wait, aware that I was probably making him feel bad. I didn't want to do it. I didn't want him to feel like I hated him.

But a little part of me did.

I was going to hell.

We walked into the new coffee store I'd heard about a few months ago, a place called Sideways. It was very cool, lots of retro lounges and chairs, with gorgeous black and white framed hand-drawn artwork hanging on the walls. The tiles on the floor were large checkers, making the whole place feel like a 50s diner.

I pulled out a chair for Dad at one of the little round red tables. He sat down and I resisted the urge to push his seat in for him.

I chanced a look around. There were only five other groups in there, three couples and two groups of four. They all looked to be in their forties, and not one of them had so much as glanced at Dad.

Feeling more confident, I walked up to the counter to place our order, my eyes trailing over to the art on the way. They were all these little scenes: a pair of shoes, a ball, a wave—but all captured in such exquisite detail, like the artist had noticed every particle of every moment and somehow jotted it down.

"One mocha and one chocolate milkshake, please," I said, too captivated by the artwork to pay much attention to the man behind the counter. That is, until I looked up to hand over my cash and found myself face to face with the strange guy from the counselling centre. He pushed his floppy hair back out of his eyes and smiled at me, dimples aglow.

"Are you following me?"

"No." My jaw dropped. "How would I even know where you worked? I saw you in a centre over an hour's drive from here."

"Relax." He gave that easy smile again. "I was kidding."

"Oh." I felt about two-foot tall. "So was I."

Liar, liar, pants on fire. But he didn't call me on it, thank goodness. He looked different here; same brown hair, same muscled physique, same liquid chocolate eyes that just seemed to go on and on forever, but something about him seemed more real, though. There was a heaviness to him I hadn't noticed at the centre when he'd been all whimsical and fancy-free.

"Been running much recently?" He tilted his head to the side and his hair fell across with it. I had an almost irresistible urge to reach over the counter and flip it back, tuck it behind his ear away from his eyes.

Almost.

"Not really," I said. "Been smoking much recently?"

"I said try everything *once*." He winked at me, reaching behind the counter and pulling out two glasses. "And it didn't capture my attention enough to make me want to try it again."

"Hmm," I said, my mind a million miles away. He'd been at the centre; what had he been there for? From what I understood, they counselled all kinds of youth there, from those whose relatives had Huntington's to parents with cancer.

I angled my body so he wouldn't see my dad. I didn't want to expose myself when he might not have any similar scars to show. "Actually, I think I might make those to go."

"Are you sure? Who are you here with? I could go on break and join you." I blinked. The offer was unexpected, to say the least.

"I wouldn't want you to get in trouble …" I dismissed his comment with a wave of my hand.

"My brother and I own this place. He's kinda the boss, though." He smiled again and walked over to the coffee machine where he started grinding some beans. I took a few steps with him, again trying to position myself so Dad was hidden from his view. Maybe, if I stayed here and talked to him, then took the drinks myself he wouldn't even come near Dad.

A quick glance over my shoulder confirmed what I'd already suspected. From here, Dad looked totally normal, sitting down, shoulders rounded, flipping a pack of sugar around between his fingers. His arm was jerking a bit, but with the sugar twirling he was doing, it almost looked on purpose.

Perfect.

"So, when did you start this place?"

"Three months ago."

"Aren't you kind of young to be owning your own business?" I wrinkled my nose.

"Aren't you kind of cute, thinking I'm so young and helpless?" A flirtatious smile spread across his face and I felt my eyes widen. *That dimple …* "I'm twenty-two."

"I'm eighteen," I said, trying to sound nonchalant. *Old enough*, was what I was thinking. "Twenty-two is still kind of young, though. Shouldn't you be travelling around the world or something?"

"We started this place 'cause we had to. Our dad passed away." His voice was soft. He bit his lip and focused on the coffee machine. "Cancer."

"I'm sorry." My hand flew to my chest. "Your mum?"

"Heart attack, ten years ago."

"Oh—God, I am so sorry, I … I …"

Ground, this is the deal. If you open up and swallow me, I'll promise to turn into lovely, earth-friendly compost.

"Don't be." The boy shrugged. The noise of the coffee machine as it spluttered into life made it hard to speak. He looked down at the jug, making the milk dance into little foamy ringlets.

While he studied that, I studied him. He was wearing glasses, thick-rimmed black ones, and I wondered why he hadn't been wearing them the other day. Perhaps he only needed them close-up. His dark T-shirt looked a little too short for his somewhat tall frame, making his body look even longer than it was. There was something about him I was drawn to, attracted to, even though I didn't know why. He wasn't the stereotypical rock-god hot like Lee, or even indie hot like Dave. He was just so—normal.

And with my current situation, maybe normal was my type.

I looked back at Dad and was struck by the reality of it all again. At least I knew now why this guy was at the counselling centre. He'd been through some horrible times, but he had his whole life ahead of him. If he were like me, with the potential to die, he wouldn't start his own business.

Would he?

And, if Dad died, would I be able to move on, just pick up the pieces like he clearly had? What would Dad's death be like?

A pang of guilt washed over me, and I hated myself for being so horrible. I didn't want him to die. I didn't.

"Is that your dad over there?" the boy asked, interrupting my thoughts. I looked where he was pointing, frightened of what I would see. Dad was sitting down, staring vacantly out the window. My stomach sunk.

"Yes." No point denying it.

"It's cool he's hanging out with you," he said, as he handed over my coffee in a takeaway cup. He walked over to the other side of the little kitchen area behind the counter and prepared the milkshake while I stood there, pondering his words, replaying them over and over in my mind.

It was cool he was hanging out with me. Cool because he didn't have a father to hang with him? Cool because old men spending time with children was nice, in general? Or cool because he'd sensed Dad was sick?

What exactly did he mean by, "cool"?

"Whatever," I said, and twisted the cup in my hands. It had one of those corrugated cardboard rings around it. I spun it from side to side. "I like this cup."

"You do?" He smiled at me again, and for a second I forgot about Dave and Dad and disease. The three Ds.

"Yeah, it feels nice." I studied the walls of the place again. "This place is really … different. Looks like a cool place to work."

"You're looking for a job?" The question took me by surprise, and I let it settle over me. No, I hadn't been looking for a job. I'd been looking forward to a summer of touring the country and making out with my boyfriend, then pursuing a career in event management.

However, now it appeared that my schedule was a whole lot clearer.

"Yeah, I am actually."

"We might have a vacancy." The boy paused. "I have a few commitments, and we both go to the counselling centre a bit more than we'd thought we would. Would you be interested in working here?"

I froze and studied him. His pink lips were slightly parted, his eyes focused. He appeared to be serious.

"But you don't even know me," I protested.

"And you don't know me." He shrugged, pouring milk into the milkshake jug.

"But I could be a terrible waitress," I said. "I'm clumsy, and I've never done anything like it before."

"Can you pass me back your coffee?"

"Um … sure." I handed him back the cup that I'd been playing with. He took it from me, gave the ring a little twist and smiled, handing it back over in a matter of seconds.

"See? You just handed me a drink. Now you're experienced." He turned and scooped some ice cream into the glass.

"It's not the same. What if I steal from you?"

"Will you?"

"Well, no, but I could, and—"

I was interrupted by the roar of the milkshake maker. The boy looked at me and mouthed *I can't hear you* over the din, all the while a wicked grin adorning his face.

"Great. I'll talk to my brother, but I'm sure we'll get you in for a trial," he said. "We'd love to have someone like you working here."

I quickly turned my back to the counter, taking a big sip of coffee. My tongue burnt from the heat. I had no idea why I was so embarrassed by that last statement. He'd love to work with me. Big deal. It was probably because he'd *love* to have a few afternoons off per week.

But what would I love to do with him …

I gave myself a mental slap. What was I talking about? I'd loved Dave; this guy had good dimples, and that was about it.

He was no replacement.

He walked around the counter, milkshake in hand, all the way to the table, and I completely forgot any reference to a job. He was taking the milkshake to Dad! I wanted to stop him, but I couldn't. It was like watching one of my horror movies. I was kind of curious to see the blood.

"Milkshake's for you, I'm guessing?" He placed the tall cup down in front of Dad, a straw poking out the hole in the top.

"Thanks," Dad said in his slightly slurred way. I studied the boy's face to see if he flinched, or gave a weird look as Dad spoke. Nothing. Not even a hint of interest.

"Thanks for stopping in, guys." He gave Dad a slight tap on the shoulder. "Your daughter's gonna be working here, you know."

"That'sh good." Dad grinned. His eyes were unfocused, darting around the room. "Kate's a—she's a hard worker."

"Not a thief?"

"No." Dad shook his head emphatically and I groaned. What was with this guy?

"Here's my number." The guy pulled a card out of his back pocket, one of the "Buy eight coffees get one free" variety. Down at the bottom was a mobile number with the words *Text your order ahead for speedy service.*

He was back behind the counter before I even had a chance to ask his name. I sank down in my chair, and took a sip of my takeaway coffee. Clearly, I was drinking in.

I was just so shocked at his easy state of unknowledgeable acceptance.

"He likes you." Dad said, in a surprisingly quiet voice. I blinked, then followed Dad's eyes to where they were focussed, on the man behind the counter.

"The coffee guy?"

Dad nodded sagely, reclined in his chair and took a giant slurp from his straw. I tried to ignore the urge I had to look at him again, to see if a quick study could reveal some potential interest in me.

Not like it mattered, anyway. No guy would be interested

in me if they knew the truth. Dave had made that abundantly clear.

I'd never stand a chance with this guy, someone who I'd have to tell about Huntington's.

Realisation: Dave had flat-out left me when he'd found out about the disease; both Dad having it, and me being a potential victim. No other guy would want to be with someone like that, someone who couldn't risk having children in case they passed the disease on.

Was this one of the seven stages of grief? Had I reached acceptance?

And if so, acceptance freaking sucked.

TWELVE

A WEEK AFTER my Gold Coast mini-break, Mum committed to working six days a week. She scheduled shift work, allowing her to be home some mornings and afternoons, but it still meant I had to be there when she wasn't.

"I know looking after him isn't exactly fun, but you're going to have to do it," Mum told me as she swept her hair up into a neat bun. She studied herself in the white light of the bathroom mirror, checking that her appearance was picture perfect, her hair centred.

"Okay." I didn't want to argue. I could tell from the click of her tongue she wasn't in a good mood.

"Unfortunately, as well as the addiction side effects, suicide is a real possibility for people in his situation. The doctor thinks we're past the time when this is an immediate threat, but still, I don't want him left alone."

I shut my eyes, the voice of the counsellor ringing in my ears. I could see why a young person might want to die, but why him? He was already on a limited life sentence, and his quality of life had deteriorated. What would be the point in committing suicide now?

"I know you said you have a job trial, but it will have to be flexible hours, as someone needs to be with your father at all times," Mum continued. I nodded, staring at the white mosaic of tiles on the floor. *At all times.*

"And about your next appointment with the genetics counsellor, has she given you the contacts to book in for your testing yet?"

"I'm not sure if I'm—ready." I frowned. Mum stopped her primping, her hands dropping to her sides. She stared at me in the mirror.

"You don't have to do it, darling. I just thought you'd want to. You flipped the coin; I thought you wanted to know."

I shook my head, confused. The problem was, I didn't know if I wanted to know or not. One moment I thought, *Yes, I'll get this over and done with*, the next I'd crumble into a quivering heap of fear. If I knew and it was positive, what would be the point? What would be the point in anything?

But if I didn't know and it was positive, why waste years of my life on college or work, on keeping friendships, forming relationships? Even if I found someone who could put up with Dad, they'd end up seeing me not as a lover but a burden.

A big, old burden.

Much like my dad.

"Yeah," I paused. "I think I do want to get tested."

"Well, good! Now, go downstairs and make some breakfast for your father. I'll be down to say goodbye in a minute." Mum placed a hand on my back and gently prodded me out of the bathroom.

I walked downstairs in a daze, heading for the kitchen. Dad was seated at the table, dressed in a plaid shirt, reading the newspaper. Or, looking at it, at least. His eyes didn't seem to be moving much.

"Morning." He grinned.

"Morning." My voice was flat, a can of lemonade opened too long, and I forced my lips to remain downturned. It was hard not to smile around him, when he looked so pleased. I wondered if, in a weird way, he was happier now? He didn't look as uptight as he'd used to when I was younger and he was working late, and he and Mum were fighting all the time. Did he know what he had lost? When he was acting in this different manner, did he know he was doing it?

They say ignorance is bliss, but maybe ignorance would suck. Would I realise I was losing control? Would I be able to make simple decisions, like what to eat for breakfast? I didn't even know what Dad would want to eat. The man sitting at our kitchen table was a stranger.

"Toast?" I asked. It seemed the easier of the two imminent problems to deal with.

"Yes." His eyes were wide, and his smile even bigger. His enthusiasm was a little unsettling. It was, after all, only toast, but he was acting like I'd offered him Christmas. I popped two slices into the toaster and flipped it on. I boiled the kettle and got out two cups with tea bags.

When the slices were ready, I buttered them, and added the water to the tea. I placed Dad's breakfast down in front of him, and went back to the counter for mine.

I don't know how it happened, or exactly what he did, but while my back was turned I heard a scream. The sort of heart-piercing, ear-splitting scream that only someone experiencing real pain can make.

I spun around and saw Dad, his face crumpled like a piece of paper, red as a lobster, mouth open wide as he expelled a volume from his lungs I didn't think possible.

His teacup was sideways, its milky-brown contents pouring over the edge of the table and onto his stomach and groin, a waterfall of boiling hot lava.

I raced to his side, and pulled him to his feet. It was like getting a young child to move—he was too involved in his pain to respond with urgency to the physical commands I was giving him. When he wouldn't move fast enough I ran back into the kitchen and grabbed a tea towel. I threw it under the ice-cold water of the full blast tap and bolted back to Dad, pressing it up against his stomach where the dark coloured stain had spread. I moved at lightning speed, but everything felt like it was happening in slow motion. I couldn't come to his aid fast enough.

Mum rushed down the stairs, half a face of make-up on. The non-painted section drained of colour when she saw the scene in front of her. Another time, another place and I would have laughed.

"Kate, what happened?" She snatched the towel from my hands and pressed it harder against Dad, her face etched in concern. Dad's wails continued, a background noise of high-pitched pain.

"Nothing. I didn't do anything, I made him some tea and—"

"This is why I told you to look after him. He can't be trusted to manage on his own," she snapped. She rubbed his back and started nudging him to the stairs. I grabbed his other arm, the one with the tea towel, and helped her. He lifted his feet after a while, still wailing.

We reached the bathroom, and I turned the shower on full blast, cold water splashing out.

"Should we take off his clothes?" I asked Mum. Despite the situation, a flash of horror ran down my spine. I did not want to see my father naked.

"Let's just get him in there," she yelled over Dad's wails. We pushed him in the shower, fully dressed, and watched as the water poured over his head, plastering his brown hair against his face, changing the colour of his shirt from check black-and-white to a see-through grey. All the while, his screaming never stopped. It just went on, and on, and on.

If you've never heard a grown man scream before, it can be very disconcerting. Especially when the man in question is your father.

Mum and I just stood there, like idiots, watching in horror.

"Should I call emergency?" I asked.

"No, I think he'll be fine."

I nodded. She never took her eyes off him, though, so she probably didn't see me.

Then, just as suddenly as it had begun, his screaming stopped. He went from full-wail fire engine to quiet as a mouse in the space of a millisecond.

A tiny whimper escaped his mouth and he raised his arms across his chest and grasped his shoulders, shaking with cold. The soaking-wet tea towel was still clutched tight in his hand.

Mum darted beside him and turned off the taps, and I grabbed a big, fluffy, white towel from the railing. We wrapped him in it, Mum and me, swaddling him, tucking it in so his arms were trapped on either side of him.

He had tears running down his cheek and his face was a pale shade of pink. The water from his eyes added to the wetness still dripping down from his matted hair.

We went back downstairs and sat him on a new chair, Mum holding his hand, me fetching water, milk, cookies, toast. It was no use. Even when the crying stopped, his body still shook with sadness and a sense of desperation. No edible comfort would ease his trauma.

I glanced at the clock. Mum should have left already. I walked over and gently took his hand in mine, forcing hers out of his baby-like grip. It was hard being angry with this man for leaving and potentially cursing me with illness when he looked so forlorn and helpless.

Mum rushed around the kitchen, quickly washed her hands and smoothed back her hair. She pointed to the fridge, mentioned something about a list, gave Dad a quick kiss on the cheek and grabbed her make-up bag on the way out.

She was kissing him again? They were back together, even though mentally, his status had changed?

The kiss seemed to have worked, however. Dad stopped his sobbing and instead just stared steadfastly at the newspaper and meagre collection of food offerings I'd placed in front of him. He was frozen, his mouth set, his expression resolute. He looked tragic and broken, a still-life portrait of the man he had become.

It wasn't hard to imagine someone like Dad committing suicide if a normal day could start like this.

THIRTEEN

PULLED THE ends of my ponytail and watched the strands of my brown hair tighten around my head in the rear-view mirror. I looked down at my gold-buttoned black shirt and tight black jeans teamed with Doc Martens. *Deep breaths, Kate.* It was only a trial, after all. Why I'd decided to arrive forty minutes early was a mystery, even to me.

When there was ten minutes till the start of my shift, I couldn't stand it any longer. I got out of my car and slammed the door, walking 'round to the front of the café.

"You're early," the boy said as I walked over to the counter.

"Not that early." I shrugged and checked my watch. I had got the right time, hadn't I? What if I was hours early or, oh God, a whole day? Had I screwed up?

"She's more on time than you, little brother," a second voice sounded. A tall guy with longish brown hair, a goatee and crystal blue eyes walked over to me, hand outstretched.

"Kate," I said.

"Johnny," he replied, pumping my arm up and down with vigour. "And you obviously already know my brother."

"Uh …" I trailed off. When I'd texted about the job, I'd hoped he would sign with a "from 'insert-name-here'" reply, but no such luck. For some reason, he hadn't signed off. Now I was standing here in front of him, and he wasn't even wearing a nametag.

"You *do* know my brother, don't you?"

I said *no*, just as the boy replied *yes*. It was all I could do not to stomp my feet. Why was this guy so infuriating?

"She means, she doesn't know my name, but she knows me," the boy told Johnny, an edge of a smile creeping up his face.

"Oh, man. Not this bullshit again." Johnny ran his hands through his hair, pulling loose threads out of his ponytail. "You'll have to excuse him. He *loves* to get all mystic and shit."

"You need to accept that life isn't about labels." The boy poured some milk from a metal jug into a glass sitting on the counter in front of him.

"Dude, are you gonna be like this all day?" Johnny raised his eyebrows.

"What is a day but a measure of time, set to control the universe, and—"

"I'm gonna grab Kate some forms." Johnny shook his head and disappeared into a door out the back.

"I'm just stirring him up." The boy looked over at me. "I promise, I'm not really like that."

"You seem kinda like that to me." I frowned. I couldn't quite figure him out. Normal guy with open-minded attitude or lecturing freak? Either way, I knew there was no way I was going to ask for his name. Not when he'd withheld it so carefully.

Johnny jogged over to us and placed a stack of papers to the left-hand side of the cash register. "All right. I have your forms here. Just fill out the emergency contact one for now; we'll get you to fill the rest out at the end of the trial."

Emergency contact? Would that be … Mum?

"I mean, if you do a good job and we decide to get you back." Johnny was still speaking, bouncing on the balls of his feet. "No wonder you look so confused."

"Thanks." I took the paper and pen he offered, and quickly scribbled down Stacey's number. If I had an emergency situation while here, Mum wouldn't be able to come; she'd have Dad.

"So, what do you want me to do?"

"Right. No small talk, I like that." Johnny nodded, and punched his brother on the arm. "I like her."

"This order needs to be taken to the table by the window." The boy shoved a tray with two cups on it toward me. "The one on the right is a latte, the other a skim flat white, and the patrons are seated accordingly."

I slid the tray to my chest and held it from underneath. No way could I balance the thing with one hand as I'd seen the professional waitresses do, and after my recent scalding-hot-liquid experience-monitoring failure, my confidence was at an all-time low.

When I got to the table and it came time to place the orders, my arm started to shake. I could feel the eyes of the two brothers upon me.

Is this a symptom?

"Hi." I smiled, in what I hoped was a convincing manner. Customer number one, a lady in a green floral-print dress who looked sort of round at the edges, smiled back at me. Customer number two, a man whose face was all hard lines and abrupt posture, did not.

"So, as I was saying, if the market keeps falling like this, we'll—what are you doing? Drop the coffee, and go." The man shook his head at me, eyes agog. I hovered with one coffee held aloft, hoping that one of them would indicate it was theirs. Did the boy say his left and right, or my left and right?

"My apologies, sir." I gave him what I thought was the full-cream drink. Granted his physique was thinner than the woman across from him, but I felt like he was the sort of guy who'd want indulgence, and skim milk was certainly not that. Then I lifted the second cup and saucer, my hand shaking as I placed the rattling drink in front of the lady.

"Thanks." The man sniffed. He fiddled with a brown, leather wallet lying on the table then placed a ten-dollar note flat on my empty tray. I nodded in thanks and quickly scuttled back to the counter where I slid the tray across toward the boy and his brother.

"You got a tip?" The boy had a very cheeky grin creeping up one side of his face.

"You know he's already paid, right? He must like you." Johnny laughed and wiggled his eyebrows comically.

"Well it clearly wasn't her service." The boy chimed in. "She gave them the wrong drinks." The boys guffawed, and Johnny slapped his brother's back, like it was the funniest thing they'd ever heard. I shuffled my feet.

I was on trial for a job. My bosses knew I was seeing a counsellor. And one of my bosses wouldn't tell me his name.

Like this wasn't already embarrassing enough.

"Gu-uys," I sighed, and tucked a loose strand of hair behind my ear.

"Seriously? A tenner on top of the coffees is a huge tip." Johnny gave a gentle smile. "It's more than the price of the drinks themselves."

"I think it was more about *this*." The boy lifted the note and produced a business card from underneath, flipping it around in his fingers. "Looks like he was hoping the ten could influence you to provide a little extra service, if you know what I mean."

"I think I quit," I muttered, the heat burning in my cheeks.

"No! Kate, ignore him, he's an ass." Johnny jogged around the counter and threw a casual arm around my shoulders. "We were just teasing. I promise I'll try be more professional."

"We both will." The boy placed a jug of water under the milk spout of the coffee machine, and it roared into life as he cleaned it. He gave me a quick wink when Johnny turned away, and I managed a smile back.

I didn't really know what to make of the two brothers and how easily they'd decided I fit in to their routine. Johnny was such a large personality, and Mr "Try Everything Once" was certainly pleasant enough. I couldn't help but fit in.

The shift was surprisingly easy. It was a simple job: take orders, serve orders, clear tables, wash, repeat. It wasn't planning a tour or organising an event, but it killed the time well enough.

"You're a fast learner," the boy commented as he watched me press buttons for the correct items on the cash register with speed.

"I'm using a computer. It's not exactly hard." I rolled my eyes, but felt myself push up my chest a little. It was nice to know that something in my life was going right for a change.

"True, but sometimes it's the little things in life, the ones you take for granted, that really are most important."

I took the coffees he'd placed in front of me and walked to the table where they belonged. His words resonated in my head like they should have meant something, something more.

"What do you mean?" I asked, when back behind the counter.

"I mean that it's the little things that make life great."

"But that's not true." I crossed my arms against my stomach. He kept playing with the coffee machine, a mysterious little smile on his face as he cleaned the milk spout and dumped the old, used beans in the bin.

"What about college and having a career? Or having babies? Or … or love, and marriage, and all that?" I blurted out. "They're all huge, massive things. And they're great. The greatest."

And they were. When I thought about life potentially with Huntington's, and the big things being taken away from me, all those doors slamming in my face, there was nothing small to take solace in.

"They're big things that are built on a series of tiny happily ever afters and tragedies." He finally put the cleaning materials down, running his hand through his floppy brown hair so it stopped hanging over his eyes. "Say, you had a friend who went to college. Say she went there, and she found love. She got married and had a child."

"Her life sounds great," I said.

"Say you did none of those things. Then, say someone announced over a loud-speaker the world was ending tomorrow," he continued, unperturbed. "Would you rush out, throw yourself into love, make a baby, and enrol in college?"

"No."

"Why?"

"Because there'd be no point. I wouldn't have time."

"So what would you do?"

"Ummm …" I paused, searching the drawings on the wall. The one closest to me showed a wave, crashing and curling. It was beautiful. "I guess I'd do whatever made me happy."

"And is what makes you happy the same as what makes your friend happy?"

"No."

"Isn't it? In the last twenty-four hours, it's the little things. You can have all the possessions and love in the world, but on your last day on earth, you and your friend will be enjoying the little things. She'd be smiling like you would, holding hands with those she loves, eating delicious food and—"

"She'd probably be screwing her husband," I muttered.

"Exactly! She'd have sex." The boy raised his finger in a very "Elementary, my dear Watson" kind of way. "A symbol of love. A smaller version of the whole. A tiny great thing that can end in a marriage, a baby, a life together."

"If it was sex with a random it wouldn't be great." I drew my brows.

"Everyone is random to someone." He smiled. "Which brings me to my point; until you can appreciate the greatness of opportunity in the small things—and I'm not just talking about sex—you won't be able to really appreciate the great bigger things that could be heading your way."

"I don't have great bigger things." I turned, and started to tidy a pile of napkins. A light sweat broke out on the back of my neck. Something about this talk made me uneasy.

"You do." The boy shrugged. "You just haven't found them yet."

"God, he's not getting all Zen on your ass again, is he?" Johnny came swooping into the service area, and all the awkward feelings that were busy swirling and churning their way through my gut dissipated.

"Johnny is a prime example of someone who doesn't know how to appreciate the little things." The boy arched an eyebrow at me and swatted his brother's thigh with a rolled up tea towel.

"That's because me and the word *little* don't tend to go hand in hand." He laughed, and faux punched his brother in the stomach. "Don't scare Kate off, bro. I really want her to be our new employee." Johnny smiled, and I felt my body relax. Weird spiritual talks aside, I'd nailed it. I guess that meant I'd gotten the job.

"Yeah, yeah." The boy nodded and shrugged the whole thing off. Something about their brotherly camaraderie made me comfortable. It wasn't stiff and terse, as things were with my family at the moment. In fact, with their over-the-top joking, there was barely a formal moment. They'd been through the ultimate tragedy, but their family bond was strong.

Why couldn't I be more like that?

The shift continued much in that fashion, the two boys laughing and teasing until Johnny excused himself when the last customer walked out, saying he had a counselling appointment to go to.

"So, what's next?" I asked. The café was empty and the streetlights had started to flicker on. Dark shadows spread across the room.

"Well, usually I stack the chairs then wash the floors." The boy lifted a chair up and stood it on the table, placing another upside down on its seat.

I watched him do one table, then start on a second. After a while he tilted his head at me, a puzzled look on his face.

"Is something wrong?"

"Nope." I shook my head and leaned back against the counter.

"You just don't feel like helping?"

"You didn't say *we* do it. You said that's what *you* do. So,

I'm watching." I folded my arms and flashed him a cheeky grin of my own. It felt good to get some back, after their teasing earlier in the day.

"You like to watch?" He walked over to the door and flicked the *Open* sign to *Closed*. He flashed a look back at me over his shoulder and I was glad for the counter's support. Otherwise, I don't know how well my knees would have handled the hot flush that momentarily weakened them.

The boy approached, taking long, deliberate steps toward me. He cleared the café in an agonising thirty seconds and I took in his tall, lean body, the olive toned skin, the glasses that screamed kind of nerdy but cute, and how they amplified the deep intent in his eyes.

"I'm glad you came in for the trial." His face was inches from mine. My heart pounded against the walls of my chest, busting to get out of my ribcage.

Was he going to kiss me? Was this really happening?

I licked my lips, and felt the heat of his breath on my face. He smelt like coffee, and outdoors, and man.

I thought about how his lips would feel, how his body would feel, how I wanted it pressed up against me. I'd never felt this sort of attraction with Dave. Maybe that was because we were meant to be just friends.

Friends. Because that's what me and this boy were. And all because of who and what my life had become.

There was no point trying to pursue something with this guy when, once he knew the truth, it'd all be over. He seemed to be okay with Dad on a surface level, but when he found out about the hereditary nature of the disease and how much worse Dad was going to get, I doubted he'd stick around. For crying out loud; he wouldn't even tell me his name. How likely was it he'd be accepting of Huntington's?

"Yeah. It's great Johnny likes me, and seems to want me back." My voice was light and airy. I pushed off the counter and walked over to the nearest table, stacking the chairs in a mirror image of what I'd just seen him do.

"Yeah. I'd say he does for sure." I couldn't look at his face.

I didn't want to see if he was hurt or—worse—completely unaffected. I didn't want to see him at all, not while I was so damn confused.

"You can take off now, Kate." I turned to him, and he nodded to the door. "I've got the rest of this."

"Are you sure?"

"I'm sure."

I walked over to the door and paused there for a second, unsure if I was doing the right thing.

"Kate?"

"Yes?" I spun around at lightning speed.

He was there, right behind me, incredibly close. I had no idea how he'd moved so fast, but his broad shoulders were suddenly at my chin level, the muscled lines of his arms visible beneath his shirt.

I slowly let my eyes roam up his body, across his chest and over his rigid jawline, over the little freckle on his cheek and deep into his chocolate eyes that were staring into mine, staring through me, like he could see every little secret I'd ever kept.

Don't look at his lips, Kate. Do not look at his lips.

I let my eyes flick down to his lips and saw they were slightly parted and wet. His Adam's apple bobbed as he swallowed, and a shiver ran down my spine.

Maybe it would be worth it after all. Maybe he'd be different.

Maybe he wouldn't call me or my family members crazy.

"Lachlan." His lips formed the word.

"Pardon?" I was jerked out of the moment, my eyes snapping back to his. I'd been about to kiss him, even after I'd decided not to earlier. I was—what was *wrong* with me?

The heat of embarrassment warmed my cheeks again, and I wanted to melt in a puddle on the floor. Why would I have thought he liked me? Why would I look at his lips, for crying out loud?

He was telling me his name. Not trying to make out with me.

Probably what he was doing before.

"My name is Lachlan," he said softly.

"I …" I gave an awkward wave of my hand. "I have to go."

I spun on my heel and ran out the door.

Fourteen

"I BET YOU didn't expect to see me back so soon." I settled myself into the tiny chair opposite Leslie's. I wondered whether she had any larger patients and, if so, if they fit in between the narrow, black arms. Maybe that was one of the side effects of having a family member with a disease: weight loss. Gosh, it'd be every female's dream.

"How are you today, Kate?" Leslie ignored my glib comment and smiled at me, hands laced gently over her knee.

"Okay." I shrugged. Torrents of water bucketed down. They coated the window, and blurred the world outside.

"Have you spent much time with your father?"

"You know." I shrugged again. At this rate, my shoulders were going to get a workout, too. The Huntington's Diet: good for weight loss and shoulder muscle building.

"No, I don't." Leslie's smile never faltered. Maybe the Counsellor's Diet involved strong cheek muscles. "When did you last spend time with him?"

I racked my brain, cataloguing the last few days in my mind.

"Yesterday, I guess," I said. "At dinner."

"And what did you talk about?"

I forced my brain to try and remember the mundane events of dinner the night before.

"I had a job trial a few days ago, so Mum asked how that went." I bit my lip. "And we talked about the medication Dad was on."

"What about how your father was feeling?"

"What do you mean?"

"Did you talk to him at all about his feelings, and the emotions he was going through?"

"Not really."

"What about you? Did you share your feelings and emotions with him?"

"It was family dinner, not a counselling session," I said. "You asked about the last time we hung out, not the last time we got involved in a deep and meaningful."

"Well, when was that?"

Silence.

I smiled. For a moment I was worried I'd have to say before it all, back when he was still my father and not this stranger living in our house. I was fairly certain that would be the *wrong answer*.

"A week ago he told me he thought a boy liked me."

"That's nice." Leslie nodded encouragingly. "And what did you say in return?"

"That he probably didn't." I thought back to the flash that had darkened Lachlan's eyes when he'd walked toward me at the end of my shift, the way he seemed to see straight through me and melt my insides.

"Was that an honest answer?"

"Yes," I replied quickly. Because once Lachlan knew the truth, it would be.

"And how do you feel about that? Didn't you and your boyfriend break up a few weeks ago?"

I exhaled, a long stream of air coming out of my nose. I stared at the water on the window again. I could only see the shape and shadow of the tree outside. No definition at all.

"It still hurts," I admitted. I gripped my hands together and gave one of my wrists a light pinch. "But I think I'd stopped—stopped loving him a long time ago. I was with him because it was easy, not because it was right." The words rang true as they left my mouth. "And thinking of him—it doesn't hurt nearly as much as all this." I raised my arm limply then let it drop. Sometimes it all seemed so big and overwhelming and scary.

"You're allowed to hurt."

I stared out the window again. I didn't need her permission to be sad. Oft times, all I felt was the weight of this oppressive sadness hovering over me. Even when I smiled with Stacey, even when I'd laughed with Johnny, it was still this niggling itch in the corner of my mind I just couldn't let go of.

Sometimes, the sadness is everything.

"How do you cope when it all gets too much?" It was like she'd read my mind.

"I don't know," I choked out. "Sometimes I can almost forget about it, get lost in a moment. Then I remember and it's sad again."

"What do you do then?" Leslie's face softened from one-thousand-megawatt smile to something more half-hearted. It was like someone turned down the sun.

"Nothing, I guess." I thought of the night I'd watched movies to forget, then the time I'd turned to a fortune teller to predict my future, then the time I'd kicked my toe to feel pain, to feel release.

Yes.

That.

"You must do something," Leslie pressed.

"Well … sometimes I just do something else," I said.

"To forget?"

"More to push it away."

"You know, forgetting this problem, pushing it away, isn't going to make it any easier," Leslie said. I steepled my hands at the bridge of my nose and shook my head. Why was this all so hard? What did she want me to say?

"Well, what's the right answer, then? Tell me, and I'll say it back."

"This isn't a test." Leslie's voice was level as ever.

"Then why do I feel like you're constantly judging me?"

"Kate, I promise you I am not judging." She shook her head. "And I'm sorry if I made you feel that way. It was never my intention."

I stared out the window again. It was becoming my solace, my escapism from the intense questions that constantly spewed forth from her mouth. I thought of the old man I'd seen walking through those gardens the other day. Was he not walking today because of the rain? Or had something happened? Was he no longer walking because he was no longer able to?

"Let's talk about why you're here," Leslie said. "You want to get tested, so I've printed out the two referrals, one for the neurologist, the other the psychiatrist." Leslie grabbed two sheets of paper from the printer and handed them to me.

I looked at the papers like they were made of fire.

"You do want to get tested, right?" Leslie's eyebrows were raised.

"Sure," I agreed. It made sense. I should get tested. There was no reason for me to not get tested.

Was there?

"You're not very convincing." Leslie gave a wry smile. "There's no rush, you know. I want you to keep seeing me through the process, regardless. And remember; you don't have to get tested just because there's a possibility the answer will be yes."

"More like a probability."

"A *possibility*," Leslie corrected.

We lapsed into silence again.

"Do you want to get tested?"

I thought back to the morning when I'd discussed it with Mum. Then I thought about everything else—my life. "Yes."

"Why do you want to get tested?"

"I feel like we've been through this."

"Indulge me." Leslie tilted her head to one side.

"Because until I know, I feel like I don't know how to plan my life. Whether I should pursue a career, date boys—God, I don't even know if I should take out private health insurance." I gave a bitter laugh.

"Well, there's an easy one." Leslie gave a soft laugh. "You should get private health cover, Huntington's or no."

"Gee, thanks for solving that." I rolled my eyes. "Sorry," I added. I hadn't meant to be so rude.

"Did you book this appointment, Kate?"

She already knew I hadn't.

"No," I indulged her.

"Your mum did?"

"My mum."

"Why?"

"Because she thought I wanted to get tested," I started, "and I do. Like I said. I'm pretty sure it makes sense. Otherwise I'm just floating in nothing."

"And she didn't book you in because she thought you could use some support?"

More silence. We were getting very good at it.

"If you have it, what will you do?"

"I'm pretty sure I have it anyway. I flipped a coin. And a fortune-teller kinda told me …"

"A fortune-teller told you?" Leslie's hand slapped down on her desk. Her face contorted into a mixture of shock and anger, the two least controlled emotions I'd ever seen her display.

"Well, not exactly," I back-pedalled. "But she heavily implied it. Said there would be sad times ahead for me and my family, knew there was something wrong with my dad's head …"

"Is that why you want to get tested? Do you feel like your chances are higher than fifty per cent?"

Yes. Absolutely.

Part of me feels like it's almost guaranteed.

"No," I lied. "I know the statistics."

"You do," Leslie agreed. "Although something tells me

you're not trusting them."

I didn't reply. The sound of her clock ticked by and the whir of the fan, despite the torrential rain outside, created a steady, deafening buzz. The background nothingness was all consuming.

The skull on her desk stared at me and I was fairly certain it mouthed the word *sprung*.

FIFTEEN

I STOOD UNDER the building's awning, waiting for a gap in the rain before I ran to the parking lot. It was a two-hundred-metre dash from the care unit, and I just didn't have anything important enough to rush home for on a Friday night. Stacey was out on another date, and Mum and Dad were home having Chinese takeaway.

If I were on tour, I'd be in Melbourne right now.

The thought was in my head before I could stop it, then all I could think about were the things I wasn't doing. I wasn't forging a career. I doubted I'd even get another shift at the café, after running off at the end of my trial.

I wasn't watching my boyfriend make it to the top. I wasn't hanging out with Lee Collins, networking with Coal's manager, trying to organise an internship or more joint events. I hadn't even lost my virginity.

I was a great big loser with no Friday night plans and no foreseeable future.

Happy Friday to me.

"Whatcha doing?" I was so stuck in my own mind I

jumped what felt like a foot in the air when I heard Lachlan's voice. What was he doing here? What were the odds of him having an appointment around the same time as mine *again*? And why didn't he run out in the rain and pretend not to see me, when that was clearly the appropriate thing to be done in this situation?

"What do you think?" I snapped, because it seemed safest.

"Looks like you're being afraid." Lachlan stepped up beside me, gazing out at the rain-drenched grass before us. "You know, it's just a little rain."

"A little?" I raised my eyebrows, gesturing at the sheets of water that were falling from the heavens. "You call this little?"

"I'm not going to make a joke about the size of my penis right now." Lachlan winked at me. I fought with my face to keep my lips straight. It wasn't even funny. And I hated boys who made dick jokes like that. Even though he'd only made a joke about making one.

I gritted my teeth and stared at the rain ahead. It showed no sign of easing up. Maybe it was worth getting soaked to the bone if it meant I didn't have to stand here with him.

"Well, I'll see you later, then." Lachlan smiled at me. He popped open an umbrella and its large red-and-white awning spread out, completely covering his head and shoulders. "G'bye." He took a step out into the rain and it made a loud smattering noise over his umbrella.

"What?" I was fairly sure my eyes were popping out of my head. "Aren't you at least going to ask me if I want to share your umbrella?"

"I've already offered you a job." Lachlan gave that lopsided smile of his again. "If I was to offer you my umbrella, you'd owe me big."

"Excuse me? I have the job because Johnny said I did well at the trial." My jaw dropped. The nerve. Like I owed him. He could take his stupid job, and his umbrella, for all I cared. Screw them both.

"Of course, I'd be willing to share if you did something for me." Lachlan stepped closer. The rain that had been dripping from his umbrella now landed on the toes of my black shoes, creating dark mirrors.

"Go on," I said, my eyebrows drawn.

"Well, I'll gladly walk you to the parking lot," Lachlan started, "if we both hop in a car together. I want you to come out with me tonight."

"Where?"

"To try something new," Lachlan said. "Remember? It's all about living in the present."

"Forget it." I shook my head. I'd rather get wet than listen to more of his psycho bullshit. I already had Leslie for that.

"Suit yourself." He shrugged and turned his back, taking long strides down the path into the rain. I watched him as he disappeared toward the parking lot, his umbrella bobbing as he walked.

I sucked in a deep breath.

It's just a little rain.

I can do this.

I gingerly put one foot forward. Rain soaked my ankle and sunk deep into my shoes. I stepped out again and my heel shot up. I stumbled backward, my hands grasping for stability on the brick pillar to my left. I jerked my foot back under the awning. I'd been out there for maybe two seconds and already I felt like I was in danger of falling over.

Symptoms of Huntington's disease: loss of balance, and lack of basic co-ordination.

God, turn it off. I needed to get out of my head.

Would spending the night with Lachlan really be so bad? He could share his umbrella, and I could lean on his arm.

And his family are broken, too. *Just like mine.*

"Wait," I yelled. "Wait!" The rain was so loud I wasn't sure he'd hear me, but, sure enough, he turned, and jogged down the path, huge umbrella swaying from side to side.

"Okay." I nodded.

"Okay …?" Lachlan squinted at me, and I slapped him lightly on the front of his shoulder. It was hard beneath my touch, much firmer than I'd thought it'd be.

Not that I'd thought about how his chest would feel at all. Much.

"Okay, I'll go on a date with you."

"Who said anything about a date?" Lachlan asked, but his eyes were alive with mischief.

"You know I didn't mean it like that. I meant, like, a friend date." I shook my head. Must he be so exasperating all the time?

"Friend date it is." Lachlan grinned at me and held out his arm. "Shall we?"

I rolled my eyes and linked my arm through his, trying not to lean too close into his body but still be protected by the umbrella.

Two minutes into our walk, and I was certain I'd made the right decision. My ankles were the only part of me getting wet, but they were so thoroughly soaked I could hear my feet squelching in water that had infiltrated my shoes, making every step treacherous as I battled not only to gain purchase on the moss-covered path, but to keep traction within each shoe itself.

"Which car's yours?" Lachlan yelled, struggling to be heard above the rain.

"Mine?" I ignored the slightly hurt voice in my head. He'd obviously gotten over the friend date idea. Not that I minded, of course. Not even a little bit.

"Yes."

"That one." I pointed. The lot had gotten very dark, and yellow streetlights highlighted its four corners. Lachlan guided me over to my vehicle, waiting as I retrieved my keys from the depths of my inky-black purse and turned them in the lock.

"Well, I guess I'll be off, then." I unlaced our arms. My elbow felt cold when it left the heat of his body.

"Off where?" Lachlan looked confused. "You owe me a friend date."

"But we're at my car."

"Yes." Lachlan nodded, like he was explaining the most obvious truth in the world. "But since I ride a motorbike—and

I doubt that's the try-something-new experience you're after tonight—I thought we'd take your car."

I blinked, my lashes sticking slightly to my cheeks, which had somehow gotten damp despite the umbrella's protection. He was absolutely right. There was no way I was hopping on a bike with him, rain or not.

That just left one option; taking him home, or out, or wherever the hell we were going, in my car.

What have I got to lose?

"Hop in." I gestured to my beat-up yellow machine. I opened the driver's door and slid into the leather seat myself, watching as he jogged around the other side and fell into the seat next to me.

"Let's go." He grinned, closing the umbrella and tossing it in the back. To my surprise, I turned on the car and reversed out of the spot, leaving the parking lot with Lachlan in my passenger seat.

And despite the persistent alarm bells going off in my head, I didn't ask him to put his wet umbrella in the plastic bag I specifically kept in the car for such a purpose.

Even though I really, really wanted to.

SIXTEEN

I DROVE TOWARD home after Lachlan insisted he would be coming back to Sydney on Sunday for Johnny's appointment and could pick up his bike then. It was an unspoken agreement between the two of us; he didn't ask what my problem was, and I didn't delve into his, even though we both could have taken a reasonable guess. He must have guessed something was up with my father, just like I knew his dad had passed away from cancer.

In some ways, I was dying to know. Why was he here? Was it just coping with grief, or was he sick, too? And, if so, how sick? How did he go about life, start a café, with that sense of impending doom hanging over his head?

Lachlan broke the silence once we hit the freeway. The skies had cleared up and were more of an omniscient dark haze, than a waterfall of doom. "So, tell me something you haven't done before but always kind of wanted to."

"I don't know." I immediately banished the obvious "have sex" from my mind. It wasn't exactly a first I was looking to break right now.

"There must be lots of things you haven't done but wanted to," Lachlan continued, like my answer presented no problem to him. "How about sky diving? Have you ever been sky diving?"

"No." My knuckles popped as I gripped the steering wheel. "*And* it's night *and* it's just been storming. I can't think of a worse idea!"

"Okay, I'll cross it off the list." I could hear the smile in his voice. Clearly he'd been stirring. Jerk.

"I'd say get a tattoo, but I already have one," I said loftily.

"You do?"

"Yep." Score one, me.

"What of?"

"A musical note." I twisted my lips into a grimace. A musical note I'd gotten with Dave, at the same time as he got his.

"I've never had a tattoo removed before," I offered brightly.

"Nice try, Kate," Lachlan said my name with delicacy. "But some scars you need to bear."

I ignored his cryptic words and concentrated on driving, weaving the car to the far lane and checking my headlights were on. It was dark, but the moon bathed the freeway in an eerie light, its orange glow providing enough illumination to make out the ridges of cliffs on either side of the empty road.

We drove in silence for a while, me concentrating on the speedometer, Lachlan with his eyebrows furrowed, his hands loosely draped over his knees.

At the sign, we took the turnoff for Lakes, and I followed the streets to my house. I waited for him to say something, to come up with some brilliant plan, or to at least tell me where he lived so I could drop him off.

For some reason, though, I didn't want to break the silence. I didn't really want the trip to end.

"Left," Lachlan said, when we were about five kilometres from my house. I shot him a quizzical look and turned off the main road onto a side street. It was close to where I lived, sure, but I'd never really been the exploring type. And I knew this street ended in bushland, anyway.

Bushland.

I barely knew this guy.

Uh-oh.

I've seen this horror movie.

Is he taking me here to kill me?

"Uh, so, where are we going?" I chanced a quick look over at him. His eyes were alive again, focused on a prize I couldn't see. He didn't look like a serial killer. My gaze trailed down his arms …

Those arm muscles look toned; like they could seriously do some damage.

Or like they could sweep me up and pull me toward him in a Mills-and-Boon style passionate embrace …

The heat was in my cheeks before I even realised what I was thinking. I quickly reached for the AC and turned it up as high as it would go, letting the frosty air cool me down to a somewhat normal temperature.

"Park over here," Lachlan said once we reached the end of the street. I pulled up to the wooden barrier and killed the engine, letting the silence of the night fill the car. It was dark here, just shy of completely black. The only lights came from my clock radio, which reflected the nine pm time, the full moon, and a streetlamp three houses from us that reflected the sheen of wetness covering the road below.

"So, have you taken me here to kill me?" I joked. Or, I hoped that was what I was doing.

"I'm relieved you're so untrusting, but no," Lachlan said and opened the car door. The sounds of the summer night came rushing in to greet me: crickets, the wind, the rush of water falling over rocks somewhere in the distance. "Come on."

He hopped out of the car and shut the door carefully behind him. I wondered what the hell his plan was. If he thought I'd never been bushwalking at night, it was true, but there was a reason for that, such as, oh, yeah, it was *dangerous* and you could easily *slip and break a leg*.

I was about to tell him all this as I met him around the front of the car when he reached out—and held my hand.

"Let's go," he said, like it was the most natural thing in the world, and started to walk. My eyes widened, and I tried to make sense of my thoughts. I didn't want to go in the bush with him. It was dangerous. And why was he holding my hand?

And why was my hand so sweaty?

We moved around the wooden guardrail and started to descend a leafy track, our way lit by the moon, and tiny white markers reflecting off the spotlight on Lachlan's phone. The ground was slippery but not unmanageable, and as we kept walking, I found myself—strangely—enjoying it.

The humid summer air bathed my skin. The sound of the wind, the crickets and the rushing of water were sharp, and the smells—the scent of rain, the hint of some native flower here, the earthy smell of mud there—it was amazing. I didn't even think to be scared.

We turned another corner and entered a clearing. Lachlan shone the light of his phone forward and I saw the gleaming lines of rocks, then the steady falling of a waterfall plummeting down to meet a silvery pool beneath it.

I dropped his hand and raced forward. I stopped at the edge and looked out. The waterfall rushed down to meet the lake in a chaos of bubbles that quickly dispersed so they were no more than ripples by the time the water met the sand. It was a living, breathing thing, this beautiful copse of woodland. I felt myself still, my whole body stone: it was without a doubt one of the most exquisite things I had ever seen.

"Is this—okay?" Lachlan asked. I didn't realise he'd come to join me but there he was, phone-light in hand.

"Okay?" I bit my lip. "It's *more* than okay. It's just—it's everything."

It felt like the craziness of the past few weeks was nothing, nothing at all compared to this intense natural wonder. I blinked and stared again, barely believing it was real. How had this beauty been so close to me for so long, yet I'd never seen it?

If I had, would I have realised it?

"I'm glad you like it." I felt Lachlan link his hand with mine again and give it a tiny, reassuring squeeze. "Because you're about to go skinny-dipping."

"What?" I grabbed my hand back, clutching it to my chest. Was he out of his mind? I turned to face him, ready to slap him from cheek to shoulder, and was met with that infuriating grin of his.

"What? You haven't done it before, have you?" Lachlan laughed, his eyes giggling with him.

"I haven't even had *sex* before, I doubt—" I clapped my hand over my mouth.

"Well, we can add that to the list for later." Lachlan smiled, then quickly added, "Kidding! Kidding!" when I shot him a murderous look.

I bit my lip. If I were honest with myself, part of me wanted to try it. I'd never been skinny-dipping before, even though I knew it was pretty much a rite of passage for every teenager in town.

But what if this guy was a creep? What if this was all some weird ploy to see me naked?

A really sexy creep …

"You don't have to if you don't want to." Lachlan stepped back. "But it's something I've never done. So, if you could please turn around …"

"Why?"

"I'm getting naked," Lachlan said the words slowly, like it was painfully obvious. I cringed and turned my back to him, burying my head in my hands in case my facing the opposite direction wasn't enough. My eyes had grown accustomed to the light, and I knew I could have made out his naked body if I'd been looking.

If.

How did this happen? Two hours ago I was furious after another shitty counselling appointment, feeling all pent up and stressed about my neuro and psych appointments, and now I was trying to decide if I would go skinny-dipping with a boy I'd only just met who had nice arms and beautiful eyes and a really hard chest and—oh.

This was not good, at all.

I heard a loud splash and spun around. The water's surface was broken, large ripples spreading out near the rocks. Seconds later, Lachlan's head and shoulders surfaced above the lake, his brown hair plastered to his face.

"I'm going to swim over there." Lachlan tilted his head toward the opposite corner of the pool. "In case this water is a little more see-through than I think." He dived under the surface, and I smiled, knowing he knew full well I couldn't see a thing under the deep black, cover.

He dived and surfaced, floating every now and then. I sat down on a rock and studied my hands, checked my phone, listened to the waterfall. But, for some reason, I wasn't as lost in the magic as I was before. And I wouldn't look at Lachlan; I *couldn't*. It was like he wanted me to, and I wouldn't let him have the satisfaction.

I checked my phone and noted the time: 10:03 pm. We'd been there for an hour. I'd have to think about heading home soon. My fingers scraped my thigh and I gave it a little pinch. Home, to Dad and Mum, before it reached curfew and Mum lost it. Although that made me wonder when was the last time Mum lost it with me?

When was the last time I took a risk?

And how bad would taking one really be?

Without time to think about what I was doing, I stripped off my clothes, leaving them in a pile near the rock. I didn't dare look to see if Lachlan was checking me out, instead focusing on speed and precision as I rid myself of the items like stripping was an Olympic event before splashing into the pool, all within the space of ten seconds.

The water was icy cold, numbing every part of my body except my head. There, it felt cool, refreshing against the heat that had been surrounding it. I pushed the water back and swam deep, deeper, until I felt my lungs bursting for air, like they couldn't hold any longer. I turned and kicked up to the surface, paying close attention to the way the water felt on every inch of my body. It was such a different sensation than showering, or swimming in a bikini, even though I knew both were incredibly similar. Something about this was just—something about this was free.

"It's great, right?" Lachlan's voice surprised me, coming from much closer than I'd imagined. His naked body. Right there. I rubbed the water from my eyes, thankful I wasn't wearing mascara.

"The best." I grinned back at him. He was an arm's length away, and I wondered what would happen if our legs met while we trod water to stay afloat. If they would tangle, bringing us closer together.

What his arms would feel like, pulling me to him, pressing my bare chest against his in the almost blackness of the night.

"Race you!" He gave a wicked grin and ducked under the water, freestyling like mad to the side of the pool where we'd dove in. I took a deep breath and followed, thankful he'd snapped those crazy thoughts from my mind.

He beat me—by ages, of course—but when I got there I called a rematch, and we went again, powering after each other through the pool, over and over until my arms were so sore, and my breath so caught in my chest.

I forgot where I was, what had happened with my family, the fact that I was naked … It was like nothing existed but the here, and the now, and this burning exhaustion in my chest, and this exuberant joy bursting throughout the rest of my body.

"I …" I started to say. I looked at his eyes, hope in them, like he expected me to call another race. All of a sudden, the whole situation seemed so funny—skinny-dipping swimming races with a virtual stranger in the dark—that a big bubble of laughter worked its way up my throat and blurted out my mouth.

"What?" Lachlan said. "What's so funny?"

"It's just—the race—and the—oh, God …" I couldn't contain it. Mirth rose through my chest and I laughed, the sort of crazy hysterical laughter that was obviously catching, as soon Lachlan joined me, too, and we were two idiots losing our minds, treading water in a pool in the middle of the night.

"I'm—I'm hopping out, now." I bit my lip when our laughter finally evaporated into shallow gasps for air. "Can you …?"

"Of course." I saw something flash in Lachlan's eyes. My stomach tingled, or was it slightly lower down? I wanted to see that flash again, so I swum closer, until his face was so close to mine I could see the droplets on his forehead, the way his hair was slicked to his head.

I parted my lips slightly. It was all I could do not to wrap my legs around him. He lifted one hand and pressed a finger to my lips. It was shrivelled and wet.

"I'll turn around now." He turned his back and put his hands over his eyes for good measure.

I trod my way to the edge of the pool until I felt the slimy surface of mud and rock beneath my feet.

"Ew!" I shrieked as my foot slipped deeper into the mud. "This is so gross."

"I know," Lachlan said, hands still clamped firmly over his eyes. I waded out of the pool and ran over to my clothes, struggling to get them on.

Once I was dressed, I felt almost more exposed than before. My hair was a mess, and I was sure the water had washed off whatever foundation I'd had left on. I wasn't one of those Victoria's Secret model-types who looked hot when they were wet. I felt even more naked than I had in the water.

"Your turn," I sang in a voice that wasn't nearly as confident as I felt. I turned my back to him and studied the leafy floor. No covering my eyes this time.

"'Kay," he said, and I tried to ignore the sound of water slapping against his skin and imagining what it would look like if I turned around.

I wasn't going to. There were a million reasons why we wouldn't work, such as the whole Huntington's thing. And if he were into me, wouldn't he have made a move while I was naked in the pool with him?

Wouldn't that have been the perfect time?

"Kate?" Lachlan interrupted my internal struggle.

"Yeah?"

"Did you have fun?"

"Yeah." I smiled. If nothing else, I couldn't remember the last time I'd laughed so hard.

"Would you do it again?"

I paused. Would I do it again? I didn't know. Probably not. How could anything ever be better than this perfect moment here?

"No."

"Okay." I heard him step closer to me, his feet squelching against the mulch underneath, the light of his phone illuminating my feet. "But it was a new experience worth trying."

seventeen

CALLED AND made my neurologist appointment a few days later, needing to make progress with the testing process. My voice scratched when I booked, as if I was on a bad line. It didn't help that I'd seen an article about Dave dating Lee Collins's girlfriend (now, presumably ex-girlfriend) in the newspaper *and* I hadn't heard from Johnny or Lachlan regarding new shifts at the café.

Not that it mattered, of course. Lachlan and I were just mates, and mates didn't stress when they hadn't heard from each other in two days. Or two days, twelve hours and eighteen minutes.

Did they?

Maybe that's why I found myself pulling into the lot at Sideways later that week, Dad by my side. I opened the door to the café and quickly ushered him to a table in the corner, trying to create as little fuss as possible. The place was busy today, the three pm caffeine-addicted crowd settling in. I prayed Dad wouldn't do anything to embarrass me.

I walked up to the counter to order and was surprised to

be met by Johnny instead of Lachlan.

"Hey, where's Lachlan?"

Cringe. Could I be more obvious?

"He took the afternoon off." Johnny nodded at the crowded room before him. "Of all the days though, right?"

"Right," I agreed. "Oh, just a milkshake and a flat white, please."

"No problem-o," he said, quickly pressing a few buttons on the machine to no doubt keep the orders coming. "Put that money away. We can do staff drinks." He gave me a wink, and I smiled back.

"So, speaking of, I never heard from you about another shift, and I …"

"Oh! Of course, yeah, right, I forgot to call you." Johnny slapped his forehead. "Sorry, mate, I've been flat-out here. But could you come in? Like, next Tuesday?"

"I'm pretty sure that's fine. What time?" I felt like an idiot. He'd just been busy, and now he probably thought I'd hunted him down in his place of work to find out more. What was wrong with me?

Oh, yeah, that's right. Potential Huntington's disease.

"Maybe from ten till close? You can shift with me, Lach is off again," he said. "Now go sit down, I'll bring these out when they're ready."

I smiled my thanks and headed back to the table where I pulled out the chair across from Dad. Just the two of us. Having a drink.

Leslie would be proud.

"So, what'd you get up to yesterday?" I asked brightly. Dad didn't so much as make eye contact with me. He kept his gaze glued to the table in front of him where he was playing with a saltshaker, tipping it from side to side in his hand. He'd tilt left, and all the tiny white crystals would slide down the glass tube. He'd tilt right and they'd fly that way, stopping when he covered the holes on top with his palm to prevent spillage. Then he'd lose control, drop the shaker, or his arm would jerk out again.

Process and repeat.

"Dad?" I spoke a little louder in case he couldn't hear me over the salt.

Nothing.

Side to side.

Palm to tube.

"We're supposed to be trying." I spoke the words quietly, and slumped back in my seat. At least I'd given it a shot. Ten points for me at my next counselling session.

"Trying?"

Of course. *That* he heard.

"Trying to act normal." He put the saltshaker down.

I studied my father, his thinning dark hair that glinted auburn in the warm afternoon sun. Wasn't it obvious? What other way would we be trying to act?

"This is normal." He slurred just the slightest bit when he spoke, but the words were coherent, at least. I finally understood that saying about being grateful for small mercies.

"Okay, so how was your day yesterday?" I tried again.

Silence.

He picked up the saltshaker and started twisting and turning it again, humming a tune under his breath. I shook my head, ever so slightly. How could I try when he acted like this? In and out, like washing blowing on the line, like one of those bobbing birds that reach for the water. Now you see him, now you don't.

"Here we go." Johnny approached our table with the sort of speed no man carrying two drinks should find possible. He placed the milkshake in front of me and the coffee in front of Dad. I saw Dad's eyes light up, and I quickly switched the drinks around. No way was I having a revisit of the spilt hot drink experience here, in a public place. Not a chance.

"Thanks." I smiled up at Johnny and ripped open a packet of sugar, letting the contents fall into my drink. "It was nice of you to give them to us free."

"For my new star employee? Anything." Johnny clapped my back lightly, tilting his head to the side.

"Y … you work," Dad said. It was a statement, not a question.

"Yes," Johnny and I answered in unison.

"What about-boy?" Dad's eyes widened, and I felt my heart sink. No, no, no. Please don't say anything about him, not in front of Johnny, not in my place of work, and not in that frustrating stunted voice.

"Which boy?" Johnny rested an arm on the back of Dad's chair, a quizzical look on his face.

"Oh, he just means Lachlan." I rushed the words together. I had a high pitch to my voice, like I was trying to counteract Dad's lower one. "We saw him here on our first visit, and Dad was quite impressed with …" I trailed off, and scanned the room, searching for something, an answer to the end of my sentence.

"His art?" Johnny asked, right at the same time as I said "the coffee." *Thanks, brain, for finally kicking in.*

Wait.

The *art*?

"He does all this?" I turned my head to look at the wall behind me, the wall of amazing, intricate images that had first drawn me to the place. *Lachlan had done this?*

There were frames of all different shapes and sizes, black-and-white pictures inside. One captured a frail hand, the veins etched deep, and lines of age and worry marked clearly. Then there was one of a ship, each tiny plank of timber knotted out in such detail I wanted to touch it, to learn more.

Something clicked in my head. The boy on the ground, notebook in hand, ready to capture the experience of smoking for the first time. These pictures were his way of capturing the firsts.

All of them.

I pushed back my seat and stood up to get a closer look. It was amazing, the fine lines that all weaved together—tiny complexities creating a simple whole. All this work was beautiful.

"He's good, huh?" Johnny came to stand by my side, arms

folded across his chest.

"He's—" I stopped. Good wasn't even the word. His pictures made me want to curl myself up and try to fit inside them, to move from this heartbreaking world to his beautiful one. "—breathtaking." I finally finished. It was, it really was.

"Does he sell these?"

"Yeah, when people are buying." Johnny nodded. "No one really knows about it, you know? He needs, like, a launch or something."

"People *should* know about these," I said, because they should. I reached out a hand and traced the feathers of a bird. Every frond was displayed. Amazing. "I organised a tour once. A launch can't be that hard." If high-school-educated me could do that, surely Johnny, who had opened a business with his brother, could sort out a simple launch.

"You think?"

"Sure." I nodded. "You'd just need a guest list of customers and media, plus maybe some art elites or bloggers, a bit of catering, some entertainment and you'd be set." Just like in music. It was crazy how easily the answer came to me.

"Great! How about in six weeks? Is that enough time?" Johnny's eyes were excited. I couldn't help but catch his enthusiasm, giving him a small grin in return. He'd be good at this. Hell, if I managed to organise a band tour with an absentee father and potential Huntington's in my genes, he'd be great.

"Yeah, I'm sure that'd be fine." I nodded, glancing back to our table.

Dad unscrewed the silver cap from the saltshaker and poured all the tiny white granules into his milkshake. My jaw clenched.

"One second." I held up my index finger and darted back to the table, hoping Johnny hadn't seen. I couldn't even leave Dad alone for five minutes without him embarrassing me. I guess I was just lucky he hadn't tried to sample my coffee.

"Dad, what are you doing?" I whispered, my eyes wide. I hoped they conveyed my hidden message of *stop it, now*.

"Sugar." Dad nodded.

"It's a milkshake. It doesn't need any."

"Does."

"No it doesn't."

"Yes. Does."

I pressed my eyes shut for a moment. It was like arguing with a two-year-old.

"Well, it's a saltshaker. It's not going to work," I tried.

"Sugar."

"No, it's salt." I tried to take the empty glass bottle from his tight grip, but he snatched his hand out of the way. I glanced back at Johnny, to see if he'd noticed what was going on. Thankfully, he was still staring at the art, no doubt focusing on the launch he was about to plan.

"Sugar!" Dad yelled, and raised his arm behind his head. It all happened in slow motion: the word from Dad's mouth, Johnny turning around, shoulders mid shrug, Dad's hand behind his head, half the customers in the store turning to face him. Then came the big one.

His arm sprung forward and he let the saltshaker fly, sending it sailing across the room till it collided with the wall right next to one of Lachlan's brilliant pieces of art, shattering into hundreds of thousands of tiny pieces on the polished concrete floor.

Now it wasn't just the half the café with their eyes on us.

It was all of them.

I felt my face turn bright red and I pressed my lips together, determined not to give in to the side of me that wanted to crumple up into a little ball and cry. I should never have brought him here. Not to my place of work, a place that mattered. In my desire to get answers, I'd jeopardised the only thing I had going for myself.

I turned back to the table and watched Dad, who now had his mouth firmly latched onto his straw, oblivious to the stares and the no doubt extra-salty taste. He was sucking it all up.

"I'll go get a dustpan," I said to no one in particular and ran behind the counter to where I knew the cleaning supplies were kept. I pulled the pan and broom out from under the shelf and ran back around the counter to the broken shaker where Johnny was standing guard.

"I got it." Johnny put his hand gently on mine. It was only then I noticed how much it was trembling.

"I'm fine." I wrenched my arm away and dropped to the floor, sweeping the bits of broken glass into the pan and trying to ignore the *everything* that was building inside me. Sad, embarrassed, hurt, angry, ashamed … there was a whirlpool of emotion stuck somewhere between my chest and my throat, just dying to spew out.

I blinked, trying to see through the thin veil of tears lacing my eyes. Every time I swept a shard of broken glass into the dustpan, a piece that was already inside fell out. It only made my sweeps more furious, harder, faster, which of course resulted in more falling to the floor.

"Kate." Johnny knelt beside me. His voice was soft and steady, like he was talking to a child. I heard parts of the tone I'd been using with Dad in him. I froze in place, staring into his pale eyes that were locked on me.

"I got this." He took the dustpan and broom from my hands. I curled my fingers. If I didn't have that to hold on to, what did I have left?

I stood back up, unfurling every notch in my spine like I was in some sort of yoga class. A few eyes still glanced surreptitiously in our direction, but most were focused back on their own conversations and coffees.

I walked over to the table where Dad was taking giant, noisy slurps from his milkshake, sucking air up the red-striped straw.

"We're leaving." I grabbed the glass from in front of him and took it, along with my so far untouched coffee, over to the counter.

"Thanks for that." Johnny moved past me on his way to tip the glass pieces in the bin.

"I …"

I'm sorry?

I guess I shouldn't come in for work again?

I can't fix this.

I don't have anything to say.

"Cool, so I'll see you next week. And start working on that art launch; Lach is going to be so excited."

I blinked, and stared at him. My forehead creased, the teensiest bit. Then common sense snapped back in and I nodded my goodbye, and walked out of there as quickly as I could.

Johnny didn't fire me. I still had a job. Somehow, through all the confusion, he'd thought I was going to plan the launch for Lach, not him.

At least it meant I could get out of looking after Dad.

We walked to the car, and I felt a little spring in my step. I had purpose again. I had an event I could plan. Something I could organise and do, all on my own. Something to make the neurologist appointment less of a focus for me.

Something I could do for Lachlan over the next week to avoid being inside my head.

EIGHTEEN

FELT LIKE life was on hold. Waiting till I had another shift. Waiting to see Lachlan. Waiting to find out if I had Huntington's disease.

I wanted to know. I liked to read the last page of the book first, just to ensure there were no nasty surprises waiting for me in the wings. Once I made up my mind to get tested, once Mum sort of said it would be a good idea, there was no stopping me.

The worst part about it was the avoiding, though. Trying not to get too excited about anything, keeping all emotions under wraps and distancing myself from the present. I couldn't afford to be there any more.

I'd gone to the neurologist appointment and it scared me. Petrified me, in fact. It was all big machines, impersonal service, lie here, look that way, we'll take that credit card, thanks.

The whole thing had felt surreal. Like it was happening to someone else.

More than once I'd wondered if this was all worth it. If I

should go through it at all, keep seeing my counsellor, visit a psychiatrist and get a blood test.

That thought only ever lasted for a second.

I needed to know.

I had to know.

"Kate. Focus." Stacey nudged me in the ribs and I snapped my gaze from somewhere out the floor-to-ceiling window and pretended to concentrate solely on the activity at hand. The activity at hand, mind you, was helping Stacey pick out the most appropriate shade of lipstick to match her dress—hardly what I'd call a task requiring 100 per cent brainpower.

Mum had the day off and was with Dad at the lake for a picnic lunch. She'd encouraged me to spend time doing "normal teenage girl things" while they did "normal adult couple things."

I'd spent the morning working on a few ideas for the launch, creating the perfect guest list, researching a theme and an exhibition name. I'd even gone so far as to get the names and contact numbers for the local art reviewers in the area.

Then I'd thought about Lachlan and his art. Lachlan … and why I just couldn't seem to stop thinking about him. Why was I so attracted to him? And would he want to be with me once he knew I could have Huntington's?

That was why I hadn't mentioned him to Stacey. Until I knew the results of the test, I didn't want to get too excited about anything.

"I like the first one." I pointed to the back of Stacey's hand that was covered in tiny pink marks, stripes of colour that looked a little like she had broken out in fifty shades of rashes.

"Really, though?" Stacey held up the tester tube next to her mouth. "Because I think it might be a little too candy, not enough pink. Know what I mean?"

I stared at the white ceiling, desperately trying to think of the correct answer and coming up with a whole lotta nothing.

"I was just walking along, thinking that this was one of the most boring days of my life, when who do I see through the window of the pharmacy? Only two of the hottest girls I know."

The deep voice cut our concentration. I turned, and saw Michael. He bounded over to us, past the sunglasses and skincare stands in his usual puppy-dog fashion, then leaned in for a hug hello. I hugged him back, trying to ignore the fact that Michael knew way too much about my personal situation, and that the last time I'd seen him was prior to being dumped by his best friend. Instead, I focused on the slightly damp feel of his T-shirt and the stench of beer exuding from it.

"Michael, just because we're out of school now doesn't mean you can touch me." Stacey endured the hug with a lot less tolerance than me. "And you smell like a brewery. Gross."

"Ah, come on, I don't smell that bad, do I?"

"Yes." Stacey and I answered in unison.

"I, uh, thought you guys were supposed to be out of town this week." I tried to sound casual, my voice light, and my eyes focussed out the window.

"Oh, yeah, well everyone else is in Wollongong, but I wanted to come home and see Mum so I drove back after the gig instead of partying." Michael froze and his mouth formed a tiny O, and then shut again. "Not that the rest of the guys are, you know, partying heaps hard. Mostly they just sit around with Lee and Coal, and …"

"Michael, it's okay." I waved his speedy explanation off. "Dave's allowed to go out and party. We broke up. It's how it works."

"Yeah," Stacey chimed in. "Kate and I certainly have been." She flipped her hair over her shoulder, the picture of confidence. I smiled, thinking of our one-off trip to Queensland and the time she'd helped me with the groceries since we came back. It was hardly the definition of party. Thank God for good friends.

"Oh, really? That's awesome. Because I have a night off and nothing to do, and it'd be great if you guys were heading out. Then we could all go out together, like old times." Michael's eyes lit up, and he shuffled his feet. "It'd be nice to chill on home turf, you know?"

"Well, we are going out for dinner tonight." Stacey nodded,

and I wondered if the action was to help convince Michael or me of the plan.

"Rad! I'd love to come." Michael tapped my shoulder with the back of his hand, like it was the best idea he'd ever heard. "So, ladies, shall we just meet out, or have a few drinks before, or …" Michael weighed up the options with his hands.

Stacey filled in the blanks since I'd developed the speaking prowess of a goldfish; I was all open mouth, shut, open mouth, shut. "Meet out. We'll go to the Thai place in Lakes at eight tonight."

"Cool, see ya there, babes." Michael winked and waved then walked out of the shop as casually as he'd entered. He seemed to lope, like every step was an adventure.

"Well … that was interesting." Stacey widened her eyes.

"I …"

"You need a new outfit. That's what you're about to say, right?" Stacey grabbed my wrist, pulling me closer to her side.

"I guess?"

"Of course you do. We need Michael to report back to Dave how hot you're looking." She moved to charge forward, and I stood there, stuck in the pharmacy.

"Kate?" When she turned around, her eyes were sparkling. She gave a small smile.

I grabbed a tube off the shelf and took it to the cashier for payment. "You forgot your candy pink."

When I'd chosen a new dress, Stacey relented and let us stop for a break. She was determined to check out my new place of employment, which was why we ended up at Sideways.

"Are you going up to order?" Stacey placed her menu down in front of me.

"No, I thought you could." I pushed the menu back toward her across the red Formica top. Johnny had seemed fine after Dad's little incident, but I wanted to keep a low profile, anyway.

"Isn't this the café you work at?" Stacey arched one of her manicured brows at me.

"Look, Dad's been a bit of a pain recently, and—"

"Kate! Hi." As per usual, I heard Lachlan before I saw him. That boy had a way of creeping around.

I glanced up to drink him in. His hips were in line with my eyes, and I could see the shadow of his torso through the thin material of his shirt. It was so close to me that I could touch it, lift it up just a little if I wanted to see what was underneath.

My hands started twitching in my lap. Apparently, a week without seeing him had done nothing to dull my attraction, even though I'd decided not to pursue it.

"And who is this?" Stacey gave me an open-mouthed grin and I felt my heart sink into my stomach. Oh, no. Not the Stacey Show today. Not with him.

Please.

"This is just Lachlan." I tossed my hand in his direction. "And Lach, this is Stacey."

"It's a pleasure to meet you, just Lachlan," Stacey purred. She held her hand out in the air and he shook it gracefully.

"I can't believe Kate hasn't mentioned you." Stacey smiled but her eyes clearly said, *And why haven't you, you selfish bitch?*

"She hasn't?" Lachlan drew his eyebrows together. "That's odd."

"I know."

"Especially since we were naked together last week."

Stacey's jaw dropped so hard and fast, I worried that she may have done some serious internal damage.

"It's not like that." I shook my head. "We were just skinny-dipping, and—"

"You went skinny-dipping?" Stacey's eyes were wide, emphasis on the word *you*.

"What's so hard to believe about that?"

"Nothing." Stacey shrugged and tapped her nails on the table-top. "It just—doesn't seem like something you'd do. You hate stuff like that."

"She really enjoyed it," Lachlan said. "Even raced laps with me."

"Apparently, there are a few things *she* hasn't been telling me lately." Stacey's eyes were narrowed now, and I shrunk back into my seat. I was going to kill Lachlan next time we worked together.

"I'll have a flat white, thanks."

"Make that two, please." Stacey smiled and Lachlan nodded, turning to walk to the kitchen. "Oh! Before you go, Lachlan, what are you up to tonight?"

No, Stacey. Stop it.

Stop it right now.

"We're going to dinner with a friend of mine—would you be interested in coming, too?" I'm fairly sure Stacey batted her eyelashes.

"I'm sure he's probably busy." I gave a sharp kick, but caught the table leg instead of Stacey's ankle.

"Actually, I'm free as a bird," Lachlan said.

"But it's probably going to be too early for you, with close." I didn't even try to hide the implication in my voice.

You are not invited. I don't want you to come.

"Not at all." Lachlan shook his head. "In fact, I'm knocking off early today. Where are we headed?"

"The Thai at Lakes at eight." Stacey smiled sweetly. "Don't be late."

As soon as he was back in the kitchen I folded my arms firmly across my chest and stared Stacey down.

"What the hell was that all about?"

"You don't think Dave hearing you're out with some hot new guy will hurt his ego?"

"I don't care what Dave thinks," I hissed back.

"Even though he's dating Lee Collins's ex-girlfriend, less than a month after you guys broke up?"

I scowled, and flicked a packet of sugar at her. So maybe I did care a little …

"And you can honestly tell me you don't want to go to dinner with that guy? I saw you, eying his stomach like you wanted to rip his shirt off right then and there." Stacey shook her head. "And skinny-dipping? And I'm finding this out *now*?" Stacey let a long rush of air escape through her glossy lips as she shook her head, and fluttered her eyes to the ceiling.

I stared down at my chipped nails. I could feel the shimmies of butterflies as they raced each other around my stomach. I was going to dinner with Lachlan, Dave's best friend and Stacey, and I was going to have to act happy and like everything at home was fine, and keep the disease specifics from Lachlan, and keep the skinny-dipping and counselling specifics from Michael and—there was no way those things in my stomach were butterflies.

The beating wings in my stomach definitely belonged to an eagle.

NINETEEN

W E WERE late for dinner. Technically, we were ten minutes early—it was just that Stacey refused to let us be the first ones there.

After picking me up and driving us to the restaurant, she convinced me we should bide our time in a public toilet two blocks away. I tried my hardest not to touch anything or breathe in any air that wasn't entirely necessary, and Stacey conducted a study of the back door graffiti, and tried to work out if she knew any of the names mentioned.

"*Emily is a slut*," she read slowly. "Do you think they mean Emily Greene, from school?"

I thought back to high school, which seemed so long ago. Emily had been known to cheat on her boyfriends.

"Maybe," I replied.

"I'd say she's more a cheater than a slut. She hasn't done everyone, she's just done the guys she has at the wrong bloody time."

I tried to stifle a laugh then pursed my lips together as the foul-smelling air crept into my mouth. *Gross.*

"Can we just go to the restaurant already?" I rested my hand against the side of a cubicle then jerked it away as I felt something sticky. I took a few steps to the left and hit the other wall, spinning around and trying to check the back of my dress for dirt.

"Come on." Stacey held out her arm and I linked mine in it, walking with her across the street to the restaurant.

Inside, the crowd was buzzing: the restaurant was near full. That is, except for the front booth. Still empty. Despite our attempt at making an entrance, we'd failed.

"Table for two?" A waitress in uniform black, asked us.

"Booking for Tomlinson, thanks." Stacey walked past the waitress to the table, slowly edging her way into the booth as if she could drag out our entrance just another second.

I slid in next to her and fiddled with my hands in my lap, wringing them together. What if I looked horrible? I looked down at my dress again, trying to remember how it had appeared in the mirror earlier that day. Not that I cared how I looked, of course. I had no one to impress.

But what if?

"What if they don't come?"

"Shush!"

"Did you definitely give them the right time?"

"Shut up!"

"Are you sure?"

This last comment earned me a stiletto-shod kick in the ankle.

Ouch. Clearly her aim was better than mine.

"Hey." Michael's gruff voice broke up our fight. He plonked a six-pack of beer and a bottle of pink sparkling wine in front of us on the table, his eyes all puppy-dog hopeful. Condensation slid down the sides of the beverages, the cardboard box holding the beer together turning soggy around the edges. "I didn't know what you girls wanted to drink, but I asked my sister, and she said sweet and sparkly was the go, so …"

"That's so thoughtful of you." I noted his button-up shirt, his black jeans and the neat way he'd pulled his dreadlocks back. This wasn't the sort of look Michael wore when he was just hanging around the house. He was definitely trying to impress Stacey. I stifled a grin, hoping his efforts would work.

"I guess we can always walk home." Stacey flagged over a waitress who popped the cork for us, and returned with two champagne flutes.

"So, is it just us tonight?" Michael slid into the booth next to Stacey, his brown eyes widening. He sat close to her, the sort of close that would freak you out if he were a stranger seated next to you on public transport, but she didn't seem to mind.

"No, Kate's friend, Lachlan, is coming, too." Stacey all but wiggled her eyebrows and I shot her another look, the kind that had daggers behind it.

"Where's Lachlan from?"

"We just work together." I studied the black table-top, the napkin in front of me folded into some sort of a crown. "That's all."

"He's a bit late," Michael said, ignoring the fact that he'd hardly been the picture of punctuality himself. He picked up the green plastic menu and studied it.

"Speaking of …" Stacey tilted her head toward the doorway. Lachlan walked in. He was wearing a white T-shirt that only made his skin appear tanner in contrast, his dark denim jeans tight, but not too tight. His hands were in his pockets and his shoulders hunched as he scanned the tables for us, then, after a few minutes, he finally settled his intense, dark brown eyes on our group.

On me.

I shuffled in my seat.

"Hey, mate." Michael was on his feet, arm outstretched. He shook Lachlan's hand vigorously, his usual effervescent self. "I'm Michael."

"Lachlan." Lachlan smiled. "Hi Stacey. Hey, Kate."

"Hi Lachlan," Stacey said. "Why don't you slide on in over there next to Kate?" She pointed to my side of the booth. This time, when I aimed my foot at her ankle, I didn't miss. At this rate, we'd both be limping out of here.

Lachlan manoeuvred his body around the black leather booth and came to a stop three inches from my right leg. He smelt fresh, and earthy, topped with a hint of coffee. No store-bought product could ever smell so good, so proper and manly.

"We should look at the menus." The words came out of my mouth in a tumble as I grabbed one of the cards from the table and started reading.

"Oh, come on, Kate, Lachlan just got here," Stacey said.

"There's no rush." I felt rather than saw his broad shoulders shrug. The butterflies in my stomach were back, snowballing their way around my lining. I was acutely aware of everything Lachlan did, of how close he was to me.

Get a grip, Kate. He's just a guy.

And until you take that test …

"Hmm … I think I'll have the chilli basil," Stacey said. "I feel like something spicy."

"You look really pretty."

I blinked.

Had Lachlan just said that, super quiet under his breath, or was I hearing things?

I chanced a quick look in his direction and was met with those dark eyes of his, rimmed with the perfect long, black lashes.

"Th … thanks," I eventually managed to spit out. I sharply turned my head back to the menu. This was not going well.

"'Scuse me." Michael frowned as his phone started to ring. He grabbed it off the table and answered, not seeing the drawn eyebrows Stacey directed at him.

"Well, there goes his chance." She turned to face us.

"Date not going well?" Lachlan said in a hushed voice. "He seems nice enough."

"He is." I eyeballed Stacey. If she could try to force Lachlan onto me, there was no reason I couldn't try to force Michael on her.

"Sorry, guys." Michael hung up the phone and turned his attention back to us. "That was just Dave."

Silence washed over the table. Michael cracked his knuckles.

"You know what we should do? Take a photo. Kate, Lachlan, squeeze together!" Stacey said in a shrill voice.

It didn't take a barista to understand what she was brewing. Take a photo, post it online, wait till Dave saw it, which of course he eventually would, and hope he got jealous.

Still, it was ridiculous. I was having a difficult enough time trying to fight my own stupid, guilty attraction-but-not-really-attraction to Lachlan, let alone having to deal with Stacey pushing me onto him, too.

"Let's not." I shook my head, and deliberately leaned towards Stacey.

"Why? It'll be cute." Stacey pouted.

"I just don't think it's really appropriate, I—"

"Well, look who it is."

The voice cut through the air, loud, harsh, and cruel. I'd recognise it anywhere.

"Dave. Hi." Michael shifted in his seat. I kept my head down but raised my eyes.

Dave slouched, one arm resting up against the dark leather of our booth. He was wearing a black button-up shirt—new, I noted—and skinny blue jeans that clung to his legs like glue. His hair was spiked up and his pale green eyes were piercing as they glared right at me.

Oh, and wrapped in his other arm was a seriously hot blonde girl I recognised from the newspapers.

Lee Collins's ex-girlfriend.

"Who are your friends, baby?" she asked in some sort of European accent, twirling a lock of her honeyed hair around a finger. Of course she was gorgeous *and* foreign, I thought. What a cliché. She swayed into Dave's chest like she was drunk.

I hated her.

"You know Michael, right?" He pulled her even closer, so there was no space at all between their bodies. "And these are just some girls I went to school with; Stacey and Kate."

The words stung exactly as they were intended to. Dave

looked over at me, his green eyes cool and calculating as I saw him size me up and judge every bit of flesh on my bones, from my waist to my crown, like I was barely worthy of breathing the same air he did. Like I was barely worthy of living.

Stacey came to my rescue. "This is Lachlan, Kate's— *friend*." I regretted kicking her under the table earlier.

"Oh, hey, man." Dave jerked his head in Lachlan's direction.

What had I ever seen in him?

"Well, this is a weird coincidence, but I guess I'll just see you tomorrow?" Michael asked. He was sheepishly studying his cutlery, like he hoped it could spirit him away to another country.

I didn't for a second think Michael had planned this, but it didn't make it any less awkward. Nor did it make him any more appealing to Stacey, who was currently staring at him with very thin lips and glittering angry eyes.

"What? You gotta be kidding me! Three old friends running into each other on a night like this? We should share a table." Dave opened his arms wide.

"You remember you two are in a band together, right?" I snapped.

"Yeah. You're going to see him tomorrow," Stacey chimed in.

"True." Michael tilted his head toward her. I had to give him credit. Going up against Dave was never easy.

"All the more reason to join you now." Dave unleashed his girlfriend from his grip and sat down next to Lachlan, leaving her hovering awkwardly next to the table. "Sit." He nodded to the seat next to Michael.

"Does she respond well to other commands, too?" Score one, Stacey.

"Yeah. She's particularly good at one special command—" Dave looked pointedly at me, "—that I know *some* people wouldn't ever do. Am I right, man?" Dave looked expectantly at Lachlan.

I wanted to die.

If I could melt into the folds of the booth, that would be great.

"I don't know what you're talking about." Lachlan met Dave's gaze, holding it without waver.

"You know …" Dave gave him a not-so-subtle wink.

"No, I don't."

"Well, maybe you guys aren't at that stage in your relationship yet." Dave laughed and ran his tongue over his teeth. "Don't hold your breath waiting, man."

The stabbing pain was real, straight through my heart. I'd thought I was over him; I knew he'd been a jerk. But still, being basically called frigid at dinner, with his new supermodel-esque girlfriend across the table, in front of a guy who I didn't-like-but-maybe-a-little did? It sucked. It more than sucked. It hurt.

"Huh." Lachlan shrugged and took a long swig of the beer Michael had placed in front of him earlier. "Guess you mustn't have been all that good at foreplay, then."

My eyes widened.

Had he just—in a weird, roundabout kind of way—implied I'd had sex with him? Or … foreplay with him?

How—sweet?

"From what I hear, he certainly wasn't." Stacey was like a horse at the gate. "A bit of a non-event, you know?"

"You are talking about the bedroom, no?" Dave's accessory opened her mouth for the second time.

"Yes, dear," Michael sounded like he was speaking to a child. Even he was getting in on the act. A smile worked its way up my face.

"Oh." She nodded thoughtfully. "He very good and—how you say—fast?"

"She means, like, fast at it, not quick," Dave said. But it was too late. The damage had already been done, and Stacey, Michael, Lachlan and I burst into a cacophony of laughter, the kind of laughter that drew the attention of people at other tables.

Dave grabbed the table, and the veins on his hands popped out. I waited for his outburst, for him to snap and leave—but it didn't come.

"Fast and hard, and lasting all night. You know it, baby." Dave stood up and walked to the opposite side of the booth where he bent over and kissed his Swedish miss. And trust me, kissing was the polite term for it.

"Chill, man." Michael shot him a worried look out the corner of his eye.

"Let him do what he wants. Who cares?" Stacey waved a nonchalant hand in their direction.

I looked over and saw Dave's tongue slither into the girl's mouth. I felt nothing but revulsion and disgust, mixed with a slight hint of "thank goodness it's not me".

And yet, I couldn't help myself.

"We certainly don't, do we, babe?" I placed a hand tentatively on Lachlan's shoulder, and looked at him out from under my lashes with what I hoped was bedroom eyes, and not desperate, crazy woman ones. I felt Dave's gaze from the other side of the table.

"Not at all." Lachlan broke into an easy grin and leaned forward, resting his forehead against mine.

I focused on the table below, then pulled away jerkily, hoping Dave hadn't noticed my adverse reaction. Having Lachlan so close, his eyes close to my eyes, his lips close to my lips—it was all too much.

"I don't know how you do it." Dave sauntered back over to our side of the table, sliding in a little too close to Lachlan's personal space for my liking. "You know; put up with all that shit."

"What are we all going to order?" I lifted my menu. *Please Dave*, I silently begged. *Please don't go where I think you're going to go.*

"I mean, you must have a really easy-going family." Dave tossed his head back and laughed, like it was the funniest joke in the world.

No.

Please, stop.

My mouth was opening and closing like a goldfish. I didn't

want Lachlan to know; not like this. I was sure he'd guessed something was up with Dad, but I didn't want to tell him everything, not until I knew if I had it, too.

"I mean, how would your family react if your girlfriend's dad was going crazy?"

The words were far too loud. Not only did our table fall silent, but several around it did, too. I slumped back in my seat.

"He's not crazy." My words were quiet. Too quiet.

"You should have seen him at our graduation. Rocking up drunk, embarrassing the school. And you know what they say: like father, like daughter …" Dave raised his brows in my direction, then took a swig of Lachlan's beer, setting it back down in front of him. "Thanks, man."

I couldn't say anything. I couldn't think. All I could see was the jigsaw puzzle of my life falling to pieces.

"A hereditary disease? You're one helluva guy for sticking around for that." Dave rested back in the chair.

The pain in my lungs expanded as they waited for me to draw breath. My bones were stuck in place. I couldn't look at anyone, at anything. My mind had left my body and was hovering somewhere above it, watching on like a rubber-necker at a car wreck. It was ruined.

Everything was ruined.

My heart slowly sliced itself in two.

"Excuse me, guys, I'm just ducking to the ladies room." I stood up and squeezed past Lachlan and Dave, not noticing how my legs brushed theirs, how the silence was still resting over the table, how Stacey's eyes were burning with anger and her mouth not yet moving.

I didn't care about any of it.

I didn't care at all.

I ran out of the restaurant, and across the street to the public bathrooms we'd been in earlier, desperate to be alone. Mud splashed up my ankles and onto my skirt, and I didn't care one little bit that I was getting my new dress dirty. Nothing mattered anymore. A tiny tear snuck its way out of the corner of my eye and I bit my lip, furious with myself for being so weak, for even caring at all.

"You would have had to tell him anyway," I whispered, as I punched my fist into the toilet door. The skin broke, and angry red blood smarted my knuckles.

I would have had to tell him, but I wouldn't have had to tell him now.

Waves of emotion made my chest shudder as I felt the pain sluice through my body, as if each pump of my heart helped the misery of my life flow till I was sad and heavy from my forehead to my feet.

I stared at myself in the mirror, balancing my clutch delicately on the edge of the stainless steel sink. My brown hair was still pulled back, little tendrils of it curling up and breaking profile in the heat. My face looked pale, my lips almost white.

Why had I thought I could do normal things?

Why had I thought a normal boy would be interested in me?

I quickly shoved my hands under the tap and gave them a speedy rinse. I didn't want to go back; I couldn't. I pressed up against the wall, ignoring the dirt and grime that was probably caked there. I shouldn't have even gone to dinner. I had to sort out problems with my family, and myself. I didn't need this in my life.

What am I doing here?

I grabbed my phone from my clutch and started texting Stacey furiously.

Hey babe, I don't feel well. I have to bail, I'll

"Kate?"

Lachlan's voice interrupted my text, and echoed through the room.

I remained silent. He'd leave soon, anyway, and I was going home. I didn't need to see him again, not tonight.

I focused on making my breath steady and quiet—long, deep breaths in, and a slow, controlled release out. I could do this. Everything would be fine.

After five minutes had passed with not another sound

from outside I finished up my text, and released my stronghold on the wall, letting it keep upright without me. I put my phone back in my purse, took my shoes off and dangled them from my hand with my clutch, ready for the long walk home.

"Kate."

When I rounded the corner, Lachlan was still there. He was leaning casually against the wall, like it was the most natural thing in the world, hands in his pockets, head tilted back.

I felt my heart pound, my pulse quicken. What was he still doing here?

"I … I don't feel well. I'm going home." I charged past him and headed across the park.

"Why?" He kept pace with me, easily matching my short, emotion-fuelled strides with his long, controlled ones.

"I just told you, I don't feel well." My eyes focused on the ground, only seeing the patches of grass and gnarled branches beneath my feet.

"Why really?"

"None of your business." I barked the words out like they were weapons. I hoped they hurt.

"Can I walk you home?"

"You'll miss dinner."

"I'm not hungry."

"I don't need you to feel sorry for me." I spoke loud, much louder than I'd intended. I turned to face him, my arms wide. "I don't need it."

Lachlan took a step back. His studied me, from my feet to my face. Not in the way Dave had earlier, judging, but with a solemn look, a firm set of his mouth, as if he were working out the answer to a problem he'd long wondered about.

"I don't feel sorry for you." His voice was soft. He took a tiny step closer to me and reached out as if he were going to touch my arm, then thought better of it, and put his hand in his pocket. "I just want to walk you home."

He wasn't angry. He was calm. I took a deep breath. He'd been through hard times too.

"Okay."

I turned on my heel and started walking again. My pace was less frantic, now, my breathing less heavy. I took it all in: the grass and the trees around the edges of the field, the road up ahead, and the houses beyond that.

We walked for ten minutes in that direction then swapped, taking a main road and walking along a grey footpath. Lachlan never faltered in pace, never interrupted my thoughts. It was good, because I had a lot of them. What did I ever see in Dave? Why was Lachlan here, now that he kind of knew the truth? What the hell would happen to me in the future? Why was I so embarrassed about it all, anyway?

Would I ever stop looking at my dad like a stranger?

When we reached the track that led to my house, the one that hugged the opposite side of the nature reserve where we'd skinny-dipped, I'd had enough.

"Can we stop for a second?" I halted in my tracks, staring down at the tiny drops of water on the long green grass spiking up around my shoes. Lachlan didn't say a word, just froze next to me. I stared at his black skate shoes, less than a foot from mine.

"So, my dad has Huntington's disease. It effects the motor system, and he basically loses control of everything." I gripped my left hand with my right one and pressed my nails in. *Hurt, Kate. Make it hurt.*

When the release of physical pain came, I felt in control again. I was able to continue. "One day, he'll die. And, it's hereditary. So I could have it, too."

For a moment, I was open. The gun was in my mouth, the trigger in between his forefinger and thumb. It was half the reason Dave had left me, one of the key factors in why I couldn't trust Lachlan's interest.

Quite simply, it was everything.

Go on.

Pull the trigger.

"I …" Lachlan started a sentence, but couldn't finish it. He opened and shut his mouth then stepped in closer to me, till there was less than an inch separating our faces.

"I have cancer."

Whoa. Not what I was expecting.

"But you're … so …" Words failed me as I studied this incredibly sexy, non-sick-looking guy. How could someone who looked so alive have cancer?

"I know. I'm in remission, and I haven't had any problems for more than two years, now," he said. His liquid chocolate eyes locked with mine. "But it could come back. I'm not completely in the clear."

"Is it the same kind your … your dad had?"

Lachlan gave a single nod, and I felt a little piece of my heart fall away. How could I be so caught up in my own shit, when he had so much more; and so much worse? His parents were both dead, and he was sick, too.

"Hereditary illnesses, huh?" Lachlan gave a wry smile, and I laughed.

We stood there on the corner, just staring, processing—learning. I was acutely aware of how close he was, how his shoulders stood just around my eye level, how the white fog from his breath hitting the night air was misting toward my face. I felt small and vulnerable, looking up at his clouded eyes, like he could snap me in two with his next sentence.

"Kate?"

"Yes?" My breath caught in my throat. My eyes were drawn to his lips, slightly parted, a wet sheen glistening there.

"You're just … you're just so beautiful." Lachlan moved closer to me, millimetres from my face. I looked at his mouth. It was so near to mine in the moonlight.

I licked my lower lip and heard him inhale, sharply, felt his eyes watch my every movement, and then the pull of tension became too much and he pressed forward and melded his lips to mine. I widened my eyes then parted my mouth. His tongue darted between my lips, and my own moved to receive it, touching it, melding with it.

His kiss was amazing, everything I'd wanted it to be. He ran his hands up my sides, over my hip bones and higher till I could feel them rest at the bottom of my bra. I thrust my hips forward, wanting to close any gap between us, needing to feel my body pressed against his solid form.

We kept going, feeling the wetness of our mouths colliding until there was no he kissed me, no I kissed him, but us, only us, making out in the light of the moon.

This was happening. Lachlan knew, and he didn't care. We were making out, and I could have Huntington's disease. My heart had gone from frozen to pumping at a million miles per minute as I lost myself in him.

"Kate," Lachlan groaned, his voice aching in my mouth. I teased the edge of his shirt up, letting my hand roam underneath and feeling the shape of his back, the trough of his spine under my hands. I pressed myself against him again and gave a slight moan into his mouth. I felt him shudder as he gently bit down on my lip. It only made me want him more.

"Kate," he said again, this time pulling back, holding my arms in his big, strong hands. My breath was coming far too fast, my chest heaving up and down.

"Yes?" I looked into his eyes. His pupils were dilated, his cheeks flushed, and I wondered if that was how I looked to him, too.

"I—this is a new thing for me." He dropped his hands and shoved them into his pockets, pulling out the pad of paper I'd seen that first night.

"What?" My mouth hung open. "You've never kissed anyone before?"

"Of course I have." I swallowed. *Idiot, Kate.* "But I've not really done anything else, like—well, with the cancer, I wasn't exactly beating the ladies off, and I just—I really like you. But I have to go now. I'm going to go home, and … and draw."

This wasn't happening.

Was I *cursed*?

"So you don't want to kiss me anymore because you need to sketch up an image that captures this first for you?"

If my eyes went any wider, they'd fall out of my head. *I was the one who was having tests regarding my mental health, for*

Christ's sake.

"No." Lachlan gave me a sheepish smile. "But I don't want to kiss you anymore in case this first turns into another first, and another, and another." A light glinted in his eye.

"I want to do this right, take you on a proper date, not make out with you on a street after your loser ex-boyfriend was a jerk." Lachlan ran his hands through his hair. "And I worry that maybe I'm taking advantage of you in your emotional state."

I shook my head, no.

"Either way, I do like to draw all my firsts. And you need them for the launch." Lachlan pulled me close, and pressed his lips gently to my forehead. "Good night." He turned away and walked down the street, not looking back.

I had no idea what I was supposed to feel. Was he making an excuse, or was he serious?

I watched Lachlan go, a lone figure on our quiet street, highlighted from streetlight to streetlight. I'd liked walking by his side. I'd liked that he didn't seem to care about Dad or my potential illness.

I wrapped my arms across my chest and squeezed tight. If he could survive—could run a business, act like a normal guy, and have *feelings* for girls—then surely I stood a chance.

TWENTY

"KATE. IS that really what you're wearing?" Mum raised her eyebrows at me. I was lying on the bed in my room, black sweatpants and grey tank on, hair pulled back in a messy ponytail. Or, it had been a messy ponytail at one point. After two hours of lying on my bed, working on Lachlan's upcoming event and wondering how on earth I'd act when I saw him next, it may have simply turned into a mess.

"Looks like it." I smiled gaily back at my mother.

"We are leaving in fifteen minutes." Mum gave me "the look"—you know, the one that says, "I'm the parent, and if you want to live under my archaic roof, you obey my archaic commands."

I exhaled slowly, letting the air puff out of my cheeks. I didn't want to do this. After the last time I took Dad to Sideways, I'd refrained from taking him out of the house. My babysitting of him was restricted to our home address, with no excursions permitted.

Which is why I was less than ecstatic to be going out on a family dinner.

O-u-t.

I clicked the home button on my phone and saw, to my disappointment, that there were no new messages. Not that I'd wanted Lachlan to get in touch, or anything, more that I'd thought maybe he'd feel he should. You know, after kissing me kind of oh-my-God-passionately, then leaving me in the middle of the street.

It had only been one day. If he really liked me, he'd text me.

Right?

I sighed and sat up, pushing my hair out my eyes and thinking about tonight.

Lachlan and Johnny make an effort to be a family.

I had to go. How could I not when they had so little?

With the weight of ten thousand Acme pianos on my shoulders I headed to the wardrobe and pulled out a dress I hadn't worn since Before.

Before my dad was sick.

I yanked my shirt up and threw the dress over my head, then pulled my sweats down, lifting them from where they pooled on the floor and placing them, along with my shirt, in my dirty-clothes basket.

"Ka-ate," Mum called from downstairs as I pulled my hair from its tie. For a brief moment it hung loose around my shoulders. I stared at myself in the mirror, brown wavy hair, dark hazel eyes. Yep, I still looked the same. When I'd been normal, when I'd found out about Dad, when an incredibly sexy guy had kissed me—somehow, I still looked the same. How did that even work? When everything else had changed irrevocably …

With seconds to spare, I grabbed my brush and slicked my hair back up again, tight, so only a few unruly tendrils could escape. Just how I liked it.

"Look … nice." Dad was sitting on the couch in the living room. Though his words were stilted, he seemed to be somewhat with it, his eyes focused instead of flitting from side to side. Maybe this would be a good night.

"Thanks," I said, suddenly super self-conscious, and pressed down my dress with my hands. This was going to be okay. Everything was going to be okay.

"Let's go, then." Mum gave a bizarrely bright smile. Dad stood up and staggered to the front door, his knee jerking every now and then.

When he reached the doorway it buckled completely and he went tumbling to the ground, a pile of bones and skin. Had he always been this underweight?

Mum rushed to his side and helped him up. He kept a brave face, eyes steady, in control. He wasn't the guy who'd screamed when the tea spilt on him at all.

Give him a chance.

I hooked my arm through his and walked toward the car, keeping time with his slower gait. I felt him smile a big, goofy grin at me, and something inside me warmed.

Maybe I could do this after all.

We all piled into the car, a slightly odd family acting like nothing was wrong, like we had every right to be out mingling with society on a Sunday evening.

Mum turned the engine and I clicked my seatbelt into place, flattening my body against the felt seat cover.

"Dad, your seatbelt," I reminded him from the backseat.

He ignored me, his eyes focused on some eye level item in the garage that neither Mum nor I could see.

"Dad." I tapped his shoulder this time.

Nothing.

"Dad." I yelled and tapped simultaneously.

"Huh?" His brow was creased, his lips twisted in a question.

"Just leave it, dear." Mum reversed out of the garage.

"But you could get fined," I protested.

"Worse things have happened," she replied, and all I could think was, *Well, hell yeah, I suppose that's true.*

We pulled into the parking lot of a restaurant a five-minute ride from our house. Bob's Seafood and Grill was a building on stilts overhanging the water, a navy-blue wooden shack with white features. We walked along the plank to the restaurant doors, the scent of garlic and herbs wafting out to greet us long before the maître-d did.

"Table for three," Mum announced when we were finally seen to.

"Is that restaurant or buffet?" The server asked.

"Restaurant," Mum answered. Dad giggled. I swallowed.

We walked through the crowded, noisy room to our assigned table and took our seats. Mum flicked her napkin out and over her lap, and then did the same for Dad. I moved mine to the side and picked up my menu. So far, so good.

"Can I get you any drinks?" A waitress approached our table, paper and pen in hand.

"I'll have a water, thanks," I said, smiling up at her.

Mum looked up from the wine list. "A glass of the house Chardonnay, please."

"Schooner of New."

Silence.

"Sure, I'll just get those for you," the waitress said, scribbling the order down.

"No," Mum and I said at the same time.

"He won't have the beer." Mum shook her head.

"I will," Dad argued. If you couldn't see his twitching, his shoulders rolling, you probably wouldn't even know he had a problem. His voice was surprisingly coherent.

Mum glared at Dad, like she was trying to project a message into his brain. He looked back, and then studied the floor, the ceiling, the table.

"He'll have a light beer," she finally said, breaking eye contact and dismissing the waiter.

"Is this really a good idea?" I asked Mum as soon as we were free from staff.

"What, dear?" She folded her napkin in half then placed it back on the table.

"A beer," I spat it out, like the dirty word it was. All I could think of was Dad at graduation, and how he'd behaved.

"One won't hurt," she said.

"Won't it kill his brain cells?" I looked over at Dad. He was following our conversation, a small smile lifting the corner of his lips.

"One." Mum carefully enunciated the word, as if I were a small child.

"You can't let him do this! He's going to embarrass us, and—"

"Kate, will you join me in the bathroom for a moment?" Mum pushed out her chair and power-walked toward the restrooms. I got to my feet, held out a finger in Dad's direction and mouthed the word *stay*, and then followed after her.

"What are you doing?" I slammed the bathroom door open. The fluorescent lights made me blink, as I took in the restroom, empty bar my mother, who was leaning over the sink.

"What are you doing, Kate?" Mum's voice was calm, a complete contrast to my own.

"I'm trying to look after my dad. Don't you—don't you care?"

"Of course I care," Mum sighed, and shook her head. "He's my husband. I love him more than—more than anything."

"But he left." I shook my head. "And he's different now."

Mum was silent for a while. She blinked, and those purple bruises under her eyes, the crow's feet in the corners, were deeper and darker than they'd ever been before.

"Kate, he's sick." I stepped in closer in order to hear her better. "And one small drink isn't going to change that."

"How can you say that?" My voice wasn't as loud as it had been before, nor anywhere near as steady.

"Because if I deny him everything, when God has already denied him so much—what does he have left?"

I turned and left the bathroom. I walked past the table; I just couldn't deal with this, couldn't understand. I saw Dad take a small sip of his beer, a smile spreading over his face as his foot tapped to a soundless tune under the table.

I didn't know. I just didn't know any of the answers.

TWENTY-ONE

Aᴀꜰᴛᴇʀ ɪ disappeared from dinner, Mum booked me another appointment with the counsellor. Technically, I only had a psychiatrist appointment to go before I could be tested, and so the counsellor shit wasn't needed.

I drove down the highway to the counselling centre and parked my car in the lot, walking the five minutes through the grounds till I came to the big, brick building looming in front of me.

I checked my watch: five minutes early. Of course I was. I was always on time for things. Why couldn't I be late, just for once?

My feet started walking, almost without my permission, and I rounded the corner of the building, finding the small courtyard where I'd run into Lachlan that first day. I walked over to the huge, old willow tree and ran a hand lightly over its gnarled trunk, the veins of the tree bulging out all over the place. It was thick, perhaps four times the roundness of my body, and tall, with branches that draped a canopy over the entire courtyard area.

Tick, tock, tick, tock.

Time was running out. I knew I'd have to go in now or miss my appointment.

Tick, tock, tick, tock.

Nothing.

I pressed my back against the tree and slid down its spine till my legs folded up and I hit the dirt floor, curling in on myself. I kept replaying the scene from dinner last night, Dad and the beer, Mum and her weird small mercies outlook.

If I had the disease, what would I do? Would I end up like Dad, throwing saltshakers, and being grateful that I was allowed one glass of supervised beer? Was that all there was?

I knew suicide was a common cause of death for sufferers. Would I be able to go through with it?

Would I pull the trigger and spare my family from another mess?

I took a stick from the ground nearby and started to trace patterns on the skin of my arm. White marks scraped flesh as I scratched the word. The tip of the stick wasn't hurting me enough, providing only a mild irritation.

C-r-a-z-y.

I knew he wasn't crazy; not in the literal sense of the word. He was sick, and nothing made me madder than when people used that term incorrectly.

But somehow, right now, thinking of what I'd gained with Lachlan, and what I feared from the future, it seemed appropriate.

I dug the stick deeper, branding myself. How would I be able to cope in the future? If I had the disease, I'd be a ticking time bomb. If I didn't, I'd be looking after my dad, always trying to hide things, trying to recover. Could I be like Lachlan and Johnny? Was I strong enough?

The stick snapped in two, brittle. I rested my head back against the tree, taking small comfort in the dull ache at the base of my skull where I'd made impact with wood. *Mum. Dad. Me. Lachlan. Dave.*

My breath came shorter and sharper, my heart beating

faster and faster as my chest tightened in on itself. This time, the panic attack was random, but it was no less fierce than it had been before. It was all consuming.

What was wrong with me?

How could I get out?

I didn't really think I'd be capable of committing suicide, not now, not ever. But what if, what if I hopped in my car and drove and, when I was driving on the highway, I just drove off a bridge? Going more than one hundred kilometres per hour, maybe I'd turn the wheel hard left, and power through the guardrail, sending my little yellow car spiralling in an almighty drop to the rocky banks of the river below?

I wasn't going to do it, of course. But would it be easier? Would it make all of this go away?

I stood up, dusted my shorts off, and walked to my car. Maybe I'd just drive and see if I still felt like that when I got there.

Would I see my whole life flash before my eyes or just certain parts of it? If I focused on memories of Dad I'd developed as a kid, was that the way I'd immortalise him in my brain? Was I strong enough?

Could I really do it?

My steps had a certain resolve to them, as though I'd discovered a purpose. Lightness gently draped around my shoulders where heaviness had cloaked me before.

I reached my car and took out my keys. They dove straight into the lock, clicked over and opened the car. It was like the universe confirmed my intentions, the signs falling into place. If this were such a bad idea, would it feel so right?

Would everything be so easy?

"Kate."

I froze, hand still on my keys.

Did this guy look at my diary and schedule his appointments for the same time as mine? How on earth was he here every time I entered the building?

"Hi." My tone was flat as I wrenched my keys from the car.

"What are you up to?"

"Oh, you know, considering driving off a bridge." The truth was surprisingly easy to say.

"Well. That's interesting." Lachlan chewed his lip, like I'd just presented him with one of the world's greatest conundrums. "Why?"

"Why not?" I blurted out, letting my emotions bubble to the surface. "If anyone understands how shit and unfair life is, surely it's you?"

"Sure is." Lachlan walked around to the passenger side of the car, opened the door and hopped in.

"What the hell are you doing?" I opened my door and stared at him. "Get out of my car."

"What for?" Lachlan tilted his head to the side.

"Because—" I felt like stamping my feet up and down. It was my car. "—because I damn well said so!"

And because I need to be alone.

"Why do you say so? Have I done something to offend you?"

I raised my eyebrows, incredulous. What was wrong with this guy?

"Truth is, I've always been curious about driving off a bridge."

I tilted my head back, and studied the clouds scudding across the twilight sky. For real? Was this guy ever anything other than bizarre and philosophical? Why had I kissed him, again?

"You know, I'm not serious." *I'm not.*

Am I?

Lachlan looked at me, those dark eyes of his never straying from my face. His wristwatch counted down the time. *Tick, tick, tick.*

"Fine." I sighed. Lachlan gave a tiny fist pump, then jumped out of the seat, slid over the bonnet of the car and snatched the keys from my hand, indicating I should take the passenger seat.

"I'm not going to make you drive to your own bridge-jumping party," he said with a wink, as he lowered himself into the driver's seat and shut the door behind him.

"Can't you take anything seriously?" I grumbled as I hopped in the car. But I was smiling when I said it. A smirk that I was fighting too hard to keep inside me, but that I knew was playing on my face—and I knew he saw it, too.

We took off out of the parking lot at speeds I never would have driven, and I found myself sucking in my breath when we rounded corners too fast, went that extra mile to speed through a red light.

"Do you drive like this on your bike?" I gasped after we flashed through an orange-nearly-red light at the same time as a truck turned across the intersection from the opposite direction. We beat it by a fraction of a second, but knowing it happened because Lachlan was obviously speeding was of little comfort.

"You ride a bike, Kate." Lachlan flashed those eyes of his over at me and I shivered, my mind temporarily off the road as I felt his gaze on my body. "You don't *drive* it."

I bit my tongue and didn't say a word. *Don't give in, Kate. Don't cave.*

We drove in silence as the sky turned darker, the first stars shining bright in the darkened sky. After a while I propped my knees up, pressing them against the dashboard so my body was moulded into the seat behind me.

Minutes ticked by, and I ran over my list of problems in my head.

Dad.

Self.

Lachlan.

It was like a broken record, cataloguing all the individual details of each one over and over till it was almost a script of made-up scenarios and emotions filing through my mind.

We kept going, speeding through the city until we reached the empty, long lines of the freeway that took us to Lakes. Almost no cars appeared in the lane going the opposite direction, a testament to the Sunday night traffic typical of the area. It was all dark, straight-line driving there and sparse, bushy countryside here, a monotonous journey I normally hated.

Despite our breakneck speed, I was intent on looking at every single thing: each bush, each slight variation in horizon height, and each tiny rock that grazed the skyline. Focussing on anything but the boy driving my car.

When we were twenty kilometres from the exit, I felt the speed drop slightly as Lachlan moved over to the far right lane. My mind ticked, calculating. Was he going to take us farther north? Were we going to skip the Lakes exit and continue on to some weird location where Lachlan would kiss me again? Give me some of his hippy counselling bullshit?

Chop me up into little pieces and hide my body?

The car moved toward a turning lane marked for police and emergency vehicles only, and Lachlan slowed the car right down. My eyes widened and I instinctively glanced in the rear-view mirror to make sure no cars were behind us.

"What are you *doing*?" I asked as he turned the wheel hard, sending us spinning into the turning bay. Thank God there was no one else on the road. We careened across the asphalt, and I heard my tyres give a slight scream of protest.

"This is crazy!"

"So is driving off a bridge." Lachlan nudged the car forward so we were officially parked on the wrong side of the highway, facing south.

"Stop!" I screamed and clutched the seat. I dug my nails in so hard I could feel the metal spine of the seat underneath me.

"I have." Lachlan was irritatingly calm.

"I mean reverse, you idiot!" A bright set of headlights bobbed in the distance, moving slowly toward us. Of course, it looked slow from here, but I knew they'd have to be going the speed limit, and that was fast—too fast to live through.

My pulse throbbed at my wrist. My eyes widened. Maybe this was it. I was going to die. Here on the highway, not of some disease like I'd been worried about, but with some crazy guy who, up until a few days ago, I'd been worried didn't like me.

"Lachlan." The lights were closer. They picked up speed with menacing intent. It was a three-lane road and we were only in one, but, oh, God, they were going so fast, and what if they didn't see us and—

"Shit!" I bit my lip hard and screwed my eyes up. It was hard to breathe. My chest was in staccato mode, blunt tiny gasps. I tried to think all the thoughts I should think about before dying.

Dad before Huntington's. Mum. Stacey.

Instead, all I saw was the crazy guy next to me who was about to take our lives in some crazy suicide pact and—

"I don't want to die," I yelled. My chest heaved in an almighty sob, a desperate gasp for air. Bile jumped in my throat. I felt the car jerk and move and I screamed, my chest still shuddering, my heart racing as my neck snapped back and then my chin slammed forward, crashing against my chest with such force my teeth grated together.

I felt removed from the situation, like I wasn't really there. Pain shot through my neck, severe pain, not the slow, escaping kind I'd caused before with the stick.

This pain was hard and fast and different.

Why, though?

Why aren't I dead?

I pried one eye open, then the other, and saw we were back in the turning bay. The gearbox said we were in reverse.

He'd reversed. When the car had gotten close, Lachlan had reversed us back into the safety of the turning bay. The jerk of motion wasn't the other car hitting us. It was his abrupt driving.

I wasn't dead. I was alive!

And I was furious.

"You idiot." I slapped him across the face. His tanned cheek was now marred with my big, red handprint.

I jumped out of the car and ran to his side, yanked open the door and grabbed onto the lapels of his shirt. I pulled him out of the vehicle, so he was standing there next to me where I could see his body was giving off tiny trembles, like he was freaking out too.

"You crazy, stupid, insane, dickhead!" Each word was accentuated with a punch to his arm, his chest, his stomach. I was still kind of crying, weird gulps and shudders, but I couldn't stop. He just took it, accepted the pummelling, while I yelled and screamed and ranted.

"We could have died."

A very small voice came from his lips. "I wanted to make you realise you didn't want to." My eyes widened further and I gave him a sharp kick to the shins. This he couldn't just take; he stumbled back and gave a sharp intake of breath.

"You could have killed us, you idiot." I clapped my hands to my face. "I wasn't serious. I would never do something like that."

As the words came out of my mouth, I realised they were true. I couldn't kill myself. Huntington's or no.

"I saw you under the tree." Lachlan's voice was wavering. He sounded upset, and I wondered if he'd been just as shit-scared as I had. "You were hurting yourself."

"I wasn't!"

"Your arm." He grabbed my elbow before I could protest and held it out under the streetlight in front of us. Dried blood ran in lines from several spots, scratches that raked from my shoulder to my wrist.

I blinked, surprised. I'd known I was after the release, but I hadn't catalogued the damage I was doing. I thought back to the other times: kicking the fence, punching the wall. Was I capable of a lot more than I'd realised?

The pain hadn't felt enough.

"You hurt yourself." Lachlan's voice was definitely trembling now. "That's a sign of someone who is seriously crying out for help. I wanted you to realise how important it is to live." He didn't let go of my arm, still holding it delicately in his grasp. "But this was not the way to go about it and—Kate, I'm so sorry."

I looked up at him and saw nothing but misery in his eyes. The streetlight highlighted the line of his jaw, and the tiny stubble glistening there. What he had done was so far from okay.

But was it so different from what I'd been doing to myself?

If you were numb to the pain of the blood you were drawing, would you have been numb to the reality of death?

Lachlan took his other hand and raised it to my face, gently tracing along my cheek. He stepped in closer to me, still holding my arm, running his hand up it so lightly it gave me goosebumps.

What was I doing? This guy was crazy. In the past four days he'd kissed me, run away, and nearly drove me into a head-on collision.

He tucked a loose strand of hair behind my ear. My chest was rising and falling, still at the speed of a freight train, and I couldn't take my eyes from his lips.

"I can't stay away," Lachlan whispered. "You're just—you're everything."

I was acutely aware of the lack of space between us as he cupped my head in his hand again. I melted into it, welcoming his touch. This time, I closed the gap to him and pressed my lips against his. At first he just stood there, a little taken aback, then he welcomed me, parting his lips and dampening them with mine.

He moved his hand from my face to the back of my head, the grip on my arm roaming to my back. He pulled me against him so our bodies were melded together, the impact of his chest against mine giving me chills.

He sucked on my bottom lip and I moaned, feeling the ache all over my body. I ran my hands up his arms, over his broad shoulders to the nape of his neck.

My heart was pounding as adrenaline coursed through my veins from the passion of the moment, a heated contrast against the stark fear of the moment before.

He took a step forward and pushed me up against the cool car door, pressing his hot body against mine until there was no space between us. I found myself writhing beneath him, thrusting my hips forward. I could feel him hard through his thin denim. I wanted him, so badly.

"Kate ..." He groaned, and I felt his hot breath on my cheek, his hands gripping my hair.

"Don't," I whispered.

"Don't?" He pulled back. I saw the confusion in his eyes.

"Please don't stop," I said in my smallest voice. He answered my question with a fierce kiss, his hands running up my sides and lingering on the spot where my bra ran under my arm. I grabbed one of his hands and pressed it closer to my chest, desperate to feel his touch.

I was lost in the moment, in him, and in me, so much so that I'd stopped paying attention to the occasional car flying past. It was just Lachlan and I, and life, glorious, addictive life.

Or, it was.

Until the siren. Then it was us, life and an unimpressed policeman.

"Step away from the car."

I jumped and ducked to the side, the crackling static of the megaphone making me jump. Blue-and-red lights flashed from a car that had pulled over into the turning bay.

Lachlan moved away from me and stood up straight. He didn't let go of my hand, though, not for a second.

"Well, this is a little embarrassing," he muttered, and I suppressed a giggle.

"What are you doing?" A middle-aged, round policeman with a very red face stepped out of the car and walked toward us, arms folded across his chest.

"We're sorry, sir." Lachlan ducked his head like he was bowing. It only made me want to laugh more.

"This is not an appropriate place to be n-necking." The officer spat the word out, as if it offended him. His face was fifty shades of red. "You could have been killed."

"We're sorry," I repeated. A tiny waver shook my voice. I couldn't do it. How could I keep a straight face?

"It won't happen again," Lachlan chimed in.

"Well, move along now, or I'll fine you for obstructing a safety lane." He nodded toward the car, and I scrambled around to the passenger side as quick as I could.

"Thanks, Officer," Lachlan said as he hopped in the car next to me, the picture of contrition.

"Just move it." The man shook his head and walked back to his car. He placed one hand on the door handle, and then turned back to us, like he'd just remembered something of great import. "And remember," his voice blared over the megaphone. Lachlan and I froze. "If it's not on, it's not on."

I widened my eyes across the vehicle at Lachlan. He slammed his door shut.

Laughter erupted from deep within me. We completely lost it. "Did he ... did he just say that?" I wheezed.

"He ... he did." Lachlan grinned. We laughed and laughed and laughed, till tears were coming out of our eyes and our sides were hurting. At one point, I was doubled over, hugging my knees and slapping my thighs in hilarity. Everything about the day was so very obscure. We laughed all the way home.

I felt different, somehow—like maybe I could handle this thing after all. And Lachlan never let go of my hand.

Not even once.

TWENTY-TWO

THE HOUSE was eerily quiet as I clicked the coffee machine on and waited for it to heat up. Odd, I thought, glancing at the clock that read seven am. Usually Mum was up and racing around the house, getting ready for work by now.

I grabbed some milk from the fridge. It was brandished with a yellow post-it note: *Call me.*

Huh? But Mum had to be home. Where else would she be?

I placed the milk carton down on the bench and took the thinly carpeted stairs, two at a time, to my parents' bedroom. I gingerly knocked on their closed white bedroom door, third on the right, my knuckles barely rapping the surface.

"Mu-um, time to get up," I sang out in the cheeriest tone I could muster. I think it fell somewhere in between Ursula, the evil octopus from *The Little Mermaid*, and Morticia Adams.

Silence.

"Mum?" This time, I slowly turned the handle and peered into the dark of my parents' room.

The bedspread was thrown back, crumpled in a heap at the foot of the bed, and sheets were knotted across the mattress.

The dresser drawers were open, a T-shirt hanging suicidally from the corner of one, and the curtains were drawn tight. Not a skerrick of light entered the room, aside from where I'd opened the door.

"What the hell?" I whispered.

This was bad. Really bad.

I'd never known Mum to leave the house without making her bed, without letting the light into her room, without leaving it so tidy you could have had a house inspection in her absence.

When had she left? Where did she go? And where was Dad?

I swallowed as a sick feeling settled in my stomach, rolling around as heavy as a bowling ball.

Something had happened to Dad and, somehow, in my blissful post-Lachlan sleep, I had dozed right through it.

I flew down the stairs and snatched my mobile up off the counter where I had left it. I hit "favourites" and clicked on Mum's number, biting my lip as I waited the eternity it took to connect, as it slowly rang that obnoxious repetitive tone.

It rang out and I tried again, muttering the words "Come on, come on, come on," and pacing back and forth, like it would actually have some effect.

"Kate, I can't talk." Mum's voice was short, like she was doing a million other things. Knowing Mum, she probably was.

"Where are you? Is everything okay?"

"Your father is sick. They think it might be pneumonia. We're at the hospital, down in Sydney, next to the counselling centre. They flew us there from Lakes early this morning after your dad—after your dad …"

"Mum?"

"Sorry, Kate. He's just really sick. And if it's pneumonia, with his condition …" She didn't have to say anything else. My heart froze.

"You didn't wake me up?" I was five years old again, bottom lip atremble.

"It all happened so quickly, my love. Everything's fine, he's getting the best medical care, and—"

"I'm coming, okay?"

"Kate, you don't have to do this. Stay there—"

I ended the call and raced back up the stairs, throwing on the outfit I'd worn the day before, running a brush through my hair to make sure that, if I had to go to work straight from the hospital, it would be okay.

Okay. Like that word was relevant anymore. Dad had pneumonia. I flashed my mind back to the things Leslie had said about people with Huntington's.

Potential causes of death: Injuries caused by falls. Pneumonia.

My heart beat at double speed, thumping deep in my throat so I could hear and feel it resonating throughout my body. I threw an elastic band around my hair, pulling it off my face, and grabbed my phone and handbag as I raced out the door, barely remembering to lock it behind me.

I turned the key in the ignition and drove, trying desperately to stay within the speed limit and not think about the worst possible outcome for the hour it took me to reach the hospital. It was hard to shut out the noise in my head.

I had my psychiatrist's appointment scheduled the next day, too. And after that, the blood test, which meant another four weeks and I'd know my fate. Whether I could have the Huntington's gene, too. Whether one day, I could wake up, my health having gone from sniffles to downright pneumonia overnight, and having my life hanging in the balance, too.

Please don't die. Please don't die.

I slammed my car in the first available spot and jogged up the lawn, through the doorway of the big, white reception area. A woman sat behind a desk, prim and proper, her hair pulled back in a stark bun.

"I'm here for my dad, Paul, Paul Tomlinson," I told the receptionist. My breath was coming short and shallow, tiny gasps that racked my chest.

"Just breathe, dear." The woman clicked away on her

computer for so long I almost wanted to jump the counter and type the name in for her.

"He's in emergency. No visitors." She looked up at me and smiled. "You can wait in the café, though, just down the hall to the left, it is."

"I'm his daughter."

"I don't make the rules, dear." She shook her head. "You might be able to see him, but he probably needs the doctor's full attention right now. It's just how it is."

"Where would my mother be, then?"

The receptionist flashed me a smug smile. "I don't know, dear. Is she a patient, too?"

I slammed my fist on the counter and stormed off, racing towards the lift. I'd follow the signs to emergency and just find him there. Surely, they'd be more sympathetic once they saw me in person.

When I rounded fifty corners and took thousands of stairs, I reached emergency and ran straight up to the counter there, noting that out of the twelve people in the room sitting on chairs, none of them were my father or mother.

"I'm here about Paul—Paul Tomlinson," I gasped to the nurse behind the counter. She smiled at me, checking the piece of paper in front of her.

"Are you immediate family, dear?" Her red hair was frizzed around her face. She reminded me of a slightly less in-control version of Leslie.

I nodded. "He's my dad."

"Your father is being transferred to the wards as we speak. I spoke to your mum just minutes ago." She smiled. Her droopy cheeks shook as she waddled closer to the counter.

"Will I be able to see him?"

"Absolutely. Just sit down and I'll call you when." She gestured to the couches on the side of the room and I walked over to them, shoulders slumped.

After the seconds ticked by and turned to minutes, I finally heard my name called and the receptionist gave me a little piece of paper with a room number on it. I took it from her hand, trying to control my shaking, and walked out of the office down a long, narrow corridor.

Room 401.

Four-oh-one.

He had a room. He wasn't dying. They wouldn't put him in a room if he were going to cark it. It was going to be okay. He was going to be okay.

I opened the door to the room and feasted my eyes on every last detail. There was Dad, hooked up to an IV and a drip, tubes running in and out of his body. His eyes were closed, a five o'clock shadow on his chin, and his hair stuck to his head, like he'd been sweating, or caught in the rain. He was in a white hospital gown, and his face was drained of colour.

My heart was doing the pounding thing again and my knees felt weak.

"Kate," Mum spoke, a quiet voice shaking with worry. Her eyes never left his thin frame. She hovered near him, clutching his hand tightly in hers.

"Is he okay?" I asked. I couldn't take my eyes off him, either.

"He's very sick." Mum squeezed, her nails gouging into his wrist. I couldn't blame her. Anything to get some feeling back into his body.

"Is he going to … die?"

The words hung between us, big buckets of space swallowing them up until they weren't even our words any more. They weren't words Mum was prepared to answer.

"Good afternoon." A lady in scrubs entered the room, giving us both a quick nod. "I'll just do a few quick checks." She looked at the machines attached to my father, comparing them to the little scribbles of writing on a clipboard she'd taken from the end of Dad's bed.

No, not Dad's bed. The bed Dad was in. The bed he would soon be leaving.

"Is he going to be okay?" My voice was trembling, even though I tried to steady it. The nurse looked over at me, past the clipboard.

"It doesn't look to be pneumonia. He has a bad case of the flu, yes, but at the moment things are looking good."

"But he's unconscious," I said, pointing to his still figure on the bed.

"Sleeping." The nurse shook her head. "I didn't mean to panic you. Even the flu is very serious for someone with a disease like his." She placed the clipboard back at the end of the bed. "Keeping him here is mainly for observation and prevention. We're trying to make sure his condition doesn't worsen. You did the right thing, coming in. Much better safe than sorry."

"Okay." I sank numbly into a white plastic chair next to the hospital bed. Dad's breathing was laboured, varying in speed from rapid staccato gasps to long, drawn out inhales. With his eyes shut, his skin so pale, cheeks so drawn, he didn't look at all like my father. It was easier to believe this stranger was the man who had Huntington's, not the guy who'd demanded a beer or thrown a saltshaker at a wall. The guys who had been alive, three-dimensional, were too similar to my dad, and too full of life to be hospital-bed sick.

This guy was nothing but a shell.

I pursed my lips, thinking how one day this could be me. I thought of Lachlan, who had kissed me anyway, and his close relationship with Johnny, despite how hard it must be.

I scooted my chair closer and rested my hand on Dad's arm, for the first time in more than a year.

TWeNTY-THree

I DECIDED TO go to work, content in the knowledge that Dad wasn't knocking on death's door. Mum was curled up on Dad's bed, asleep. They looked cute together; like a young couple.

Would Lachlan get sick again?

One day, will I curl up on his hospital bed? Or will he curl up on mine?

The thought didn't upset me like I'd thought it would. Instead, it was a morbid curiosity that plagued me for my trip from Sydney back to Lakes.

I pulled into the parking lot beside Lachlan's bike and raced in through the back entrance, hoping no one would notice how fifteen-minutes-late I was.

"Sorry," I muttered under my breath as I jammed an apron around my waist and tied the ribbon in a bow at my back. Lachlan just shrugged and smiled, throwing me a tea towel.

"It's okay." He took out some milk and filled the beaker next to the machine as I lined up a few fresh cups. A string of receipts were lined up in front of him, and I wished I'd kept a better eye on the time. Clearly, he'd been busy.

"I was visiting the hospital," I offered, as I added tiny cookies to the two cups of coffee he placed in front of me. "I won't be late again, though."

I placed my hand under the first saucer to lift it up and deliver it to its rightful owner when I felt a firm grip on my wrist. I widened my eyes as Lachlan pulled me closer to him, ever so slightly. The milk trembled in the glass.

"Is everything okay?"

The passion, the intensity of concern burning in his eyes went straight through to my soul. I shivered.

"It's fine." I took a step backward. I had to break the connection of his flesh on mine. He was making me feel much more than I wanted to, much more than I was able to.

I delivered the coffees, cleared a table, delivered more coffees, and cleared another table. Soon I'd fallen into a seamless rhythm. I was like an actor in a play, never once deviating from her script. It went something like this:

"Hi, how are you today?"

Insert mundane answer here; usually "Good thanks" "Fine" or, in some cases, complete ignorance of the question.

"What can I get for you?"

This is where they would ask for X cups of coffee and X sides, and please make sure it was low-fat/extra-sugar/came with a dash of caramel/weak-strength/double-shot/not too hot/scald-your-mouth burning.

"Fantastic. That's X, thank you, I'll be right out with your order."

I tried to stick to my script as well as I could, reciting word after word after word. After the emotional rollercoaster of the last month, I just wanted things to be easy.

When we finally slowed down, Lachlan and Johnny were both at the counter. Johnny was drinking a coffee as he hunched his shoulders over the receipt book, his thin frame creating a hulk-like figure.

"We need to start buying more beans," he noted, to no one

in particular. I walked over to the wall and straightened one of Lachlan's framed pieces. It had been hanging on a slight tilt, ever since someone had come to check it out earlier that day. I took out my tea towel and polished the corner, removing the offending fingerprint from where the person had touched it.

"Oh, and Kate, I have the art show down for four weeks from tomorrow still, is that cool?"

"Yep, that's fine." I spun around to face them, making a mental note to chase the remaining RSVPs and confirm the catering.

"Great. I've spoken with a friend about getting a temporary liquor license, but is there anything else you need from me?" Johnny consulted his notepad, checking items off as he spoke. I tried to think. I'd chosen a menu, and sent out the invites, and even hired security.

"If it's too much, you don't have to do it," Lachlan offered.

"No, it's fine. I said I would." My pride held up, and I straightened my posture.

Johnny nodded and gathered his things, saying goodbye to us as he left the café. Lach and I were closing.

I checked my phone before starting the cleaning procedures. One new message.

Hi darling, no change with Dad but they want to keep him overnight. I'll stay here and see you tomorrow evening. Love Mum xx

Observation.

That was okay. Surely, that was okay.

Still, the idea of sitting in the house alone, all night, by myself, really didn't speak to me. The idea of driving back to Sydney for a night spent in a cramped hospital lounge chair held an equal amount of appeal.

"What are you up to tonight?" The words were out of my mouth before I had time to second-guess them.

"Me?" Lachlan asked.

"No. The coffee machine." I rolled my eyes, referring to the only other object in between his body and mine.

His body ...

I had to stop doing that.

"Nothing, why?" Lachlan smiled lazily, one corner of his mouth twitching up.

"My parents aren't home, and I was thinking maybe you could come over and we could have a few drinks, and watch some movies," I announced the plan as I made it up in my head. A few beers, some movies … things normal people did. That was what I needed; a quick dose of normality to take my mind off over-thinking everything.

Lachlan included.

"I'd love to come." Lachlan nodded. "Do you need me to bring anything?"

"Just yourself and some beers." I picked up a chair, stacking it on the table in front of me. I felt Lachlan's eyes on me and turned to look at him.

"What?" I asked.

"Nothing." His smile made me itch to lift my lips in return. I wanted to throw myself at him, but managed to retain some self-control.

Maybe tonight would be *the* night. Maybe I'd finally have sex, with a guy who hadn't suggested it once, but who I liked more than enough.

Funny how you can be with some guy for two years, and love him, but not want to give him your all without ever really knowing why. And how, on a day like today, you can be so sure that the broken boy in front of you is the one.

TWENTY-FOUR

LOOKED AT myself in the mirror for what felt like the thousandth time, studying my appearance. I'd gone from jeans and a tank, to a dress, to jeans and a tank again, and still I wasn't sure about the final combination.

I dusted some bronzer over my cheeks, looked at the ceiling and pursed my lips as I applied a think coat of mascara to my lashes. I wanted to look good, but not like I was trying too hard. My father was in the hospital, and I was having a boy over, for crying out loud. I felt like a naughty kid, sneaking around without her parents' permission. Mum had always been fine with me having Dave over, mind, but something about me having a guy over while Dad was in hospital made me think she wouldn't approve. Especially if she knew what I was hoping we would be doing.

The knock on the door made me jump, and I shoved my mascara back in the top drawer. After a quick final pout in the mirror and adjusting of hair, I ran downstairs to answer it.

"Hi." I smiled as I swung it open.

"Hi." He grinned back. He looked good, his hair flopping

over his face, highlighted by the moon. He was wearing a white collared shirt, pressed evenly, and blue denim jeans that hugged his body tight, but not too tight.

I could smell his cologne, mixed with coffee, mixed with just … just him. I inhaled a deep breath and managed to stop myself leaning closer. It was intoxicating.

"Can I come in?" He thrust a six-pack of beer toward me, and I realised I must have been staring like an idiot for far too long.

"God, yes! Of course, of course." I stepped back and let him through the door, trying to cool the red I could feel heating up my cheeks.

"Thanks." He smiled slowly, all dimples, and walked in. I could tell he wasn't teasing me this time—perhaps he'd been just as lost in the moment as I had.

"You've got a nice house." He walked into the living room and I saw his eyes roam over our couches, the stack of magazines on the coffee table, the big, black sound system, and the television in the corner.

"Thanks." I closed the door behind him. "Let me put those in the fridge for you." I went to grab his beers just as he moved them away, resulting in this weird dance where he went to hand them to me, then take them away, then repeated the pattern again.

"Sorry," he said, as he handed them over eventually.

"It's fine." I took them from his hands. "Just … sit somewhere." I gestured to the couches then turned on my heel and fled to the kitchen, eager to escape this awkward moment as soon as possible. How had we gone from normal and flirty at the café to this uncomfortable moment here?

I put his beers in the fridge after taking two from the pack and removing their lids. I pressed my back up against the door, studying the wooden panelled ceiling.

Get a grip, Kate.

You're not a little kid.

I forced myself to take a few slow breaths, then picked up the beers and walked back into the living room, a smile plastered over my face. Lachlan was sitting on one of the two-seater couches, somewhere near the middle.

Was I supposed to sit next to him, up close?

Or was he doing this so I'd sit somewhere else?

I bit my lip as I weighed up the options, and realised he was staring at me again. I'd probably let the moment go on for far too long, like I had at the front door.

Kate, snap out of it!

I walked to the table as casually as I could muster and placed the two drinks down, then turned to the cabinet beneath the television and started yelling out movie names, waiting for him to pick one.

"Your choice," he interrupted, when I read out the third one.

"I don't mind." I shrugged.

"Me neither," he said. I studied the stack of shiny cases in front of me. This wasn't going well. Shouldn't he just choose something? Why wasn't this easier? Was this date a failure?

Was it even really a date?

I ended up picking the case on top of the pile and opened it, jamming the disc into the side of the television then walking over to the couch that Lachlan wasn't on, curling myself into a little ball on the end of it. At least there I wouldn't do anything stupid, like get so caught up in staring at him I forgot what I was doing again.

I snuck a quick glance over at him, looking at his face, so intent and serious, focused on the television. One hand rested under his chin and I saw a faint tattoo line sneaking out from under the sleeve of his shirt. How had I not noticed that when we were skinny-dipping?

I found myself itching to get closer, to roll up his sleeve and see more of the tattoo. Or to take the shirt off and see the ink on the complete canvas …

"Can I sit with you?"

I blinked. Lachlan had caught me staring at him *again*.

Oh, red face, please don't do this to me now …

"Sure." I tried to sound as nonchalant as possible. I was so sprung.

He moved over and sat on the opposite end of the couch from me, his body leaning against the armrest. I tucked my chin in closer to my chest, hugging my knees. It didn't matter how far away we were. It wasn't like this was a date. We were just friends, who knew the particular details of each other's family health situations, and who had sometimes twice before kissed.

There was nothing suspicious about that.

The movie started, and we drank the six-pack of beer, not venturing to each other's territory on the opposite side of the couch.

I don't think I heard a word of what was said by the actors on screen. I didn't even really know if it was a romantic comedy or a slasher film, I was so preoccupied with this boy on the other side of the lounge and his distance from me, emotionally and physically.

"That was good," Lachlan said. The movie had stopped. The credits had even finished playing. I swallowed, trying to wash out the dry sensation at the back of my throat. Why couldn't I act like a normal person?

"Yeah," I lied. "I really liked … it." I settled on, unable to recall a detail in my favour.

"Me too." Lachlan smiled at me. Silence stretched out between us.

"Is this awkward?" He finally broke it.

"A little." I nodded.

"Or a lot." He widened his eyes. He shifted his body a little closer to mine. "I don't know why this is so weird. We've hung out quite a few times, and—"

"You've pretty much seen me naked."

"We've almost been arrested for making out!" We burst into laughter and I slumped further into the couch.

"Kate." Lachlan swallowed, and the air was still again. I bit my lip. "I think you're amazing."

"Ha!" I snorted. "Yeah right."

"Seriously." Lachlan inched closer, scooting across the

couch till his leg was touching mine. His eyes were dark, and I felt a shiver rush through me. "Dealing with everything; with things with your dad. You're not ashamed of him, you know? You take him out in public, regardless. You're amazing."

A feeling of guilt washed around in my stomach as I thought of how wrong Lachlan really was. How I did it, but I wasn't proud of it, and I certainly wasn't as "good" a person as he thought I was.

"I'm not … I don't like doing it." Lachlan leaned closer to hear my words.

"You're not expected to like it," he said, in that easy way of his. "It's not about life being easy, remember? It's about how you roll with the punches, how you deal with the shit.

"I've had some crap things in my life, you know? Fuck, there's rarely a day that goes by when I don't remember, and feel, and just—just hurt, and get mad. What the hell did I do? Why me?

"But then I look at you, and how you deal. Whether you're hurting on the inside or not, you're still moving forward with your life, you're still taking your dad out and buying milkshakes. And I think you're doing it well."

We sat there in silence as I studied his face. I lifted a hand and pushed that floppy piece of hair back behind his ears.

"I couldn't imagine being you, doing what you do. And I'm nothing like that! Both my parents are still alive, but I'm struggling. You're the amazing one here, not me. You're just—" I looked at him, in awe once again. He had it so wrong about me. I was a fraud, wanting to be in control of my life, but struggling, one day at a time.

How he got out of bed, ran a business, had a good relationship with Johnny. "—you're everything I one day want to be. The thing is," I paused. I looked at the cream suede beneath us, marred with those little scuffmarks suede gets. *Guilty secret time.* "Sometimes … sometimes I don't like him. He's like a kid I have to look after, but then, at the same time, he's me. Everything he does could happen to me, and I think that's why I've distanced myself. It's when I dislike him the most. Because one day, that could be me, too. And I hate the idea of being that me."

Lachlan reached over and grabbed my hand, pulling it closer to him. He unstretched all my fingers from the fist they'd been making, and rubbed the little lines in my palm, caused when I'd dug my fingers in a few seconds earlier.

"See this?" He waved my pinky finger in front of my face. I laughed. "It's perfect. See how you have—" he paused, and counted, tapping each of my appendages in turn. "—one, two, three, four, *five* of them."

"You should see my other hand." I gave a half-smile.

"You have five perfect fingers. And these scars you're giving yourself," he said, running his finger over the little indents in my skin where my nails had burned me, and I shivered. "They're temporary. In one hour, one day, one week—they're going to fade. But nothing's gonna change these perfect fingers."

"So you're saying that, even if I have Huntington's, I'll still have good hands?" I raised my eyebrows.

"I'm saying that, deep down, nothing will change your perfect."

In that moment, I forgot about everything. I could handle my future, whatever it may hold. Someone believed in me.

And I was head over heels for him.

"You've made me try new things," I whispered. "Even if I do test positive, and you have cancer—I don't know that I've ever been so involved, or felt so aware of my life."

And I did. Every cell in my body was buzzing as he slowly reached his hand over and trailed a finger along my jawline. I bent my head into it, wanting the moment to go on and on, to fall into his embrace completely. His lips were close now, so much so that I could feel the soft heat of his breath on my face, my lips.

"I'm falling in love with you." He moved his hand to the back of my neck and gently pulled my head toward his, closing the gap between us and pressing our lips together. It was familiar and yet different all at once, passionate yet romantic, as I felt the heat of our emotion and the stress of the past few weeks rush through my body. I clung to his shirt and pulled a fistful of it to me, enjoying the firm feeling of his chest as it collided with mine, his shoulders caving over me.

I let my tongue explore his mouth and felt my chest heave against his as he gently sucked on my lip, and then swirled his tongue around its edge. His hands were playing with the hem of my shirt and I itched to be closer to his him, to feel him against me.

I pushed him gently back and lifted my tank up, raising it over my head and letting it fall to the floor.

"Kate." Lachlan swallowed. I went to press myself against him and he pushed me gently back, checking me out from my hips, to my bra, to my eyes.

"You are so beautiful." He smiled sweetly as his eyes took in my body, his naked desire plain to see.

I moved closer and pressed against him, my mouth greedy for his. His hands roamed up my body and lingered over the lacy edges of my bra, gently moving toward my breasts. His fingers teased my nipples and I arched into him, the sensation shooting heat between my legs.

"Let's … let's go to my room." I pulled apart from him for a second. Mum said she was spending the night at the hospital, but on the off chance that she came home unexpectedly, I didn't want to send her straight back there when she suffered a heart attack induced by seeing her daughter naked on the couch with some guy she'd heard of, but never met.

And I really didn't think I could trust myself to keep the rest of my clothes on for much longer.

"Mm," Lachlan groaned. He placed his hands on my shoulders and exhaled deeply. "Okay." He stood up and turned his back to me, picking my shirt up off the floor and throwing it at my chest. "You're going to need to hold that there, or I'm not going to make it."

"'Kay." I stifled a smile and held my shirt to my chest as instructed as I led him up the stairs. I was buzzing. This was really happening. I had a guy, who liked me, who completely got the hereditary-disease thing, and who turned me on like I'd never thought possible. I couldn't wait to get him into my room.

Once we were inside, I shut the door behind him. He walked over to my bed and sat down on the edge, taking everything in: my alphabetically-organised DVD stand, my clothes hanging in colour-coded order in the wardrobe.

"You're very neat." He observed, his gaze resting on my empty trashcan.

"It's hereditary." I smiled, glad to be admitting to one family trait that was substantially less embarrassing than the last hereditary incident I'd confessed to.

"I'm going to turn on the radio." Shirt still at my chest, I flicked the switch on my sound system, suddenly a little bit nervous again. The sound of mindless advertising filled the room and I inched my way toward the bed. Lachlan was looking at me, his eyes wide, like I was the most amazing thing he'd ever seen.

"Can we … lose the shirt again now?" He sounded eager, hopeful, all at once.

I dropped the shirt, letting it fall to the floor. He gave a tiny gasp and I felt my heart start to race again, the heat of his gaze setting my pulse on fire.

His hands reached out and grabbed my thighs, pulling me close to the bed till my stomach was at his eye height. He placed his big, strong hands on the small of my back, pulling it closer to him as he kissed my stomach, over the hollow of my belly button, soft, wet, heated kisses that made me tingle on the inside.

He popped open the top button of my fly and gently pulled my zipper down, tracing a soft finger over my lace panties that were now partially exposed. I shuddered with anticipation, my breath hitching in my throat. It was all I could do not to thrust further toward him.

He slid my jeans off, pulling them down my legs and gently tracing the inside of my thighs with his fingers. I shivered, goosebumps lining my body. He was moving so slowly, not touching anywhere even remotely forbidden, and the anticipation was killing me.

"Up next, we have a killer track from hot new band Dave & the Glories; You Crazy Bitch."

The words broke through my anticipation and sent my blood running cold.

What. The. *Hell.*

Surely it was just some stupid song they'd written that was tongue in cheek, nothing to do with me. Why would Dave write a song about me? And Michael would warn me if such a song existed.

Wouldn't he?

I was vaguely aware that Lachlan was kissing the inside of my thigh, but I could barely concentrate as the opening guitar riff ended and Dave's voice kicked in.

"*She was the girl that I wanted, the girl of my mind-blowing dreams,*" he sang in that nasal twang. "*But she's blown it all up, she's made a big crazy sce—ene.*"

My heart started to thud. He wouldn't.

Would he?

"*Yeah, her dad, he's insane,*" the bridge rang. "*Yeah, all lost in his brain. Yeah—it'll happen again!*"

My knees were weak, and not from Lachlan's kisses. He moved his hands to the line of my panties and I covered them with my own, preventing him from taking the next step.

"Stop," I whispered. He looked up at me, a slight frown marring his smooth olive forehead.

"What's wrong?" His voice was equally quiet, but even if he'd yelled, I wasn't sure I would have heard.

"*She keeps her room so clean but she's messy insi-ide, her brains going out with the outgoing ti-ide, she holds back what I want, never scratches that itch, and yeah … O-oh yeah! You crazy bitch.*"

I sunk to the bed next to Lachlan, holding my head in my hands. Everyone from school would hear. They had to know it was about me, after Dad's performance at graduation. He'd written a song, airing all our dirty laundry, all *my* dirty laundry, for the whole world to hear. Not everyone was as understanding as Lachlan. Hell, *I* wasn't even completely accepting of my father yet.

How could I expect the rest of the world to be?

"Is this—is this your ex?" Lachlan asked. He placed a hand gently on my back.

"*She keeps her room so clean but she's messy insi-ide, her brains going out with the outgoing ti-ide,*" Dave sung again as the chorus went a second time around.

I couldn't look at Lachlan, couldn't bear to make eye contact. It was one thing him knowing the truth about my dad, and another him having to listen to my ex-boyfriend sing about it on the radio. My blood boiled. *Dave* …

"*She keeps her room so clean but she's messy insi-ide,*" the chorus kicked in again.

Something within me ticked over. I couldn't handle this. Nothing about this was okay.

The adrenaline mixed with a few beers coursed through me as I leaned over and grabbed clothes from the hamper, scooping them into my arms and throwing them across the room, a sea of soft fabric floating through the air.

"Kate … Are you okay?" Lachlan asked, as I blindly walked toward the centre of my room.

I grabbed another handful and emptied my arms into nothingness. White socks, black underwear, coloured bras and T-shirts, all kamikaziing towards the floor. I had to make it dirty. Then none of it would be true.

"*She keeps her room so clean …*"

"This isn't exactly how I imagined the first time you threw your panties at me." Lachlan gave a wry grin as he peeled a lace thong from his shoulder.

I felt my face redden and I snatched the G-string from his hands before he could examine it closer.

After throwing it on the chair I walked over to the bed, pulling the quilt from the mattress and letting it fly, an arc of black and white sweeping through the air and coming to rest, half on my desk chair, half on my bin.

The DVDs were the next victim of my rampage. I grabbed a handful and lifted them, carefully balancing my way over to the middle of the room where I could dump them with maximum effect.

"Kate?" Lachlan asked. He stood in the corner, looking very uncomfortable. I didn't have time to think about that. It wasn't important right now.

I managed to drop the first pile of DVDs on top of my quilt cover. I returned to grab a second, confident I could repeat my actions. I could mess up this room. I could change it. I could be messy here and then maybe on the inside I'd be clean, and I wouldn't be the girl in the song. I wouldn't be that "*crazy bitch*".

With the DVDs balanced between my hands, I started the precarious walk over to my bookshelf, ready to finish this, to separate my new life from my old, clean one. I took one case from the top of the pile and slammed it against the wall, a grey mark appearing where it made impact.

"Kate!"

I don't think it was his voice that did it, more a combination of me being slightly drunk and dizzy, and misjudging the force with which to hold the DVDs. All I know is, one moment I was holding them and the next they had spewed out from between my arms and were flying through the air, landing all over the floor, a mass of colourful covers and shiny discs.

I dropped to my knees. It was all too much. I had to pick them up. Pick them up.

A loud, gulping sob broke from my lips as I tried to capture as many DVDs as I could in my arms, watching as they slipped out of my grip again and back onto the floor.

"*You … c-crazy bitch*," I sung along to the final line of the song, my breath catching with each sobbed word.

"Kate." Lachlan was on the floor next to me, grabbing DVD cases in both of his hands and stacking them into a pile. He got a nice collection together then started a new pile, making towers of DVDs on the floor around us.

I gave up trying to help and instead drew my knees to my

chest and turned my head down, the tears and pain consuming me. What was I doing? It was too much.

After a few minutes I felt Lachlan place an arm around my back and another one in the gap behind my knees. He scooped me up and carried me over to my bed. I was so emotionally vacant, so worn out from being so upset, I barely noticed the fact I was dressed only in underwear and he was fully clothed.

He placed me gently on the bed and went to get my quilt from the floor. He shook it out and let it float gently down to rest on top of me. He switched off the radio and turned out the lights, and I heard the sound of clothes rustling about over my shudders, my racking cries of pain that wouldn't abate.

I fell asleep, emotionally exhausted and completely drained, my almost naked back pressed up hard against Lachlan's stomach.

TWENTY-FIVE

W HEN I woke up, the sun beamed through the window. My lids were heavy, stuck to my cheeks like glue. I stretched my legs and arms as far up and down as they could go, rolling over to hide my eyes from the sun.

That's when I heard the gentle rhythm of breathing, saw the hulk of the quilt, his delicate neck, and remembered.

Lachlan was here.

In. My. Bed.

My eyes widened, and I ran my hands through my hair, smoothing it down, running my fingers under my eyes to try and rub away any mascara that had no doubt caked there after my crying the night before.

I was a mess. Why had Dave written that stupid song? Why did I flip out? Especially when there was a good-looking boy in my room, who was now next to me in my bed?

I jerked my hand over to him and stopped an inch away from his back. Could I do it? Could I just put my arm around him?

I gently placed my hand on his shoulder and pulled my

body closer to him, marvelling at how smooth his skin was, how it felt against my mostly naked body. The sun was dancing in his dark-brown hair, and I reached my other hand up to touch it. It was just as soft as I'd imagined. I trailed my finger down the nape of his neck, past the shorter hairs, over to his broad shoulders that rippled with muscle.

There was a boy in my bed!

I leant forward and gently kissed the part where his shoulder met his neck, a soft kiss, almost to prove that he was real.

"Morning." His muffled voice sounded, causing me to clasp my hand back to my chest in shock.

"Morning." I spoke into the folds of the blanket. I was fairly certain I had morning breath, and that was not how I wanted him to think of me.

"Why'd you stop?" His voice was small and sleepy. Sexy.

"Stop?"

"You were kissing me."

My heart thudded, *bang, bang,* against my rib cage.

"Oh."

I moved forward again and gently started to kiss his neck, moving up to his ear where I took his lobe in my mouth, rolling it gently against my teeth. My hands wrapped under his arms and felt his bare chest, his abs, firm and tense under my grip. I wrapped one leg around his, aching to be as close to him as I possibly could.

"Kate," his voice croaked and he grabbed my hips, pulling them over his while he slid underneath me till I was no longer behind but straddled on top of him, my legs wrapped around his muscular thighs.

I looked down, really taking him in: the sculpted lines of his chest, the strength in his arms, and the sheer, naked desire in his eyes. I swallowed. I could feel him hard against me—and in nothing but lingerie, it didn't leave much to the imagination.

"You are amazing." Lachlan emphasised each syllable as his eyes raked up and down my body. It didn't make me nervous, or uncomfortable. I felt special. Even after my freak out he was still interested in me. In *us*.

I'd never felt more turned on.

I leaned down to kiss his neck again, pressing my hips against his thighs as I went which elicited a groan of pleasure from him. I chalked it up in my head, a devious smile on my face. I was going to enjoy this. And then we would face the ups and downs of the world together.

"Kate, we need to—oh, God, Kate." Lachlan placed his hands on my shoulders and tried to push me away, but I didn't want to be pushed. I couldn't. I needed this.

"Kate?"

I froze.

"Kate? Are you home?" Mum's voice rang through the stairwell.

My heart quickened. Mum couldn't know I had a boy in my bed.

"Get in the wardrobe," I hissed, jabbing my thumb toward the opposite side of the room.

"Wha—"

"Are you still in bed?" Mum's tone was upbeat. I heard her footsteps on the stairs.

"Now!" My eyes almost popped out of my head as I watched him scramble back from the covers, his body naked in front of me, barring a pair of tight-fitting jocks. Even though we were in emergency status, I took the time to check out his arm definition, that tattoo I'd seen creeping the night before, and his chest, even better in full view, with his flat stomach ending in a well-defined V that pointed down and disappeared inside his pants.

"Honey, are you awake?" This time Mum's voice was quieter as she knocked gently on my door. I forced my eyes away from Lachlan's retreating body and dived under the covers, hoping she wouldn't have heard the noise he made. I pulled the quilt up to my chin to hide my almost naked state.

After a few moments of silence, the door creaked open. Mum poked her head into the room, her eyes first going to the mess on the floor then to me on the bed.

"Hi, Mum." I tried to muster up a croaky, small-mouthed I'm-just-waking-up voice. I'm not sure that it worked.

"Hi, dear." Mum narrowed her eyes at me. "What happened in here? Are they marks—did you throw something at the wall?" Her mouth turned into a small *O* of horror.

"Accidental," I said into the sheets.

"I know you're upset and angry, but you really need to stop hiding and start dealing with this." Mum opened the door and cleared a space at the foot of my bed, right near my feet. I was careful not to prop myself up too far, in case she noticed my non-pyjamas. Oh God; his clothes! Where were Lachlan's clothes?

"I agree." It seemed like the easiest, quickest route to getting Mum out of the bedroom pronto.

"I know you missed your counselling appointment two days ago. Leslie told me," she continued.

"It was a mistake. I'll make sure I'm on time in future." I looked down at the quilt.

"And she mentioned your neurologist appointment went well, and said you're off to the psychiatrist today."

Insert sense of impending doom here. My shoulders went heavy, my eyes hooded. How could I forget good ol' Huntington's test number three?

"I know you don't find out your results till next week, but I was thinking maybe the three of us should have a nice dinner out somewhere."

"What?"

"A nice dinner," Mum repeated.

"Not—not now."

"Well, then, maybe we could have a girly spa day tomorrow."

"Mum! It's not a celebration."

"I'm just trying to—"

"To make this a special occasion? 'Oh, Kate, you're probably going to have Huntington's, your ex-boyfriend wrote a song about it, but at least we can have a goddamned *mani-*

pedi?'"

"Kate, that's not what I meant. And Dave wrote a song?"

"Well what *did* you mean?"

Silence filled the room. I ran my hand through my hair, pulling it back till it hurt.

"I was just trying to make things … easier." Mum stood, and smoothed down her skirt. "I'll be at the hospital with your father when you get back this afternoon. And—for what it's worth—I'm sorry."

She left the room, without another word.

It only took about twenty seconds for the guilt to set in. Why had I been so angry? She was only trying to help. It wasn't her fault. I'd attacked her when she'd been trying to make things easier for me.

They needed a guidebook on this, not just for the symptoms, but how to deal emotionally with everyone suffering from it.

"Kate?" Lachlan poked his head out of the wardrobe.

"I know." I sunk back onto my bed, my hands clasping either side of my forehead. "I'm a complete bitch."

"Kate." Lachlan's voice was soft. "It's okay."

"God, I just—I just get so caught up in it all, you know? It's not fair! And then I remember it's not just me, then I feel things again and—sometimes, I wish I didn't feel."

Sometimes, I wish I were dead.

No.

No I don't.

Do I?

"Feeling is good. It means you're still experiencing life." Lachlan smiled.

"Is this the part where you give the 'try new things' speech?" I mustered a wry smile.

"I believe it would be a crime not to."

"How do you do it?" I sighed, resting my head back against the pillows and studying the ceiling above.

"You just … you just do." Lachlan walked over and carefully lay next to me. He knew exactly what I was talking about, without me having to form the words. "It's hard; I've had days where I think it's unfair, days when I can't handle it all."

I reached out my hand and wrapped his in it, giving him a gentle squeeze.

"That's why it's the little things, Kate." His voice was choked. I turned to see him blink back a tear. "If you don't celebrate the little things, the ... the biggest thing will get you down."

His words resonated within me. The little things, versus death.

"Are you afraid to die?" I gulped.

"No more than I am to live."

Silence coated the room, marred only by the sounds of life I heard from the kitchen downstairs. I stared at the stark white ceiling above my bed and counted to ten, trying to gain some perspective on the situation.

My ex-boyfriend released a song about me being crazy. *But was I really that in love with him in the first place?*

Lachlan knew every one of my dirty, selfish secrets. *But he was still here.*

I had an appointment with a psychiatrist later today, then a blood test to see if I had Huntington's. *But there was still a chance it would be negative.*

There was a half-naked boy in my bed. *There was a half-naked boy in my bed!*

"Lachlan, will you ..." I bit my lip. Nerves washed over my body.

"Will I?"

"Will you have dinner with me, and my family tonight? It might be in Sydney; I don't know if Dad will be out. After my test." I rushed the words. I just wanted him to be a part of my life, to help me through—and I wanted to help him through, too.

Huntington's or not.

"I'd love that." Lachlan smiled, those damned dimples lighting up again, and I couldn't help but smile back. This beautiful boy—how did he break through my walls?

"Katie, Breakfast," Mum called from downstairs.

"Go," I whispered to Lachlan, my eyes darting toward the window.

"Kate!" His eyes were harrowed.

"What?"

"My clothes."

Oh.

I flipped up my quilt and found his shirt and jeans under the sheets. I felt the square imprint of his art notepad in his jeans pocket as I rushed them over to him, and then turned my back to him while he changed. Somehow, even though I'd seen him walking around in a pair of jocks, it seemed polite.

Seconds later, his warm hands laced around my waist, linking in front of my stomach.

"Good luck today," he whispered, and gave me a quick kiss on the cheek.

"Thanks." I smiled. We stood there like that, bodies close, all smiles for a few minutes, till eventually he unlocked his hands and turned to the window.

"Message me after your appointment?" he asked, one hand on the window frame.

"Done." I nodded. I ran to the window, even though it was sappy as hell, and watched as he climbed down the tree, anxious to make sure he didn't fall. When he got to the lawn, he looked back up at me and gave me a wink, those dimples highlighted as he darted to his motorbike, parked just down the street.

I felt tingles rush through my body, replaced by a sense of—of nothing. No stress, no impending doom, no worry about what everybody else would think—just nothing.

Was this what it felt like to be normal again?

TWENTY-SIX

A FTER LACHLAN left, I couldn't stop smiling. I ate breakfast with Mum at the kitchen counter, a grin plastered over my face.

Next, I threw myself into the planning of the art launch to compensate, determined to make the night perfect. I'd gotten most of the RSVPs back and, to my surprise and delight, most of them had said yes, even the local media and art buyers I'd invited. I was excited, looking forward to everything about the event—and that was the weirdest part. It had been so long since I'd actually looked forward to something, been excited about having an event in the future that was important, that I felt a renewed sense of energy.

The energy was enough to keep me going in the car, all the way to the psychiatrist's appointment—even when Dave's song came blasting onto the radio a second time, and I got a text from Michael.

> He recorded it without me. I've left the band, for what it's worth. You know I wouldn't have let it happen if I'd known. Michael x

The thought was sweet. At least someone could see what a jerk Dave was being. Sure, it still felt like I'd been stabbed, with a severe and rusty knife. It still felt like everyone was pointing and laughing at me, like the drivers of the cars I overtook on the freeway were all turning their heads and grinning, realising I was the one the song was about, the one who was apparently going crazy.

But I'm not.

I pulled into an unfamiliar parking lot and walked inside a small red brick building, confidence adding lightness to my step.

"Kate Tomlinson," I told the receptionist. Her hair was pulled back so tight it looked like it was stretching her eyes, ever so slightly, and her lips were pursed in a strict no-nonsense kind of way.

But even she couldn't dampen my spirits. Lachlan had spent the night in my bed. He'd made me feel worthwhile, like maybe the way I was handling things with Dad wasn't so bad, after all. Any worries I'd had about him not liking me were clearly unfounded, especially after the song incident.

All I needed was one tiny you-don't-have-Huntington's test result, some more time with Lachlan in my bed, and everything would be fine.

"Ms Tomlinson?"

I looked up. Apparently, this was the one doctor's surgery that ran on time. Standing to my left was a short man with grey tufts of hair bordering his ears, thin-rimmed glasses and glittering eyes. He wore a pale blue shirt, finely pressed, and tight pants that were the sort of *too* high that reminded me of a bad 80s film about nerds and revenge.

"Yes." I smiled.

"Come through." He gestured with his clipboard to a doorway behind him, and I followed.

This room was painted white, a giant image of a waterfall framed on the furthest wall. The desk was spotless, with a darkened computer screen, and two stray pens the only things marring the otherwise clutter-free surface. A window was behind the monitor, but the blinds were drawn and shut.

It couldn't have been more different from Leslie's if it had tried.

"Okay, Kate." The doctor rested back in his chair, as if the very act of standing and walking to the door had taken far more energy than he'd intended it to. "Why are you here?"

I hated this. It was such typical psycho-babble bullshit, like he hadn't spoken to Leslie and found out exactly what my problems were.

But everything was going to be okay.

I was okay.

"Well, my dad developed Huntington's, and I want to be tested." I smiled and clasped my hands over my knees, sitting up straight.

"Okay." The doctor scribbled notes on his clipboard, again reminding me how different from my normal counsellor he was. "And how do you feel about this?"

This, however, I had expected.

Typical Psych 101.

"I was upset, and angry," I admitted, surprising myself by telling the truth for once. "But now, I just—I feel like I'm coming to terms with it, you know? I still want to find out if I have it, but not with the same ... the same *desperation* I felt before."

"So if I told you there's a two-year wait, how would you feel?"

"Frustrated, I guess." I tilted my head. "But okay."

And as I said the words, I knew it really was okay. I answered all his questions succinctly, let him take my blood pressure, and even told him that—heaven forbid—I had wanted to hurt myself physically to release my inner demons, but now the pain wasn't anywhere near as bad. It wasn't stabbing anymore.

Now, I was ready.

"I have an item here saying you missed your last counselling appointment." The psychiatrist's eyes flicked to his sheet of paper then to me, acutely analysing my reaction.

"I just forgot about it," I lied. "But I did make my

neurologist appointment, and I'm happy to see a genetics counsellor again."

"Good," the psychiatrist scribbled a note. He shifted his weight and I felt him look at me, as if he could see my insides—the sort of study you know is deep. "I think it's time you took the blood test, then."

It seemed ridiculous that, after more than a month of stress and worry, after neurologist and psychiatrist and what felt like endless genetic counselling, the test to find out if I had Huntington's or not was a simple blood test, done at a pathology lab, just like any other.

I found the closest one on the way home and stopped there, eager to just get it over with and find out. I squeezed my eyes tight while the nurse drew the blood, and then booked my results genetic counselling appointment to get the results three and a half weeks later, the day of Lachlan's launch.

Part of me thought it could be a mistake, but I also thought it might be a good thing. If I was positive, it meant I had something distracting and all consuming to do; if I was negative, well, hey—party!

I drove home and felt so much lighter, as if someone had lifted a weight from my shoulders I hadn't known was there.

I drove past the spot on the freeway where Lachlan and I had made out, the café, the street where we'd gone skinny-dipping and smiled—how could my future be grim when all these good things kept happening? Everything was going to be okay.

I pulled up against the curb and all but skipped to the front door. I grabbed the door handle and yanked it open, walking inside. I'd go to my room and message Lachlan, see if he was still keen for tonight. Hey, maybe I'd even spend this afternoon hanging out with Dad, if he were out of hospital. I felt like I could, no matter his mood right now. Everything was fine.

Peace had taken residence in every corner of my body. Peace, and a giddiness, caused from feeling something I hadn't felt for a long time—happiness. I was like a little kid. Since when was life this full of potential?

Spinning around, I pulled my hands from the door and twirled into the living room, about to head upstairs when I saw her.

Mum.

Sitting on the couch.

When she should have been in the kitchen, cooking. Or the bathroom, getting ready for dinner. Or the hospital, sitting with Dad. Or just—anywhere but here.

She was never the kind of person to just sit on the couch.

"Mum?"

"Kate." Mum swallowed. Her eyes were rimmed with red, and there were dark bags underneath them. "Sit down." She patted the space next to her.

I knew then that something was truly, horribly wrong.

"What happened?" I walked over all zombie-like, and sat on the couch next to her. Dad had gotten even sicker. The disease had gotten worse. The pneumonia was confirmed. Oh, God, oh no. And I hadn't even gotten a chance to take him out again. Not since I'd worked out that I was doing okay as a daughter.

Please, don't let him be dying.

Well, any more than he already is.

"There was—there was an accident." Mum studied the suede material beneath us. I furrowed my brow.

"An accident? Like a machine at the hospital …" I trailed off, unsure what could possibly have happened. Did machines have accidents? Did a doctor make a mistake? And, whatever it was, why was Mum *here* instead of *there*?

I felt my mind float somewhere above my body, looking down on me at the scene. He had to be … he had to be dead.

No!

I hadn't had the chance to make things okay.

He couldn't be dead yet.

Could he?

"He's … he's dead," Mum confirmed my fears. She placed a delicate hand on my shoulder. I felt the colour rush from my face. How could this be happening? When I'd been such a bitch to him, not even tried to understand?

I felt the heat of tears behind my eyes. Oh, God. This was horrible.

"I'm sorry, darling. Lachlan is dead."

What?

Thump.

Thump.

Nothing.

"There was an accident—his bike, slid out around a corner and hit a tree—a man named Johnny called, said to tell you. I said you didn't really know anyone named Lachlan, you've never mentioned him, but he seemed adamant you'd care, and I remembered the café boy, and—"

"No." The blood drained from my face. My eyes felt dry. "There must be some mistake."

"I'm sorry, dear." Mum placed her hand on my back and gave it a little rub.

How could … how could Lachlan, who'd been in my room that morning, whose parents had both already suffered cruel and tragic fates, who was already suffering from a potentially fatal illness, Mr Try Everything Once Lachlan, be … be dead?

"Are you … are you sure?" I pursed my lips. Maybe she'd heard wrong. Maybe she was indulging in some cruel joke, and this was some final test to see how I coped with grief, and would impact whether I got my results in three and a half weeks.

"I'm—darling, I'm so sorry." A tiny tear trickled its way from the corner of Mum's eye, over the ridges of her crow's feet and down her sallow cheek. Seeing that, the tragedy of a single teardrop, made it real. It was my undoing.

Pieces of me came apart, falling from my body onto the couch till I was a mess of me and tears and heat and hurt.

Lachlan was gone. The guy who'd understood me, who'd

wanted to be with me.

The *only* guy.

He was dead, gone forever. He was supposed to die later, from cancer, or sickness, or something. Not from a motorbike accident. It wasn't supposed to happen yet. He didn't survive cancer to die *now*.

How could this have happened?

Why?

A wave of pain crashed over my head, sucking me under till it filled my lungs, drowning me in its all-consuming horrible hurt. I opened my mouth to gasp for air, to try and come up and breathe, but all that came out was my pain, great, big tears of hurt spewing from my eyes.

I ran to the door, rattling the handle, trying to open it. I'd go to my car, and I'd drive. I'd find him, I would. It was all a mistake, a great big misunderstanding. Or a joke.

Yes.

Johnny and Lachlan always played practical jokes.

"I'm just going …" The words trailed from my lips, extra fast in between sobs I didn't know were mine, as I swivelled the handle round and round. Why wouldn't the *stupid* thing open? I gave it a tiny kick with my ankle, relishing the pain that shot up my leg.

That hurt, but Lachlan was alive. That was my pain, now he could be living.

"Kate." Mum's hands grabbed my shoulders and she pulled me from the door, spinning me round to face her with a force I didn't know she had. "I'm sorry, but he is. He's—he's dead."

The world came rushing in with my breath, all the pain and heartache of everyone, everywhere, contained inside my body. It roiled in my gut, tore at my heart with a physical ache that made me clutch my sides in desperation. I couldn't take it. How could anything be okay, ever again?

"Nooooo," I howled, my chest shaking with pain as the sobs gulped from my mouth in ugly spurts. "No. No. No."

It seemed easiest just to keep repeating that word, over and over. He couldn't. It wasn't. It didn't.

Did it?

The pain, the feelings of hurt I'd thought I felt before? Nothing, compared to this huge, empty void taking up space in my heart. It was shaped like a knife, serrated and hard, so that every time I moved my body the stab went a little deeper.

It hurt so damn much.

Why? Why did the one good thing I have …?

Why did the one good thing Johnny had …?

I sat there for hours, crying and crying, Mum rubbed my back, making tiny comforting noises, small apologies I cared nought for, and that consoled me even less.

At some point, I fell asleep. I woke up on the couch, wondering if we were still watching a movie, if Lachlan was still here, if he were in my bed, when I would see him again.

Then I'd see him leave my house, hop on his bike and ride, crashing straight into a car, a truck, oncoming traffic, off a bridge. Every time I saw him it would be his face that stuck, red foam at his mouth, and life leaving his body. He was a limp, ragdoll of a man, and I'd try to shake him back to life, begging him to come back. I'd give him mouth-to-mouth, but his teeth would fall out, then his tongue lost the warmth of humanity and turned icy cold and I was trying to revive a corpse, a long dead memory of man. I'd wake, realise it was a dream and I'd fall asleep again, the dream always the same but different, the pain never any less real when I woke up.

After waking to my sixth scream I felt a glass being shoved into one hand, a small, round tablet into the other.

"Please, Kate." Mum folded my fingers over the white pill. "To help you sleep."

I gulped back the pill and choked water down my throat. She didn't need to say please. She didn't need to ask. I only wished she'd told me where the rest of the tablets were.

Because if things like this could happen, if someone who already had a time limit on their life had it cruelly ripped away … if Johnny could lose everyone, if I could mentally lose my dad and physically lose the only man I'd thought would ever understand me, then how could staying awake be worth it?

I wanted to sleep forever.

And ever.

TWENTY-SEVEN

L IFE WAS a blur. I lost track of time, became aware only of the numbness that overtook my body, interspersed with regular hits of pain when the sleeping tablets or the anti-depressants Mum gave me wore off.

She kept saying I was in shock; this was perfectly natural. She even had her GP come and do a house call, checking my blood pressure and all the other vitals. But nothing could make it right. This wasn't a blood pressure thing. It was my heart that needed to be gauged.

It was everything, and it was not, it was the world and it was my life, all rolled into one. And it was crumbling in pieces around me.

On the third day, the doorbell rang. Two giant bunches of flowers were delivered. One was all expensive, foreign-looking things, snapdragons and tulips and strange, round coloured buds, the other simple white roses littered with baby's breath.

"Don't you want to know who they're from?" Mum asked, taking out vases from some secret vase cupboard I knew nothing about and distributing the flowers, cutting the stems for display.

"Don't care," I grunted and rolled over. I preferred facing the cream surface of the couch. The world was too much for me.

"One is from a guy named Lee," Mum continued. I shook my head. Who the hell was Lee? Clearly she hadn't read the card correctly. "Yes, he says he's sorry about the song, and that he's dismissed the writer from the tour."

I blinked.

Oh.

That Lee.

Lee-*freaking*-Collins.

For some weird reason, the thought brought on a new flood of tears, until the wetness leaking from my eyes dampened my T-shirt and turned it slightly see-through. In the real world, someone had realised Dave was a jerk. A singer from a famous rock band had sent me flowers to apologise for his support-band's lead-singer's stupidity.

I pressed my thumb and forefinger to the bridge of my nose.

"Oh, and the one with the roses," Mum continued, splaying the stems out so each of the flowers settled into the perfectly balanced display, "it's from Johnny."

Johnny.

Johnny, who had also lost Lachlan.

Who didn't have anyone else.

He'd sent *me* flowers.

No wonder all these horrible things kept happening to me. I was a truly selfish person; I deserved to have Huntington's.

I don't know how, but I escaped out the front door without Mum noticing. The keys to the Corolla were in my hand, tightly fisted, ready to aid me in my mission.

The engine turned without any protest and I was off,

driving at a slow pace down the road. There was the street corner where Lachlan had walked me, the very first time we'd kissed. There was the cul-de-sac where the bush track branched off to the skinny-dipping pool.

It wasn't on my way, but I drove through town, noting both the Thai restaurant where we all went to dinner, and the toilet block where Lachlan had waited outside.

Even then, he'd gone above and beyond for me. So why had he left me? What had I done?

I took the freeway exit, and cruised five minutes down the road till I saw the turning bay. I pulled my car in, conscious of the dimming light around me.

I remember reading somewhere that a majority of car accidents happen at dusk.

6:01 pm, the clock read.

Looked like the timing was perfect.

I waited and waited until finally I saw the bouncing headlights of a car in the distance. I didn't know how big or small it was—it really didn't matter. I turned the car and inched out, making sure it was only just my side in the line of impact. I didn't want to hurt the driver of the other vehicle. I was the bull's-eye in this game.

"Lachlan, I'm sorry," I said to the empty car. Tears were wet down my cheeks.

"I really liked you, and you—it's not fair," I gulped. "You were just—you were everything, and you'd been through so much, and *you weren't supposed to die!*"

The headlights beamed closer, so close I could trace their path till impact.

"I don't kn-know that anyone else will ever see in me what you did," I choked.

Five seconds.

"You set me free," I whispered. Now I could make out the shape of the vehicle, a four-wheel drive. Perfect. They would most likely pull through, and I would undoubtedly be ruined. Survival of the fittest. Big car versus small car.

Three seconds.

"I—" The headlights were close now. I braced myself for impact, my heart pounding in my chest, my body already numb to the impending pain that was rapidly descending upon it.

Two.

Shit.

One.

When I opened my eyes, I was back in the turning bay, the car in reverse. I blinked, staring at the little red *R* light, as if it were a joke.

Had it been me, all along? Was I the one who didn't want to die?

I turned the car on again, heard its throaty rumble, and drove home.

TWENTY-EIGHT

I'D CALLED Johnny to see how he was doing, but he'd closed the café temporarily, so it went straight to voicemail. I was on full-time Father duty, a task that seemed a breeze compared to my recent life drama.

Dad set himself down in the living room in front of the television and I got us both some snacks from the kitchen. I could have started on dinner but it was only five, and even if it felt like I'd started to live in a pensioner-care house, I figured I didn't have to eat like I was in one.

I put a can of soda and a bowl of chips down in front of the television, then took a separate bowl and can to the kitchen counter where my laptop was set up. It was easier this way. This way I didn't have to connect.

I didn't want to connect with anyone.

I pressed the start button and checked my emails, noting that some final running orders had come through from the caterers on food to be provided, and timing for the launch. The launch, for the guy who was dead.

I hit the reply button, ready to cancel it all. The words were stuck in my mind. How do you say, "Sorry, but the event I planned? The star of it all died. So, do we lose our deposit?"

I felt more tears well in my eyes and I pressed them tight together. Why wouldn't it stop? I just wanted the pain to stop.

"Kate."

Dad stood in the doorway, his hands by his side. His drab, brown shirt was creased from sitting on the couch too long, and his hair was sticking up. I wondered if Mum had taken him out at all today, and fervently hoped not.

"Yes?" I snapped my eyes back to the screen. I'd just gotten him some snacks and a drink; what could he possibly want now?

"W … want to watch TV with me?"

I blinked, staring at the document on my screen so hard that the words all blended into a bright, white light. Did I want to write the body of this email?

Or did I want to watch TV with my father?

Why would I? It wasn't like we talked much. We hadn't seen much of each other at all, ships passing in the ocean of our house. Sure, I took him out when I needed to, but it wasn't like we were friends. We weren't proper "father and daughter", and I saw no reason at all to stop that now.

Except that, one day, he's going to die.

Like Lachlan.

Like, maybe, you.

"Sure." I pushed my chair back and stood up.

What are you doing?

One part of me was screaming at myself, tsking and shaking my head as I went to waste time with someone who wouldn't even remember it tomorrow.

The other part of me grimaced and plonked myself down on the couch, trying to feign an interest in *The Price Is Right*, a television show I'd never really cared for.

"How—is work?" Dad's eyes were glued to the screen. I ground my teeth together.

Work has been on hold since Lachlan died, thanks for asking.

But he didn't know about that.

"Fine," I said. On the television, a new contestant had come up to play the Higher or Lower game. He was super excited, as all the contestants were, big smiles and bright eyes. I wondered if they had problems like we did in their real lives. Real problems.

"Are you scared?" I turned to look at Dad. His head spun and met mine, a serious look on his face. There were parts of him that were the same as the dad I'd known before, the father I'd grown up with, mixed with new lines of age, a slackness of the jaw, a skinniness of the cheeks.

"Of what?" Dad spoke slowly, and I felt him really watching me, like he was judging everything behind my eyes. I was worried about what he might find—and what he might not.

"Everything." I shrugged. "Dying, what people think, what will happen in the future …"

"But—everybody dies, Katie." Dad reached a shaking hand out to grip my knee. "Everybody." His voice was soft, and I looked into his steely eyes and saw what I thought was an understanding there; knowledge of the situation, answers about the future. I reached my hand down and squeezed his.

"Lower," Dad urged the contestant on screen to drop his price. I smiled.

"But what about … what about how it feels? What about pain?"

"It … it hurts, sometimes." Dad nodded. When he looked at me, it felt like he was looking through me. I shivered. "But everything hurts."

I thought about Lachlan. All his first-time tries.

There has to be an element of hurt, or it isn't worth it.

As he'd said, something small and good was a part of a greater whole. It was all a complicated, intricate series of good and bad.

"But don't you think it's unfair? And what about what everyone else thinks?" I blurted out.

"Ish—it's not fair." Dad said the words with care, correcting himself. "But life never is."

It never is.

Ever.

But it started me thinking. Maybe fair is relative. Maybe pain is relative. Maybe, my hurt now, and the depths it had given me, the capacity it had shown me to feel pain for others? Maybe that meant the happiness I'd feel, one day, would be great.

Maybe.

"As for what the other p … people think," Dad shook his head, took his hand and placed it back on his lap, "fuck 'em."

I widened my eyes.

"Pardon?"

"You h … heard me." Dad gave a wicked grin. "Fuck 'em!"

I couldn't help it. I cackled with laughter, for the first time in almost a week. It was so ridiculous. Dad smirked, too, and I knew he was proud he'd made me laugh. I leaned closer to him, rested my head against his arm like I'd used to when I was a little kid. It felt nice there.

It felt safe.

"Lower again," I chimed in, as the contestant on the screen went to a cheaper price bracket. It wasn't cheap enough. The contestant lost the prize and I clasped my hands to my head, pretending to be disgusted with his choices. Dad grinned at me.

We were going to be okay.

"He's an idiot." Dad shook his head.

"The biggest," I agreed.

"Do you think $20?"

"For sure."

We watched the screen, anxiously awaiting the price announcement. When a big two zero flashed up on the screen, Dad cheered. He clapped me on the back, and I caught his enthusiasm, grabbed it with both hands. I was—*surprisingly*—okay.

When the ad break started, I excused myself to run upstairs. I grabbed some of my horror movies and took them down to see if he wanted to watch them with me. It had been so long since I'd spent quality time with Dad, without being forced; maybe it didn't have to be all embarrassing moments, and duty of care. Maybe we could co-exist, in some sort of crazy harmony.

As I walked past my parents' room, I noticed the door was shut. *Funny*. Mum never shut the door unless they were sleeping, and I was almost 100 per cent certain I'd left it open when Dad had finished dressing earlier today.

I swung open the door, intending only to let the air in but stopping in surprise last minute. Mum was on the floor next to the bed, curled up in a foetal-like position, her hands tying her legs to her chest.

She was still in her work clothes, her freshly pressed suit skirt from this morning crumpled, her blouse untucked, her neat bun hair frayed and curling around her shoulders. Mascara streaked from her eyes, and her cheeks were the colour of the flesh of a blood orange, a sort of orangey red that implied heat and terror all at the same time.

"Mum."

She looked at me with her red-lined eyes, and, even though she must have heard the door open earlier, her face was all shock.

"Are you okay?"

I pulled the door to behind me and slowly walked to her side, kneeling on the floor next to her. She sat up, smoothed her hair down and smiled at me, the kind that doesn't reach the eyes. My mother, the cool and composed control freak was sitting here, freaking out.

"I didn't see your car," I said.

"I parked around the corner. I didn't want you to know I was home."

"You left early?"

"Yes."

I rested my hand on her shoulder, feeling uncomfortable about playing the grown-up to one of my parents for the second time that day. Mum shrugged me off and I placed my hands in my lap before getting to my feet. Maybe she hadn't wanted my help after all.

"Kate, I'm sorry."

"It's okay." I paused. From up here, she didn't look like the woman she'd always been. She just looked sad and fragile.

"It's just—he's my husband. And it's him, but it's not him, and I love him, and sometimes he doesn't even remember who I am, but ..." Mum trailed off into a series of silent tears, her body shaking with each word. I didn't know what to do. I placed an awkward hand on her shoulder, and this time she let it rest there. "If you have it, too ... and your friend ... I don't know that I can keep this up."

She'd been faking it? The whole time, her acceptance of him back into our lives, her permission for Dad to have a beer—deep down, she'd been just as scared as me?

"We're going to be okay." I hoped it was true. God, I hoped it was true. Mum nodded and looked up at me, those big, red-rimmed eyes raining black.

I turned to walk away and froze at her hand on my wrist.

"Kate."

I tilted my head in confusion.

"You're—you're doing so well." Her lip wavered. "I've asked so much of you and you've given, and given. I feel like I'm falling apart all the time and you're just ... you're handling this with aplomb."

Mum stood up, placed her arms around my neck and held me.

Why haven't we done this before? Why hadn't we *talked?* We were both sharing the same problem, yet all our communication had been so surface level that the deepness hadn't been touched. And now, here we were, both of us in tears over a life we both didn't have all that much control over.

But then again, did anyone?

TWENTY-NINE

SAT ON the cold, stone bench seat in the park. In front of me was a metal table, the kind that was cold as ice on wintery days and hot as the sun in summer. I'd spread out a chessboard in front of me, black and white pieces all ready to go.

I checked my watch, anxiety creeping in. I was nervous. Very nervous. He should have been here by now.

"Kate," Johnny said. I looked over at him, strolling toward me. The green of the park blurred into the background. His long hair was pulled back, his goatee thicker than normal.

His skin was a pale white, the deep purple bags sinking under his eyes a heavy contrast. The whites of his eyes were rimmed with red and his cheeks looked sallow, like he'd lost weight.

I rose to my feet and threw my arms around him, noting how skinny his frame felt against me. His body shook a little and I blinked back my own tears.

It hurt, God, it hurt.

But it's supposed to.

"I'm … I'm so sorry," I whispered when I pulled back.

He gave a curt nod then moved to the other side of the table, seated opposite me. He clasped his hands together tight, and I saw the whites of his knuckles.

"Sorry about the—about the, uh, lack of shifts at the moment." Johnny attempted a weak smile.

"No! Don't you dare …" I shook my head.

"I knew you'd understand, I just …" Johnny let his hands finish the sentence, drifting them across the table into space. "This is fucking hard, you know?" He touched the bridge of his nose, pressed there for a few seconds. "It's so fucking unfair."

I reached a hand across the table, knocking over a few pawns in my way. I grabbed hold of his wrist and squeezed, squeezed tight. Because it wasn't. It wasn't fucking fair, and nothing I said would change that.

"He just—he told you he had cancer, right?" Johnny's brows raised, and I nodded. "He was *supposed* to be okay. He was in remission, and he was going to live." Johnny's lower lip wavered and I felt a hot tear slide from my eye.

It was the same thing I'd thought, over and over again. He'd already survived a deadly disease. Why let a freak incident take him now?

"I have grandparents alive, but my proper family, my mum, my dad … he's all I had. All that was *real*." Johnny broke down, his shoulders shaking, big, full body depressions over the table. I ran to the other side to hug him, to try and make it stop, but only ended up joining him.

My legs couldn't support me so I knelt beside him and we wailed, loud, ugly, noisy tears, meshing together in the stillness of the park. I felt the gaze of people walking by. I felt the curious stares of children and the judgmental glares of the elderly and, most of all, I felt pain, great, big shuddering heaps of pain.

Pain for Lachlan.

Pain for Johnny.

Pain for my dad.

And pain for me.

"I … I really liked him," I said. "I don't know if you knew, but we were—he was—"

"Kate, I knew," Johnny said softly into my hair. "He was coming back from your house when—"

"Don't!" A sharp gasp of air jolted through my body. I didn't need to know. I couldn't know. It was too much.

"He was—amazing." I finally pulled away. Tears had dampened the chessboard in front of us.

"He was." Johnny gave a sad smile. "An annoying little shit, with all his psycho-babble crap, but he was—he was amazing." His clarity was contagious. I took a deep breath, sighed.

"And he has a pretty great brother." I nudged his arm, and then winced. *Had*. Not has. Johnny just pushed me off, but I could feel him smiling a little more, his happiness gently touching his eyes. Not enough to numb the pain, but perhaps enough to dull it for a while.

"I'm stalling on sorting out a freaking funeral." Johnny's hands writhed against each other. "I'm just—I'm sick of doing it, you know? So tired of death."

"That's actually why I wanted to meet you."

"To organise a funeral?"

"Not exactly." I took a deep breath. "I thought … what if we combine it with something we already have?"

Johnny slowly leaned his head to the left, his tired eyes studying mine. God, they looked nothing alike, but they were so the same. A fresh wave of pain washed over me again, and I tried to swallow it away.

"We have the launch coming up in two weeks, now. What if we made it a celebration of his life? A tribute?"

Silence.

I peeked open an eye I hadn't realised I'd scrunched shut. Johnny was staring at the chess pieces in front of him, his face blank.

"Is this why you bought a chess set?"

"What do you mean?"

"You win, we have your event. I win, we don't?" Cold, hard, rage boiled in Johnny's eyes, and I wished I could take back what I'd said.

"Sorry, just forget it." I shook my head.

"Why would I want to do that?" Johnny spat. His hands flew to his sides as he tried to contain his anger. "Why would I hold an art launch for my dead brother, Kate?"

"It was just an idea." My voice was choked with sobs. I didn't want him to be mad. I hadn't thought he would take it like this. "Because it's a nice way to commemorate his life."

"In the way that dead people's art is worth more?" Johnny stood up, pushed his body from the table. He gripped a handful of his long, brown hair in one hand, like pulling it helped the pain. "I thought you really liked him."

Something in those words sent fury sparking through me.

"I *did* really like him!" I said, jabbing my finger into Johnny's chest. "I still bloody *do*. I don't want to make money from this, I just thought it might be an easy way to help you organise something to say goodbye, without having to …

"Lachlan wasn't about goodbyes. He was about learning, and growing, through pain and joy. I thought you'd think this was really kind of *him*, but forget it. I'm sorry."

My hand trembled as I brought it back to my side. I understood his reaction. I was prepared for it, even. Why was I so upset?

"I don't even want to organise a funeral. I just—do you get how hard this is?" Johnny's eyes were desperate, needing me to understand.

I realised I couldn't. Sure, my life sucked.

But I could never truly understand the gravity of his.

"I don't." I shook my head softly. "But he was one of the good things. He made life okay. And I—I just want to celebrate that."

"I'll text you," Johnny mumbled and walked off, his shoulders slumped, his stride slow.

I sank back down to the table, pulling my hair at the sides. Had I made things worse for him? I'd thought it was a nice idea. I didn't mean to hurt him, not more than I already felt he was hurting. I tried to imagine the relativity of his pain scope in comparison to mine.

It ran pretty damn deep.

I fiddled with the little men on the chessboard for twenty minutes, a game against myself. Was I doing the right thing? Was there a right thing, or a wrong thing, or anything?

"Kate."

"Michael." I mustered up a weak smile and stood, accepting his tentative hug. "Thanks for meeting me."

"S'okay." He shrugged, taking the chair opposite mine. "We playing chess?"

"Kind of." I bit my lip. "I've never played chess in a park before."

"Cool." Michael moved one of his pawns forward. Relief washed over me.

I could do this.

I could still do new things.

"So, I heard about Lachlan," Michael said, taking the rook I'd let venture too close to his knight. "I'm sorry."

"It's not your fault," I replied automatically. "And the stuff with Dave—the song—I know that wasn't your fault, either." My eyes locked on the chessboard, trying to figure out how to take his queen. He was a skilled player, well protected.

It was only when I heard a sniffle I looked up.

"Michael?"

"I'm just—I feel so bad." He shook his head, wiped his nose with his hand.

What was wrong with me today?

I'd made two men cry at the same park bench.

"I can't believe I didn't know what he was doing with the … the song," Michael gulped the words down, like he was internalising the pain they clearly bought him.

"It's not your fault," I repeated. "Honestly, right now, the song seems like such a tiny part of my problems."

"Oh." Michael cocked his head to the side. "So what did you want to meet for?"

The guy had a point. Sure, we'd been friends through Dave for years, and he'd been hanging around, near and off Stacey at every opportunity he'd gotten, but we'd never clocked up any solo time together. This was entirely unusual.

"Well." I pursed my lips together. I needed to choose my next words carefully.

"I've been asked to join Coal." Michael blurted out the words, his eyes lighting up with excitement. "Lee was furious when he found out what Dave had done. He dumped us as a warm-up, but his bass player had quit the band, and he asked me to join in his place."

"Congratulations!" I broke out into a smile. That really was amazing news.

"I'm stoked, y'know? I gave him your address," Michael continued. He knocked my queen over with his bishop, easy as you like. "Dave told him about your dad, clearly, and when he heard the song he wanted to send you some flowers. I hope that's cool. He's a really nice guy." Michael's eyes lit up, and I couldn't help but grin along with him. I'd seen the flowers from Lee, but it just hadn't seemed real. Nothing seemed real lately.

Even a celebrity sending me flowers.

A tiny shiver ran down my spine. Lee-*freaking*-Collins had sent me flowers! The me of three months ago would have been ecstatic.

Today, I was pleased. Not knee-shaking, heart-racing pleased, as I'd been when I'd met him, and nowhere *near* as pleased as I'd been when I first stared at Lachlan's lips, when I didn't even know his name—but I appreciated the gesture.

Wow. I'd changed.

"It's fine," I said. I moved my rook across and took his queen. Maybe I could still win this thing after all.

I placed my hands on the table, on either side of the chessboard, and felt a vibration rumble through them. *My phone.* I picked it up, slid the screen to unlocked to see what it would say.

The launch is on. I need to do this. Johnny.

A rush of relief swept through my body. I needed to do this, too. I needed to do one last thing for the boy who'd done so much for me. The boy who'd shown me things, like no other.

The boy who'd been cruelly stripped from me.

"Sorry, you were speaking." Michael ducked his eyes back to the chessboard.

"Yeah," I continued. "It's about Stacey."

"I'm all ears." Michael knocked down his king in surrender.

I pursed my lips together.

For the first time in months, it was my move.

THIrTY

IT WAS D Day. I woke up for the eighth time since I'd fallen asleep the night before, nerves gnawing at my innards like gnats at a dead thing.

In a way, I was. Parts of me still felt dead. I physically ached when I remembered losing Lachlan, losing the whole man I'd called my father, and losing a part of me. The feeling of sorrow roiled around in my stomach, pounding me from the inside.

Other parts of me felt numb. I was dead in the sense that I wasn't here. I could look down at my actions and think *Well, that's what someone who is supposed to be mourning does.* I was distant from finalising the caterers, from buying groceries, from fixing Dad breakfast. I was just going through the motions, and keeping on keeping on. Surviving.

The thing was—and this really got me—there was a part of me that wasn't dead *or* numb. A tiny spark was alive inside of me. It wondered if I had the disease or not. I was curious about the future, about doing more events, going to college, trying to find someone who'd understand my condition just like Lachlan had.

I felt guilty when I indulged it, when I let that little spark breathe and gave it some air. I didn't want it to become a fire. I wasn't ready for that. The pain was too much, the dying inside of me too all-consuming.

But still.

There was a little light.

"Do you like it?" Leslie's eyes were wide. She nodded toward the large, blue chaise lounge in the room, stretched from one end of the window to the other.

I walked over to it, squashed its surface with my hand. It was firm underneath, yet soft to the touch, a suede material covering the exterior. It was bright blue, a hideous colour that almost hurt the eyes to look at.

"It's pretty good." I nodded. I gingerly sat on the edge of it, my fingers gnawing at the stitching. It figured. I'd badgered my genetics counsellor to get one quality item to make my experience more relaxing, and now I was too hyped up to use it.

"How have you been?" Leslie's eyes softened. She must know, I deduced. Figured. Johnny saw one of the other counsellors at the centre.

"There have been better months." I studied the flecks of coloured stone on the tiled floor. *Better*. That was putting it mildly.

"I'm sorry."

"Why do people say that?" I ran a hand through my hair. Keep it together, Kate. "You say 'I'm sorry', but it's not like it can change things. Nothing can change things."

Except maybe time.

"People apologise as a way to try and convey their condolences." Leslie clasped her hands over her knee. She was wearing a taupe nail polish. It was funny, the way every acute detail about her imprinted itself to my brain. "It's also to make them feel better, too."

"You apologised to me to make *you* feel better?"

"A little." Leslie shrugged. "That's who we are as humans. We seek ways to feel better."

I turned to face the window. The old man was there with the young woman, the same couple I'd seen on my first day at the centre. She held his arm as he limped across the garden, their shadows running long against the deep green grass.

Funny. I thought he'd have died by now.

He's alive and Lachlan is dead.

"It's not fair, Leslie." I searched her face for something. Anything. I needed answers.

"You've heard the one about life not being meant to be fair, right?"

"You think?" I arched an eyebrow.

"There's supposed to be a patient/client confidentiality thing in place." Leslie's eyes darted to each corner of the room, like she was worried someone would duck out from behind the chaise lounge with a recorder or something. "But I want to tell you something."

I shrugged, giving her permission. What could she have to tell me that would change anything now? After all that had happened?

"We talk about death a lot in this centre." Leslie tapped a pen against her armrest, making a sharp, clicking noise. "And people always see it differently."

I looked outside. The old man and the young woman were sitting down now, his back propped up against the gnarled tree trunk, her shoulders hunched as she crouched down next to him. He was smiling, a huge, gap-toothed grin. Her face was terse. She had the weight of the world on her shoulders.

"One of our more … recent patients." Leslie's voice shook, ever so slightly. "He had encountered death a lot. Lots of his family members had died, and at one point, it looked inevitable that he would die soon, too."

I wanted to mutter something smart, like *Gee, I wonder who that could be.* But, I didn't. I didn't want to enough.

"We'd talk about death, and we'd ask him if he were afraid. If he were worried about pain, about the unfairness of it all, about what would happen beyond," Leslie said. "And do you know what he said?"

Another arched eyebrow.

"That he'd lived a good life."

Huh?

"That it sucked. And he didn't like it. But he'd experienced lots of things, he'd met a lot of special people—" At that, I think her eyes flicked pointedly in my direction, "—and that how could he regret life when he'd been given so many blessings?"

I bit my lip and pushed my feet up, reclining against the soft chaise lounge. It was cool underneath my hot skin, firm and supportive. I didn't want to speak. Did she think I was an idiot? That I didn't get what she was doing here?

It was all a ploy to make me feel better. He would never have said something like that, and if he did, he wouldn't have believed it.

Although he did tell you pretty much the same thing.

But he wouldn't have meant it.

Would he?

"Now, would you like to learn your results today?" Leslie must have sensed my shift in mood as her hands busied themselves amongst the papers on her desk. I nodded, but it felt like my mind had left my body.

Oh, God. Did I want to do this, really and truly? Knowing there would be no Lachlan there to support me if it was positive? That I might never work, or find love, or be happy again?

Or would I?

My mind flashed back to the first day I was here, when I'd thought all those things, no matter what my results would be. Then I thought about Lachlan, Johnny, Dave, Stacey, planning the art event, and everything else that had happened in between. I'd thought back then it was going to be a yes, and look at all I'd achieved. I thought about my *dad*.

The little light sparked brighter.

"Kate, I have the results. A score of thirty-five or less is fine, forty and—" I shook my head.

"Can you just say positive, negative, or somewhere in between?" All of a sudden, I had to know. *Now*.

Leslie produced the paper like it was a grand scroll, waving it in the air. "Are you ready?"

"Go on." I screwed my lids shut. I needed darkness for this. *I did want to know, I didn't want to know, I was negative, I was positive, I was scared, I was frightened, I was confident, I was alone, I was—*

"Kate, it's negative," Leslie shrieked and I bolted upright, inhaling sharply. Negative.

Negative!

"Negative?" My voice was all breath. I gripped the lounge, carving my nails into the material. Did she—did she mean *negative-I-don't-have-the-disease* negative?

"Negative." Leslie's face looked like it was going to crack open; she was smiling that hard.

It was negative.

I didn't have Huntington's.

I'd have to care for my father. I'd have to live life without Lachlan—but I didn't have Huntington's disease.

I leapt from the chair and threw my arms around Leslie, and squeezed tight. Seconds later she embraced me back, no doubt shocked I'd made physical contact after months of emotionally keeping my distance.

"Congratulations," she whispered. I bit my lip. It wasn't like I'd studied for this test. I hadn't had to do any preparation.

Or had I?

"Thanks," I whispered back. The sheen of tears veiled my eyes once more.

THIRTY-ONE

STOOD IN the shower with the hot water pounding against my body and the steam fogging up the glass. I thought about the events of the past few months: Dad coming back, Dad being sick, Dave and I breaking up, Lachlan, counselling, the café, no college, wanting to hurt myself, reaching out to my father, wanting to die, wanting to live … everything. I was emotionally drained just thinking about it all. I wished I could wash it all away, like the cherry blossom scented shampoo I was using. If only it were that simple.

Instead, it hurt, but there were glimpses of sunshine. I was dirty and clean, all at the same time.

I got out of the shower and slowly dried my hair, combing through the long brown strands to separate them from one another. I rubbed my towel against the mirror and cleared a spot so I could see my reflection clearly. *Ugh.*

I went to my room and chose my clothes with the care of someone attending a funeral, settling on a short black slip underneath, and a brilliant blue lace dress that hugged my figure in all the right places on top, ending just above the knee. I blow-dried my hair and let it hang in loose waves down my back, tiny curls licking up at the ends. I dabbed on some foundation, mascara, and a red-tinged lip-gloss, trying to ignore the churning of my stomach.

"Knock, knock," Mum said, as she pushed open the bedroom door.

"Well, that kind of defeats the point in knocking, doesn't it?" I teased, not unkindly.

"How are you feeling?" Mum sat down on the bed, looking me up and down. "Nice outfit, by the way. You look beautiful."

"I don't feel it." I made a face, giving my hair one last tweak. "I feel sick. What if it's a disaster? Or if no one turns up? What if too many people do?"

What if this isn't the tribute I want it to be, but instead an epic fail?

"And you're sure you want to be an event planner?"

I spun around, ready to rip her to shreds, only to see a small smile playing on her lips. "Katie, I'm joking. Everything's going to be fine. It's your first ever event, and your dad and I— we're really proud of you."

A warm glow swelled in my belly.

"I was thinking—I'd like it if you came tonight." I bit my lip. "As in, both of you."

"Darling." Mum stood and stretched her arms out. I ran to her embrace, taking my second hug of the day. "We would love nothing more—as long as you're okay with it." She kissed the top of my head.

"You know what?" I pulled back, and studied her eyes, mirrors of my own only older, wiser. "I really am."

THIrTY-TWO

W^{HEN I} arrived, the café was dark. I switched on the overhead and watched as the tiny spots in the ceiling flickered on, illuminating the place. Chairs were stacked on tables, the counter was clean, the coffee machine off.

Nothing had changed, and yet nothing was the same.

I stowed my clutch under the register and ran a hand through my hair. There were so many things to do; it was overwhelming.

"I wanted you to help me put them up."

Johnny.

He stood in the doorway, a giant cardboard box in his hands.

"He'd been working on some new pieces for the exhibition." His voice was flat as he walked to the wall and placed the box down, like it weighed a tonne. Someone had already removed the old art. I wonder if that was done Before or After. If, perhaps, it were so painful for Johnny to see, that he'd asked someone to get rid of it.

"Thanks for coming." I crouched down next to Johnny and

the box and squeezed his arm. There were no words adequate enough to say, *I'm sorry/I know it hurts/I'm hurting too/You're hurting more/I can't make this go away*.

None.

Instead, we worked in silence. Johnny would frame an image and hand it to me, and I'd find a spot for it on the wall.

At first, I focused on getting the job done, just tacking the images up wherever I could without stopping to absorb their contents. After a while, though, I slowed down. I noticed Johnny run his hand over each image, like he was trying to take something from them.

Then I realised he was.

The first sketch I slowed on was a small pool, a waterfall at one end. The detail was intricate, everything from the gleam on the rocks to the splashes of the water as it fell from the sky, depicted in finely tuned black and white. It was our pool, where we had skinny-dipped.

Even without being here, he had the power to take my breath away.

Next was a hand holding a cigarette, tilted back, hovering over the grass. You could see each blade, singled out in glorious detail, and I felt a tiny smile creep up my face. I remembered that day, all right.

The pictures continued; some I recognised, and some I didn't. There was a picture of a stuffed toy that Johnny held for a particularly long time before passing over to me. Then there was a sketch of headlights, piercing tunnels that arced toward the viewer as if in a scene from a horror movie.

There was a pair of lips, full and plump, a sheen of light highlighted on the lower one. I snatched it up greedily and scoured the image, taking in every line and wondering how a picture of lips could be made so detailed.

I'd found what I was looking for. The streetlight in the corner. The date it was drawn.

The night of our first kiss.

A flush of happiness flooded me, followed swiftly by sorrow, then guilt. It was confusing, the emotions, the actions and the words. It was confusing just to *be*.

"Kate," Stacey said as she flew across the room, her body colliding with mine. She enveloped me in an almighty hug, crushing my arms to my sides in the warm autumn light.

"How are you?" I breathed as she let me go.

"You idiot." She pinched me gently in the side. "How are you?"

"Fine," I mumbled. I didn't feel right complaining about the numbness inside of me, the more-than-sad, guilty feeling that had taken up residence in the motel of my body. Not in front of Johnny. It just wasn't fair.

Stacey must have seen my sidelong look, because one moment she was by my side, the next, she was ambushing Johnny, pressing him to the ground in the sort of bear hug that would make a, well, bear proud.

"You must be Stacey." Johnny's voice was squashed under Stacey's enthusiasm, but I could tell he was smiling. Just a little.

"This sucks." Stacey pulled back and looked at him, straight in the eye. My heart went out to her. Good on her, for getting that "sorry" just wasn't going to cut it.

"Hell yeah." Johnny gave a weak smile.

"I think this is a nice idea, though," Stacey continued, surveying the art lining the walls. "He was such a talented bastard."

"Stacey!" My eyes widened. She gave me that, *Whatcha gonna do?* look she'd perfected on teachers at our high school, time and time again.

"Hey, hey," Michael said, walking into the café. He was dressed in a white shirt, and black jeans, with a black suit jacket over the top. His dreadlocks were pulled back in a tie, his chocolate eyes alive with enthusiasm.

"Michael." I smiled. "Thanks so much for stopping by to help." I could feel the daggers Stacey was shooting in my back.

"No worries." He nodded. "I think this is just such a nice—hey, man." Michael stuck out his hand in front of Johnny who slowly took it and gave a single pump. Two guys with long, brown hair, one with a tan, dreadlocks and all this energy, the other with paler skin and a heart buried somewhere underground. So similar, and yet so very different.

"Okay, well, I need you two to go through the guest list and make a check sheet for the bouncers, then sort out a musical playlist," I said. "But Johnny and I need to concentrate, so I'll need you in the backroom." I gestured toward the little room at the back of the café.

"Do you think I'm an idiot?" Stacey raised her eyebrows.

"Nope." I shook my head. "I think you're a good friend, who'll do what I ask in my time of need."

I saw the guilt flicker across her eyes as she followed Michael into the room. He'd brought his laptop, as I'd requested, to help pick the songs and hook them up to the sound system I'd hired.

When the two of them were inside the room, I reached over to the door, and slammed it shut behind them.

"No coming out till your jobs are done," I instructed, a tiny note of glee in my voice. Maybe some time alone together and a common goal would finally push them into admitting how they felt for each other.

Or maybe Stacey would strangle Michael with his laptop power cord.

Either way, should be an interesting experiment.

The prep time ended all too quickly, and soon Johnny and I were standing in a sea of caterers, some carrying platters of finger food, others with ice boxes and knives and other prep tools they'd need to make the hot food selection.

I watched as women in black shirts polished champagne flutes till they shone in the late evening sun that was quickly being marred by thick, storm clouds. Butterflies were crashing into my stomach lining, along with an overwhelming tidal wave of sadness.

Why wasn't he here for this?

"Kate." Johnny walked up to me. Outside we could see a few people stop to linger, some waiting next to the door for the security guard to permit their admission, others unashamedly exercising their right to stickybeak by covering their hands over their heads to peek in the window.

"Yes?" I asked. I touched his arm, feeling how slender it was, how very breakable this man in front of me had become. Yet he was still standing.

Some people are just strong. That's all there is to it.

"Thanks for doing this." Johnny nodded around the room, his eyes travelling over the paintings on the wall, the sound system Michael and Stacey were manning—together, I noted—and the few waiters who were lining up wines and beers ready for service. A steady hum enveloped the room. "I think it's exactly the sort of … the sort of service he would have wanted."

I raised one side of my lips in a sad smile. It hurt. It hurt like hell.

But I knew that, as opposed to an event where they mourned his death, Lachlan would have liked us to celebrate his art and his life instead.

It was a first he would have wanted to achieve, after all.

"Let's do it." I nodded to the security guard we'd hired, and he swept open the door.

The five people who'd been lingering outside walked in and headed straight for the wall with the art. One was clearly a reviewer, judging by the notepad and paper she held in her hands. She made a beeline for the wall and started to scribble down notes, and it took all my self-control not to linger over her shoulder and check she was writing only good things.

"This looks amazing." Stacey grabbed my elbow. "You did it!" Her eyes were alive with enthusiasm.

"So, I guess this means you're okay with me forcing you to spend time with Michael?" I scrunched up my nose.

"I guess." Stacey narrowed her eyes at me. "But don't let it happen again." I was about to ask further questions when Michael came up behind her and threw a hand around her waist. She sunk into his support and I stepped back, a little shocked.

"It was that easy?" I asked. "I just had to get all *Parent Trap* on you and shut you in a room?"

"Apparently." Stacey rolled her eyes at Michael. "He's really persuasive, okay?" Michael nibbled on her ear and I shoved her arm away.

"Oh, guys! Come on. Gross." I shook my head. Who knew I'd created such a monster?

I looked across the room and saw it filling up. People were everywhere, and now there was a definite line outside waiting to be ticked off the list and get in.

It was a success. Lachlan's event, something I'd planned, was a success!

It just sucked, a constant stabbing pain, that he wasn't here to enjoy it.

"Ka-tie." Dad wrapped an arm around my shoulders. He was dressed in a suit jacket, shirt and tie, the sort of get-up I hadn't seen him wear since well before he'd left us. "Looksh good."

"Thanks." I let him hold me close for a few moments before pulling away. A few people looked in our direction when they realised his voice was a little larger than life, but they soon went back to their own business.

"You've done a great job." Mum smiled. She looked tired, the lines at the corners of her eyes sunken deep, but she was smiling. It was going to be okay.

"Thanks." I nodded. The room was completely packed now, people milling around the display wall, waiters circling the room with drinks and snacks, moving in for the kill as soon as someone looked ready.

Lachlan would have loved this. He would have been talking to people in that carefree way he had, telling them about the theory behind his drawings, making people laugh and smile and—

Tears welled in my eyes and I tried desperately to blink them back. It was still so fresh. God, why did he have to die?

But you are going to live.

The voice was small, and I felt a new wash of guilt over me once the thought was fully processed.

But it was true.

I'd liked him, so, so very much. I learned from him, more than I'd ever imagined you could learn from someone so close to your own age. Life sucked without him—more than I'd thought it ever could.

But I had Mum. I had Dad. I had Stacey, Michael, Johnny, a career and responsibilities.

I was going to be okay.

Not today.

But some day.

"Kate, it's time." Michael emerged from the crowd and nodded toward the microphone and amps we'd set up in front of the art for me to do my speech at. He'd been keeping an eye on the clock to make sure it happened exactly half an hour after the event started, for optimal coverage.

I took a glass of sparkling from one of the waiters and shouldered my way to the front, trying to focus on the little things: the scent of women's perfume, the colours of people's shirts, the shine that reflected from their shoes.

Just not on what I was about to do.

Say goodbye to a dead man.

I finally reached the front and stared down my nemesis, the black microphone and the stick it rested upon. I chewed my lip, nervous. Was I ready for this?

"Ahem." I switched the instrument on and cleared my throat, right at the same time as a clap of thunder exploded outside. I looked nervously over the crowd. Some were turned to me, expectation written all over their blank faces, others were still conversing, continuing their lives like nothing had happened.

I felt my knees weaken and my heart speed up till it was pumping adrenalin through my body at what felt like eight times its normal rate. I searched the room for a friendly face, seeing only blank stares where I wanted to see smiles.

Why had I decided to do this again?

I shuffled my feet together and cleared my throat. Rain opened up, thundering against the tin roof, and I saw more eyes look my way, felt the ripple of attention float over the crowd and land on me.

I saw Dad, hands shoved in his pockets as he swayed back and forward on the balls of his feet. He gave a subtle thumbs up. My heart warmed.

I saw Johnny. His eyes were sad, darkened by a heartache I could never experience. Still, he was here, beer in hand, standing next to a journalist I recognised from the national paper. He gave me a tiny smile.

If he can do it …

"Good evening." The words were out of my mouth before I knew I'd spoken. Instantly, the people who hadn't been looking looked, arms folded expectantly, eyes alive with demand.

Shit.

"Thank you all for coming here tonight to celebrate the works of Lachlan—Lachlan Smith," I said. A few people golf clapped.

Cringe.

"I had the pleasure of knowing Lachlan on both a professional and personal basis." My voice was shaking so hard I worried that the words would stop coming out, broken up by all the emotion I felt welling inside me. How could I do this without him here? *Why* had I thought this would work?

Why?

"Yesh!"

My heart sunk.

One hundred pairs of eyes shifted from me to the back of the room.

Dad.

Fan-freaking-tastic.

"A good man." Dad nodded enthusiastically. He pumped his hands together. "A good man."

I chewed my lip. Of all the times for Dad to have a moment

…

"He was a good man," I repeated. Eyes flew back to me. I froze, unsure of what to do next. I opened and closed my mouth. I hadn't thought people would let the idea of my sick father go so easily.

Continue your speech, idiot.

"He was a really good man. One of the best," I said. "He loved to create art, although he'd never really admit it was art. To him, it was all experiences." I gave a wry smile, and a few people in the audience laughed. I saw Leslie at the back of the room. Johnny must have invited her.

Or maybe Lachlan had.

"The thing about Lachlan was—he was so intent on experiencing life, on trying new things and appreciating everything," I said. I glanced behind me at the wall of images, each just as overwhelming as the next. "He didn't believe in good, or bad. Everything was a tiny awesome component of a greater scheme."

I caught my breath in my throat. Tears welled in my eyes and I knew I stood no chance of holding them back. Not right now. Not with all this.

But it was okay.

I didn't have to.

"It's hard … it's hard to see the good in his passing." I gulped down a sob, but a new one choked up my throat to replace it. An army of crying came forward in little sobbing breaths. I pressed my lips together, hoping to supress it, yet failing. "But I know he would have said s … something like everything happens for a reason, or it's bad he died, but it was part of a good experience as a whole, or … Or …" My shoulders started to shake and I couldn't stop the tears. They overtook my body and I knew my eyeliner was running, my mascara giving me the worst case of panda eyes ever, but I didn't care.

Why? Why had he died and why had I decided to do this stupid event, anyway?

I felt an arm snake around my shoulders and I gratefully sunk toward it. I needed an arm right now, any arm. I rested my weight against this rock, who was there for me when I needed it most, and cried, in front of one hundred members of the public, some known to me, others not.

It only lasted for ten seconds, maybe fifteen, but it felt like an eternity of my pain in the spotlight, ripped open for everyone to see. Eventually, though, I opened my eyes.

And saw it was Dad who'd supported me.

Dad who was standing next to me.

I took a deep breath and stepped forward again, moving toward the microphone.

I can do this.

"Lachlan's whole philosophy on life was no regrets," I said. My voice wavered, but I continued. "And I know he would have loved for you all to see his artwork today. He captured a series of moments that I know were special to him—that were special to lots of people in his life—" I caught Johnny's eye again, and we shared a knowing look, "—and I think that's why he made such amazing pieces. He saw the good in everything. He wanted to share those things he held dear, and let others feel the magic of his life, his experiences, and his very being."

I paused. Every eye in the room was focused. A strange sense of calm washed over me.

"And, if you walk away from here with a desire to try things like he did, to share things like he did—" I bit my lip to stop the tears that threatened to overwhelm me again. "—then I'm sure he'd say his job was done. Thank you."

I pushed out of Dad's hold and walked away from the microphone. I shouldered through the crowd, desperate to reach the security of the backroom.

Behind me, the crowd erupted into a cacophony of noise, giving the rain that was pelting down on the roof a run for its money. As I walked past people I didn't know I felt eyes looking at me, judging me, not unkindly. It didn't matter. None of it mattered.

I just needed to be alone, and to hurt for a while.

I reached the door to the staffroom and twisted, ready to walk inside when I heard my name.

Over the microphone.

"Kate did an amazing job putting this together here tonight."

I spun around, my dress flaring around my knees.

Michael.

What?

"And Lachlan was a really special guy," Michael said. His eyes were alive with empathy, sad and pure. He gripped one hand around the microphone, like he was singing into it. I guess he'd seen more people do that than speak into one of late.

"As a way to commemorate his life even further, we'd like to invite a very special friend of mine to the stage to play a small tribute. This is a total surprise; Kate, your lovely event planner, doesn't even know about it."

My eyes widened as I scanned the crowd. He wouldn't have invited Dave to sing. Would he? Why would he do that, after everything, and—

That's when I saw the man with the guitar walk over to Michael. He was tall, with dark hair, piercing blue eyes and a five o'clock shadow that would send any girl weak at the knees.

"Introducing, Lee Collins, everybody."

The room burst into applause. Everyone knew the lead singer of Coal, and a host of camera flashes went off as people surged forward, trying to get closer to the makeshift stage, closer to Lee Collins.

Instead of throwing myself through the open door and locking myself in solitude, I pressed my back up against it.

Michael had gotten Lee-*freaking*-Collins to play at Lachlan's event.

I blinked back another tear.

Could this day get any more emotional?

The strains of a guitar reached my ears as I saw Michael plug in a second microphone he'd obviously brought with him. The notes were sad and pure, as old and beautiful as time, and I lost myself in the notes Lee played.

"*No time but now*," he sang. His voice was soaring and raw, coursed with pain. It felt like he knew the deep cut of loss, like he'd felt that sword stab before.

"*Every day, the pain it goes on,*
Every day, telling right from wrong.
And it hurts, knowing what is right,
And it's hard, to stay alive inside.
But it's the shadows that make the man,
And it takes love to understand …
Every day, love is found,
For every hurt, random kindness goes around.
You will find someone who believes,
Who holds you, helps you when in need.
And you will—never be alone,
You will—always have a home.
Always …
Always …
Always …"

Everyone in the audience was focused on him. I saw some people wipe away tears, and wondered if they knew Lachlan personally, or were simply touched by Lee's song. Either way, it didn't matter.

All that mattered was the here and the now.

And the firsts.

"*It hurts now, and it won't heal,*" Lee sang. "*And scars will form on you. And when, nothing seems to be re-ee-eal,*" Lee's voice cascaded over a scale of notes, "*Your strength will shine on through.*"

I blinked back a new crying assault and was thankful again for the support of the door behind me. I was a fairly big Coal fan, and I'd never heard this song before. It felt so real, so right for the moment—I couldn't have planned it better myself.

When he finished, the audience erupted into a tsunami of applause. I saw a few women smack their lips together and I held back a wicked grin. I knew he was about to get assaulted and seduced, in the way that surely, only seriously famous and sexy rock stars can.

Wait.

I'm smiling.

I pulled my lips back into a straight line.

"Lee! Sign my bra?" I heard a voice trill over the rest of the crowd. This time when I grinned, I showed some teeth.

"That was Lee Collins, ladies and gentleman." Michael was back on the mic, proving himself quite the emcee. "He has graciously conceded to do some signings here tonight, and will give away personalised autographs on an exclusive new EP to anyone who buys one of these stunning works of art for a purchase price of one thousand dollars or more."

My eyes widened.

One thousand dollars?

To my surprise, people surged forward, one or two credit cards already waving in the air. I saw Johnny stagger in shock as Leslie pushed him toward the register, and I smiled. I knew it wasn't about the money to him; but if he could raise his brother to celebrity artist stakes, help make a living now he was forging it on his own, surely it was a good thing.

I pushed off from the door and fought my way through the crowds. It was thickest near the wall with the paintings, dozens of people pointing and eyeing them off. I grabbed the artwork with the streetlight, *our* streetlight, and lifted it gently off the wall.

"I was going to buy that." A woman in a sequinned black dress jabbed a finger into my arm accusingly.

"It's not for sale." I tucked the piece protectively under my shoulder, quickly walked around the bar, and shoved it under the counter. Some things, you needed to hold close.

"Rain dance."

The words rang out through the room, a screeching, masculine cry over the shrill female voices that were now humming to the tune of Lee Collins.

I pursed my lips.

Really?

"Rain dance time!"

I looked to the source of the noise and saw him standing near the door, his eyes glazed and wide, focused on the downpour outside. Mum was standing next to him, her lips a mirror of my own, her fingers gripping Dad's arm like he was about to take off.

I forced my way through the crowd, determined to get to him before any more damage could be done.

But I was too late.

It was too late.

Dad freed himself from Mum's tight claws and pushed open the door, rushing into the rain outside. He stopped, right in front of the window where we all could see, like the hundred people and I were watching a movie, starring him.

"Raaaaaain dance." I heard him shout.

I was at the door now, my eyes wide, my heart thumping.

Why?

Why was he ruining everything?

I heard the voices still as everyone focused on the man with the disease in the rain. A few cameras flashed.

"Hmph! Crazy," a woman next to me said, nudging her friend's arm.

I felt something warm inside me. A fire, one I didn't know was burning. I thought of how Dad had been there for me as a kid. I thought of how Dad had comforted me on stage, only moments before.

Dad.

I pushed past the woman, not caring how my shoulder jolted hers, causing her wine to spill from her glass and splash on her dress. I moved forward, placed my hands on the door, ready to shove it open.

"Come on." I looked at Mum. Her jaw was around her shoulders, her eyes alive with panic.

"It's okay," I said. I held out my hand, offering her company.

Because if this was crazy, we were in it together.

And there's nothing like a first in the rain.

Mum delicately placed her hand in mine then stepped toward the door. Without waiting for further encouragement I shoved the door open, letting the noise of the rain further infiltrate the judgmental silence that was now inside.

I pulled Mum through the doors and together, we ran out into the rain.

Droplets of wet beat on me, slicking my hair to my head. In seconds, I was drenched. My dress clung to my knees, my shoulders, until I could barely separate the wet of my skin from the wet of the material.

We jogged over to Dad who had his arms outstretched, welcoming the clouds, and the rain, and the everything.

What was the point in fighting it?

Sometimes you just had to let the rain in.

I giggled, a stupid laugh that I knew looked crazy to those inside, and Mum gave my shoulder a squeeze. She got it. I knew she did.

Dad stripped off his jacket and let it drop to the gutter where it quickly amassed in a puddle. His white shirt had gone see-through, and his chest hair was just visible. His smile was radiant, stretched from ear to ear, as he embraced all that Mother Nature had to offer.

"Rain," he called. I'd never heard him so exuberant.

I wondered if he'd ever been this happy before.

I grabbed his hand and pulled it toward Mum's. She shyly accepted, and I saw Dad squeeze, giving her a look that was so full of love I felt like crying again.

I sniffed, holding back a tear. Wearing formal gear in the rain? It was a first Lachlan would have loved.

"Kate!"

My name made me turn. I looked at the café, at the hundred sets of eyes staring at us, and saw Stacey and Michael. They were right in the doorway, exchanging some furious words. I bit my lip. Was now really the time?

Then they were running toward me, hands tightly gripped, Stacey letting out a tiny girly squeal as the rain made contact with her face.

"Woo!" she screamed. She threw her hands up in the air, a smile on her face so wide it almost matched my dad's. Michael grabbed her by the waist and planted a kiss on her cheek, the smacking sound audible even over the thunder above. My cheeks were hurting from love, and life.

Next came Johnny. He opened the door and calmly walked out into the rain, without the enthusiasm of Stacey and Michael, but with the determination of someone who gets it. Someone who knew what was going on, and knew he had to be in on it.

He linked his arm through mine and we stared at the ominous sky above. I watched as drops of rain sluiced their way down his face, over his nose, shining as they caught in his goatee.

"We're gonna be okay," he said. His voice was so quiet, I almost wasn't sure he spoke.

But he did.

I knew he did.

"Kate."

I tore my eyes from Johnny's, and saw Lee Collins walking across the pavement.

In the rain.

Lee-*freaking*-Collins!

"You all right?" He stood in front of me. He was wearing a white T-shirt, and I could see the definition of his body beneath it. I was fairly sure about one hundred pairs of eyes inside could see it, too.

"Fine." I wasn't even sure I was speaking, but I heard the voice and I knew it belonged to me.

"Cool." Lee nodded, and stood next to me, on the other side. We were a line of seven, all facing the open window of the café. All grinning, stupid wide smiles that I knew must be contagious. I saw people inside mirroring us.

"I hope it's okay I sent you flowers." Lee tilted his head toward me. "My dad has Parkinson's. I get it."

"I'm sorry," I said automatically.

"Don't be." He shrugged. He nodded at Dad, smiling. "Looks like he's having fun."

Dad had both his arms around Mum's waist and was trying to coax her into dancing to a tune only he could hear. Mum sidestepped to the inaudible beat.

I couldn't help but smile.

"You know, I'd love to hang out sometime," Lee said. I felt his hand on my arm. It was warm, wet, and sent tingles down my spine.

I glanced at Johnny and he gave me a wink; subtle, but there.

I looked back at Lee, studied his chiselled jawline, his high-set cheekbones. God, he was sexy.

But I wasn't ready. One moment I was full of misery, determined I would never be happy again, that I could never get over Lachlan, the only boy who would ever like me, take me for who me, and my family, were.

Then I looked at the clouds, at Dad, at the café, and I remembered Lachlan's enthusiasm for life. His firsts.

Finally, I looked at Lee. He was looking at me like I was something special; even though he knew about Dad.

I chewed my lip. Rain seeped into my mouth.

"Lee," I started.

He was a rock star. I thought of the frisson of excitement that had coursed through me when I first met him.

Why did I let Dave make me think I would never find another guy again?

"I was kind of involved with Lachlan, the artist." I jerked my head toward the building.

"Oh, I'm sorry." Lee nodded, a frown marring his face. A smile broke out a heartbeat later. "But a gorgeous, unique, tour-organising, newly single girl like you; you can't blame me for getting in before the masses find out you're available, right?"

I turned fifty shades of red.

Lee Collins thought I was—things! And he knew I was the one who organised the tour.

"You know what?" I turned to face him. I saw Mum spin into Dad in the background, and Stacey and Michael share a passionate kiss. Johnny just stared at the café, a small smile playing over his face.

A rush of warmth spilled through me.

We'd get through this.

We'd all get through this.

I thought about Lee's sentence again, asking if I blamed him for trying to ask me out. I looked down at my feet, and thought about the way Lachlan made me feel. Like I was desirable. Like I was *worth* something.

I grinned.

It was an easy answer to a complicated question.

"You'd be crazy not to."

eleven weeks

Crazy in Love #2

Seven shots

Five siblings

Two boys

One heartbeat …

Stacey is good at pretending.
She pretends that the boy she's in love with doesn't exist.
She pretends that she's happy to live and die in this small town.
She pretends that her life is carefree while her best friend's world crumbles before her very eyes.
But Stacey's got a secret …
And it's going to ruin everything.

WAKE TO the sound of a drill-saw attempting to channel through a concrete pylon right next to my head.

"Why?" I grunt. Only it sounds more like "arrggghhh", even to my ears. Apparently being woken by a drill-saw seriously impedes my ability to form words. I reach my hand out and slam something in front of me, presumably the drill-saw, most likely a clock radio. Regardless, the action makes the noise stop. Thank hell.

Ugh. While the blast of noise has stopped, there's still a ringing in my head of dizzy-making proportions. Not to mention that my tongue tastes like I've been eating roadkill. Yuck.

I squint one eye open and then scrunch my lid shut immediately. Harsh yellow light screams through a window framed by black, floral curtains. What fresh hell is this? Who has opened my—

Shit.

I don't have black, floral curtains.

I inch open my lid at a snail's pace, this time preparing myself for the assault of light from the left of the room. Yep. Black, floral curtains still there.

I open my eyes wider and take in more of the room in front of me. Aside from the window, there's a black bedside table with a digital clock on the top of it, right next to a red lamp. The floor is covered in a shaggy cream carpet, with a black skirt and a red lacy bra lying on top of it.

Oh, no. Please, please no ...

I slowly raise the white sheet from my body. Yep, exactly as I'd suspected.

My black skirt and red bra.

This, of course, leaves only one question. But do I really want to look? Can I?

I rack my brain, trying to put together the pieces of the night before. There was the party at Joe's. I'd gone there with Kate, because Dave and the band were playing. Michael. I saw Michael. Tequila. *Lots* of tequila.

I glanced down at my hand. Seven little lipstick lines

mar its surface. One for each shot. At least I can remember that.

But how the hell did I get here? And, more importantly, *where is here?*

With my body still firmly positioned toward the left side of the room, I gently inch my foot behind me.

One inch: nothing. Just cool, crisp sheet.

Two inches: still nothing.

Three inches: so far, so good. Hopefully I'm alone. I just went to some stranger's house, took off all my clothes, and slept solo in a random bed.

Four in—*shit!* My big toe makes contact with something warm, hairy, and distinctively human. I jerk my leg back toward me. My heart thuds in my chest, a million miles a minute. What the hell have I done? And who am I in bed with?

My mind races through the potential options. Grant, my ex, hadn't been at the party, and he sure as hell didn't have black, flowered curtains. There had been Joe, the older guy whose place the party was at. He'd definitely shown an interest in me, in particular when I'd told him I was eighteen tomorrow.

Today. Technically, I am eighteen right now.

"Hoooaaaawwwwr." The creature behind me groan-yawns.

It's like a bullet from a starter gun. I fling the sheets back and jump from the bed. I dive for my clothes, pulling on my underwear, throwing my shirt over my head and hoisting up my skirt like this is the Olympic event for sprint-dressing and I'm the lead contestant.

I grab my bra from the floor and thank the god of hangovers that my mobile is hidden underneath it, along with my flip-flops, which I promptly slip on.

"Hey," a deep voice calls from behind me. A voice I don't really recognise. It sounds like a million male voices, all rolled into one.

I freeze. Is it better to know and deal with it, or run and hide in shame?

Only there's not really a question.

I'll take the shame, thanks, my legs tell my brain as they sprint toward the door. I wrench it open and then slam it shut behind me, the mystery man calling something in my wake.

I'm in a living room with black leather lounges in front of me, and a giant flat-screen TV to the left. Windows with more of those hideous curtains let in cruel, natural light and next to them—*thank you, thank you, thank you*—a door, the kind of thick, wooden thing that clearly screams *exit*.

I dart toward it, screeching as I step on some small, sharp, red object in my path, twist the door handle, and then run out into the street. I slam it shut behind me and run, run down past the trees, the gravel of the unsealed road digging into my feet.

I run until my breath comes in short, sharp gasps that make my chest shudder. I run until water seeps from the corners of my eyes, streaking out past my temples, no doubt giving me that desirable panda effect.

I turn left, I run; I turn right, I run. I go straight through several intersections until the stitch in my side is stabbing and the throbbing in my head, merciless. I double over and rest my hands on my knees, trying to slow my breathing, to gain some semblance of control over my body. I have no idea where I am. I have no idea where I've been.

"One," I whisper, holding my breath for the imaginary *one thousand*. "Two." *One thousand.* "Three." *One thousand.*

By the time I reach ten, my breathing is a distant cousin of normal, and I straighten up and try to think again.

I dial Kate's number, but she doesn't pick up. I think about calling a taxi, but I don't have my purse on me, and what would I say, anyway? Please pick me up from number four I-Have-No-Freaking-Clue Street? Do you accept pretend payment?

Think, Stacey, think. I massage my temple with my left hand, my right still clutching my phone and bra.

Noise. Head toward traffic, then you can work out what

street you're on, and try figure a way to get home.

I shut my eyes and concentrate on the noises around me. The chirping of birds—not helping. Traffic. The sound of cars, yes. Coming from … from the right. Yes. The right.

I pick up my pace, trying to ball my bra into a fist-sized package. The underwire makes it a little difficult, and for the first time in my life I curse myself for buying a bra that's sexy instead of practical. Seconds later, I banish the thought from my brain and send up a mental apology to La Perla for ever thinking that way.

Still, it gets me thinking. Sexy lingerie. Something I wore in the hope someone would see it and now, judging by all the things that have happened so far this morning (read: naked wake-up call, strange man in bed next to me, slight ache between my legs, and lips that feel a little bee-stung, potentially from too much kissing from a guy who possesses a great deal of chin stubble), yes, someone did.

Did we even use protection?

My stomach swells and a surge of bile makes its way up my throat, rolling into my mouth. I double over and swallow it down, determined not to vomit in some random person's rose bush. I may be hungover and doing the walk of shame—well, in my case, run of shame—but there is no reason I can't have standards.

The rumble of an engine working its way down the street has me jumping over to the footpath to avoid imminent death. *Nothing worse than having a one-night stand with a mystery guy and then being run over, on your birthday …*

The engine slows down, chugging along behind me. I keep my eyes firmly fixed on the pavement, my pace fierce.

Still, the car moves along just behind me. My heart, which had slowed from the excessive running, starts to pick up again, building to a march. Is someone following me? Who?

What if it's the guy from the house?

Rationally, I know the thought shouldn't scare me.

This guy has seen me naked.

What if it's someone else?

I mentally change my list from having a one-night stand with a mystery guy and getting run over on your birthday as being the least impressive annual occasion ever, and replace getting run over with being stalked, kidnapped, and chopped up into tiny pieces.

Yep. Not panicking.

Frick!

I insert a small skip into my step, trying to seem as casual as an eighteen-year-old girl skipping can be. The car keeps pace just behind me.

My eyes scan the street till I see a small alley three buildings away. I could run down there. The car won't be able to follow me. And the lane is even leading to my right, toward the sound of cars and hopefully familiarity.

I take a quick glance to my left—safety first—when the car engine stops.

It just *stops*.

Damn.

Before I can run, though, I hear my name. "Stacey."

I spin around. The car following me is an old mint-green Valiant. And the guy sticking his head out the window I know only too well.

"Michael." I give a rueful smile and turn my head away. I don't know if the fact I know him makes this better or worse.

"Whatcha doing?" he asks.

Oh you know, just the walk of shame home from a guy's house, one who I probably slept with and who, judging from the ache between my legs, I'd say has a medium to sightly above average-sized penis.

THE
PROBLEM WITH
Heartache

The one thing he can't forgive.
The one thing she can't forget.

Crazy in Love #3

The problem with heartache is that you can dream about
the could have—the should have—but when you wake, nothing
will console you.
Because seconds later, you remember he's dead.
And remembering is the worst pain possible.

KATE IS running from her family. It's intertwined with everything that went wrong. When she lost her career. When she lost her sense of self.

When she lost the boy she loved.

Now, she's got a second chance, travelling with rock-star Lee Collins and his band, Coal, on the road. She wants to forget, and she wants to fall in love.

Now.

Lee will do anything for family. It's why he hired Kate. It's why he donates thousands of dollars every year to the foundation that supports his father.

It's why he keeps his secrets; and it's why he cannot, will not fall in love. Not with Kate—not with anyone.

Ever.

THE PROBLEM with heartache is that you can't mourn forever. You can't walk around the streets, wearing black, carrying holy water on your person in the hope that you'll stumble upon a miracle, be able to use it and bring that person back. One day, you're gonna forget that tiny vial, and you're not gonna realise until it's too late.

"Are you done?" Mum enunciated each syllable like it weighed a ton.

"Give me a second." I threw my arms behind my back, fiddling with the straps on the bra.

A solution for heartache, however, appeared to be running. Or, it seemed to be for me. I'd been jogging on the beach every day for six months now, and slowly but surely, I was getting better mentally, becoming able to function again.

Even if it meant that my boobs were getting smaller. Hence the new sports-bra shopping trip.

"Are you having fun?"

I cringed. *Really, Mum? Fun?*

My fumbling finally resulted in success and I shook the bra off, quickly shrugging my normal one over my shoulders and throwing my T-shirt on top of that. It hung loosely over my hips, the grey speckled material suiting my mood to a tee. *Ha. See what I did there?*

Making bad jokes to yourself: a potential symptom of heartache. Thankfully, not a symptom of Huntington's disease.

I grabbed my purse from the little seat the staff at the lingerie store so kindly provided its change room patrons, and walked to the front of the store to the checkout area, sports bra in hand, ready to make the purchase.

The guy in front of me at the counter was taking a really long time. He had six different sets of lingerie to put through. I couldn't help but check around his arm to see what. Black lace, red silk, black pleather ... and was that something with fur I could see?

"Stop stickybeaking." Mum slapped my arm, and I snapped my head back to my chest.

"It's a public place," I whispered. The transaction in front of me continued. Hopefully, underwear-fetish guy hadn't heard.

"People don't like you to look at their knickers, Kate." Mum tutted quietly, shaking her head.

"Well maybe *people* shouldn't buy quite so many pairs. And besides," I hissed, raising my eyebrows at her. "We don't know that he's going to wear them all at once."

"Ahem."

Of course. You whisper three fairly innocent sentences, but the one about the guy in front of you being a cross-dressing lingerie wearer, he hears.

"Sorry." I studied the ground.

The man turned around to face me. He had maroon leather shoes, scuffed, like they'd seen better days. My gaze travelled up his black jeans, over his red-chequered shirt with the triangular collar, the black scarf around his chin, covering his lips, his nose—but not his eyes.

Holy hell, did the man have eyes.

"Kate."

I blinked. *What?* How did this guy know my name?

"Yes?" Mum replied, and I jabbed an elbow to her ribs.

"That's me." I smiled brightly. "Sorry about the panties-wearing comment."

"To be fair, this does look a little weird," the guy said. *You can say that again …* "We just have this film clip tomorrow, and the stupid wardrobe guy said the models won't fit any of the … you know …" The man jerked his thumb toward the counter, indicating the underwear the checkout chick had now finished ringing up.

Cogs clicked in my head. This wasn't—

"Lee?" I silently added *freaking-Collins.* If he was going to the trouble of wearing a bad scarf by way of disguise, I doubted he'd be keen on me screaming his full name in a crowded shopping centre.

"Yeah?"

Silence.

"Kate's just so happy to see you, is all," Mum said. She took a step closer. "Hard to recognise, behind that scarf there."

"That's kind of the point." Lee gave her a wink. I swear, my mother blushed.

"Well, we'd love to have you over for dinner sometime, since you're in town," Mum was saying, her hands clasped together. She opened her mouth to continue speaking.

"But being a really busy guy, we wouldn't actually expect you to come." I overlapped.

"Well, if we invited you formally, we would," Mum said, giving me a strange look.

"I mean, I could." Lee spoke the words softly, taking a step closer. "So long as you don't tell anyone about my secret identity."

Mum giggled like a schoolgirl. *Help me, God.*

I looked past her. Two men in dark jackets stood at the entrance to the store, no doubt Lee's security. He'd get mobbed if anyone figured out who he was. One of them was fiddling with some flimsy looking bra on a stand out front, and the other observing people who walked past in the shopping centre, and—

Him.

I dropped the sports bra and ran, shouldering Mum as I surged forward, out the doors of the shop.

Left?

Right.

I could just make out the brown hair bobbing in the distance.

I bolted, as fast as my legs could carry me, darting around mothers with prams, old people supported by walking frames, and teenagers making their way to the food court in an achingly slow fashion.

Turning the corner, I could see the hair again, but it was still too far away. My knees raised higher, my feet hit the ground harder, and I gave it all I had. I couldn't let this opportunity get away. I had to take it. I had to *make* it.

This time when I turned the corner, he was almost within arm's reach. Ignoring the stares I was getting from the lunchtime food-court crowd, I dove, reaching out and grabbing onto the denim of his jeans as I fell.

I hit the ground, hard. Tiles smashed into my ribs, my knee, the side of my jaw. Everything went black for a few moments, and I blinked, trying to clear my vision.

When I could focus again, I looked up. Faces hovered over me, voices yelling things, asking things that I couldn't quite make out.

I need you.

Then I saw him. The blue jeans, the white shirt. The brown floppy hair.

I blinked, and concentrated all my brainpower on focusing on his face. *His face, Kate. Look at his face.*

"Lachlan?"

I blinked again. An old man wearing a chocolate-coloured beret stared back at me.

Shit.

If you enjoyed this book, you may also like:

Shh!
By Stacey Nash
www.stacey-nash.com

What do you do when you're asleep?

Olivia Dean has the perfect reputation, the perfect boyfriend, and an increasingly perfect CV. She has it all, until Christian breaks up with her in public, calling her out as a self-gratifying sexoholic: the kind that plays solo. But Olivia doesn't masturbate all night—the only thing she does is sleep … right?

Now all the boys on campus seem to want her attention for the absolutely wrong reason—including resident hottie, Logan Hays. He's pulling out his best moves to gain her attention, so resisting his sexy charm is hard work.

With rapidly slipping grades, a disturbingly lurid reputation and demanding parents, Olivia must discover the truth behind her rumoured sleeping problem. If she doesn't, the perfect life she's worked so hard for may slip away, including the one person who has Olivia breaking all her rules—Logan.

SAVANNAH and I were making our way down the skinny path, the lines of trees ringing the open paddock around us. We'd walked in silence for a few moments when Savvy cleared her throat. "How are things with you and Christian?"

"Fine," I said, scrunching my brows. "That's a weird

question."

"It's the start of a new year, you know …" She trailed off, leaving me wondering where the question had come from. Christian and I were pretty rocky lately, but it wasn't like I'd spoken to Savvy about it, nor was I about to now.

"Are you coming tonight?" I asked in an attempt to divert the conversation.

"Of course," Savvy squealed. "I heard that Dane Beaumont is going as a bodyguard, and I'm not missing that glorious sight."

I cringed at the high pitch that shot out of her, but a smile tugged at the corner of my mouth. Good lord, I loved this girl's enthusiasm.

We were almost home now, and I looked both ways before we crossed the road into the car park. "I've got the best nurse outfit. Are you dressing up?"

"A sexy nurse, I hope." She waggled her brows.

I slid my phone out of my pocket and checked the time. "Shoot. Sorry, Savvy, I've only got ten minutes. Better run. I'll see you tonight."

"Bye." She waved her fingers as we walked through the gates of Oxley College and into Back Courtyard, then I peeled off toward Front and ducked into the stairwell that led up to my block. Each block was home to two floors' worth of students. The dorms weren't overly fancy, but I loved living here, surrounded by friends. I also loved not being a freshman. The more senior students got the pick of the rooms and my second floor room was certainly spacious when compared to many of the others. I shoved my key in the lock, tossed my bag on the floor and ran for the floor's communal shower. Lucky it was empty.

In four minutes flat I was back in my room, twisting my long, damp hair into a bun at the nape of my neck. I slipped into the white dress, and pulled my heels on, then tucked my key into my bra as I dashed out of my room and down the stairs. The costume looked pretty good, since the uniform was authentic; pocket watch and all. *Thanks, thrift store.* I ran straight to the dining hall, nodding and smiling at everyone I darted past on the way.

Voices wafting out of the back room meant the rest of the committee had already arrived. And with words including *keg* and *goon* in the air, it sounded like they were sorting out drinks. I pushed the door open and came face to face with Christian, a keg balanced on his shoulder. Gee, he looked fine tonight, his biceps bulging through his thin T-shirt from the weight.

"Hi, hon," I said, and stepped out of the way.

With the world's tightest smile, he manoeuvred around me, Dane close behind him with a second keg of beer. Sure enough, Dane was dressed security-style in black from head to toe. A two-sizes-too-small T-shirt stretched across his toned chest like he was sculptured art. He also had some kind of earpiece connecting his ear and mouth. Unlike Christian, Dane met my gaze with a wide smile and a wicked wink. Good lord, the guy was a flirt.

Tonight my job was armbands, and I needed to hop to it. It would take two of us to get everyone covered. Lucky for me Ella was already there, her long auburn hair brushing over the printout in front of her. She and I had been in each other's lives forever. Our parents ran in the same social circles, and when we'd both been accepted into UNE we'd chosen to live at the same college. If Oxley offered twin-share rooms, we would have been all over it. Maybe then we wouldn't have drifted apart.

"How are we looking?" I asked.

"Pretty good. There are one hundred-ninety-eight people confirmed, which is just about everyone in college. What's even better is I think we've got some ex-collegians, too. Not many though."

"Awesome. Sorry I'm late. Where are we up to?"

"You're right on time." She glanced up and pointed to a small box in the corner. "Grab the bands and we'll go set up."

I grabbed the box, and Ella stood, pushing her dead-straight hair over her shoulder. This was a courtyard party, so we'd set up registration near the college shop, right at the corner of Front Courtyard. It would be easy for everyone to find us and there was plenty of room for a line to form.

Ten minutes later we'd dragged a table outside, set up two chairs behind it, and were poised with highlighters, ready to verify attendees. We weren't a moment too early either. The first group stopped by on their way back from dinner, and after that people kept coming. Our job was to make sure only those who had paid actually got tagged. There'd be no free grog here tonight. It was the perfect job for me, because I got to socialise and work at the same time. Two boxes ticked; making sure everyone saw me, and fulfilling my committee duty.

I glanced up at the person next in line and saw a face I didn't recognise. His dirty-blond hair hung over his bright blue eyes in a way that was entirely too sexy, a tiny coating of stubble—not quite a beard, but more than one-day growth—lined his strong jaw. And his lips, smooth and pink, and tipped up at the corner as if he was in on a secret … ah, flip. I'd totally been caught checking him out.

"And you are …?" I managed to keep my voice level.

"Logan Hays."

"You're not from here."

"No," he said. "Alumni. I lived here a few years ago, but I've got a place in town now."

Sweet Jesus, that was a good thing.

"Loges!" Dane swaggered up to the table, baton bumping against his hip. He slapped Logan on the back. "He's cool, Livia, let him in."

Then the dirty flirt winked at me again. What was with him tonight? Sure he liked to banter with all the girls, but usually not with me. Christian would have his 'nads if knew. The fact that he was slurring and obviously half tanked wouldn't save him. My gaze flicked back to Logan.

His stomach, right at my eye level, was covered with a loose-fitting shirt, but the material fell over his body in such a way it was obvious there was muscle rather than flab underneath. My gaze travelled up to meet his. He still sported that teasing half-smile, his eyebrow now raised.

"R ... right." I dipped into the box for an armband. The whole thing toppled off the table, spilling blue plastic tags all over both me and Ella.

"Flipping heck." I shoved my chair back. Staring and dropping things—I was an embarrassment tonight. Scooping the tags up, I dumped them into the box, then popped back up. Logan was still watching me, his smile now full-blown.

"Flipping ... heck?"

"Yeah, she's twelve," Ella said.

"Here's your armband. Have a great night." I shoved the thing at him. Hopefully he'd disappear into the growing crowd of partygoers before I had the chance to do anything else crazy.

"Drink?" Savannah appeared beside me, wearing next to nothing. Her skimpy black dress rode all the way up her thighs, and fit her curvy form snugly. Tonight's theme was occupations, and well, she was dressed as a stripper who was acting out every guy's cop fantasy. She shoved a plastic cup at me, its contents splashing over the side and staining the tablecloth sickly yellow.

"Thanks." I took the cup before I wore whatever was inside it.

When I looked up she was gone, swallowed by the crowd.

A little while later the line finally petered out, so I grabbed my untouched drink and swept my gaze around the now full courtyard. Music blared through the air, bouncing off the chocolate-coloured brick walls and people shouted over it, trying to hold conversations. A couple leaned against the wall of A block, her body pressed between him and the bricks. I averted my gaze. I had no issue with steamy PDA, but these two looked as if they were one kiss away from ripping each other's clothes off and going for gold right here in the courtyard. That was a sight I could do without. Now, where was my sexy boyfriend?

It only took a few moments to spot Christian, standing higher than the crowd. Balanced atop one of the wooden picnic tables, he pointed at Dane who stood beside him, holding a glass stein. Dane had his head tipped back and beer coursed down his cheeks as he chugged it down. A thick ring of guys surrounded them, singing a drinking song at the top of their lungs. Good thing my parents had never seen this side of Christian, or they sure as heck wouldn't approve.

Someone jammed into my shoulder and I was jarred backward.

"Oh … I'm … I …" The girl scooped my cup off the ground, rose and tried to shove the now empty cup into my hands. "Olivia … I didn't …"

Her eyes were fixed on my hands. Her hair, which hung in two long plaits to her waist, when coupled with her flannel shirt gave her a cowgirl appearance. Or something. She'd lived in the room next to mine last year—super sweet girl, but not exactly socially confident. She mostly stuck to herself. "It's okay, honestly, I wasn't going to drink it anyway."

"I'm sorry," she said again.

"How was your summer break?" An attempt to deflect the conversation worked. She actually met my gaze, and a wide smile broke out across her pretty face.

"It was awesome. I—"

"Olivia," Dane's voice boomed across the courtyard and he swayed, dangerously close to falling on the people crowded below the table. *Holy heck.* My stomach jumped into my throat but Christian saved him from falling off the table just as Dane yelled, "Let's hook up, babe. I'll make sweet love to you aaaall night long."

"What the hell?" The curse slipped out before I had a chance to self-filter.

And Christian just stood there, doing nothing. *Double what the flipping hell?*

I pushed through the throng of partygoers, focused on my boyfriend and his mate who were now both laughing while the guys around them joined in. If they thought this was funny, if it was some kind of a joke, it was really, really, lame, and there was no way it was going to continue. I was not joke material. My fingers dug into the cup which was now crushed in my hand.

"Livie, Livie, likes to—"

I reached up, and fisting my hand in Dane's shirt, reefed him down off his makeshift stage. Still co-ordinated despite the drunken appearance, he landed square on his feet beside me and dropped his arm over my shoulders.

"You have exactly two seconds to remove that, Dane." I looked up at Christian. "Do something about him before I do."

Christian just shrugged.

Dane laughed.

"Now!" I said, my hands clenching at my sides.

"We're over, Olivia." Christian finally looked my way for the first time all night. "I can't do this anymore. You're—"

My heart stopped beating then took up again way too fast. *Over?* This joke had gone way too far. My glare settled on Christian and I ground out, "Inside. Now."

Christian shook his head and downed the rest of his beer. Then his gaze turned icy. "I can't compete with your sex-ploits. Not. Doing …"—he flicked his hand between us—"this anymore."

"My … my … what?"

Now the ice was in me, curling through my veins and settling in my tummy while all sound disappeared into a dull hum. This breakup wasn't happening right now. In public.

Dane made a disgusting gesture with his fingers and tongue.

Oh my God. This can't be happening. Why in heaven's name was Christian doing this? He knew how important reputation was and now … well, now everyone was staring.

And laughing.

Tingles swept up the back of my neck and my chest tightened. Christian loved me. He'd said so a million times. Sure he'd been cold lately, but that was something we could talk through.

There was no way I was going to let this go down in the middle of a courtyard filled with all of our friends. "Not here," I bit out.

"It's done. There's nothing more to say."

I did the only thing I could. I ducked my head and like lightning, I shot out of there, not stopping until I reached my room where I slammed the door closed and slid down it, my mind reeling as I tried to make sense of what just happened.

This night had gone from bad to catastrophic.

ABOUT HUNTINGTON'S DISEASE

Huntington's disease is a genetic, neurodegenerative disease that causes brain cell death. While the author has endeavoured to portray the suffering of real patients in this book, she understands that no fictionalised story can really grasp the pain and the difficulty these people and their families go through in everyday life.

Victims of Huntington's disease can suffer from involuntary movement, memory difficulties, mood disorders, hindered coordination, difficulty with problem solving, some issues with swallowing, and personality changes.

Following the onset of symptoms, the average life expectancy of a Huntington's disease sufferer is between fifteen and twenty-five years.

There are many great support bodies out there for those affected by this horrible illness. The author would encourage you to contact your state organisation or body, should you wish to learn more.

EDUCATIONAL MATERIAL

Discussion topics and educational questions on themes, structure and characterisation are available for school groups studying this novel. Please contact Lauren K. McKellar for more information via her website at laurenkmckellar.com.

ACKNOWLEDGEMENTS

As writers, we're often our own worst critics. It's not often I put pen to paper, or fingers to keyboard, in this case, and don't hit the delete button straight away.

The Problem With Crazy, though, is the story I just haven't been able to quit. I started it more than a year and a half ago, when I met someone who suffered from Huntington's, and wasn't able to let the idea go that such an unfair disease can receive such little attention in the media.

This story wouldn't have ever left my computer if it weren't for the help of four very special beta readers. Rebecca Berto, you snapped me out of it. You told me to cut the crap, and you were right. Thanks for sticking with me. Anabel Gonzalez, you picked up on those little things I wouldn't in a million years have ever noticed. Stacey Nash, you read, you reread, and then you reread again; your patience knows no bounds, and you made me believe in myself as a writer. And Emily Tippetts, you gave me clarity in the changes I needed to make, when I most needed to make them. Thank you all.

My fabulous cover designer, Rebecca Berto of Berto Designs, you are a gem, and I love what you've created. E. M. Tippetts, you have done a fabulous job with my formatting, and I can't thank you enough. Also, thanks to Kylie from Give Me Books for helping out with my promotion, and all the lovely bloggers I've met along the way—you guys *rock*, and I want to send you all virtual cupcakes for the support I've received.

I also need to thank my lovely family and friends who put up with me always being late for everything, for waking up too early, and going to bed too late, and for understanding that my Saturday nights are often me, my laptop and my puppies—no socialising allowed.

When it comes to thanking people, I couldn't go without thanking Peter. You're the one person who leaves me lost for words. You laugh with me, you support me, you feed and water me—and for some crazy reason, you love me. Thanks, lover.

Last, but by no means least, thank **YOU** for reading this book. Thanks for sticking with Kate and hearing her story. If you enjoyed this, I'd love it if you left a review on Amazon or Goodreads, and, if you'd like to know more about Huntington's disease, I'd highly encourage you to contact your nearest organisation. Thanks so much for making my dream a reality.

ABOUT THE AUTHOR

Lauren K. McKellar is a writer and editor of fact and fiction. She has worked in publishing for more than eight years, and recently returned to her first love: writing books that make you feel.

Lauren loves to write for the Young and New Adult markets, and blogs with Aussie Owned and Read, as well as vlogging with the YA Rebels.

In her free time, Lauren enjoys long walks on the beach with her two super-cute dogs and her partner-in-crime/fiancé.

www.laurenkmckellar.com

This paperback interior was designed and formatted by

www.emtippettsbookdesigns.blogspot.com

Artisan interiors for discerning authors and publishers.

www.ingramcontent.com/pod-product-compliance
Lightning Source LLC
Chambersburg PA
CBHW020238180626
46810CB00006B/2261